I0775763

Trapped in Once Upon a Time

Kristy Dixon

Meegore Publishing LLC

For Rylee and Harper

Every author needs super fans.

Chapter 1

Lottie sat on the edge of her bed and held her head. Something was terribly wrong. Ever since Ella ran off and married the prince, Lottie had been confused. Strange dreams were plaguing her at night, and she often woke up with a headache. Sometimes she wasn't even confident about who she was.

Lottie's sister Mara had quickly followed Ella's example and fallen in love with Stephen, a man who used to be their hired hand. Lottie's mother, Lady Anna, disowned her and was in such a mood these days. Lottie tried to stay out of her way as much as possible.

Lady Anna had been past furious when Ella married the prince. She'd hoped that the prince would fall in love with Lottie, or at the very least Mara. For a while, Lottie had wanted to marry the prince just as much as Lady Anna wanted her to. But now, everything was different. These strange dreams and weird headaches were about to consume her.

To add to the misery, Lottie needed to figure out what to do about Rodney, the Duke of Aldertown. Lady Anna was determined to have Lottie marry him, and Lottie only came to terms with it because the duke had money.

Money and position were the only things Rodney had going for him. The duke was disgusting. He ate with his mouth open, often dropping food onto his lap. His hair was greasy, and an awful body odor trailed after him. Lottie used to think she could be happy marrying anyone so long as they had enough money, but that was before Rodney.

A duke would be someone that would thrust Lottie into the public's eye. That used to be Lottie's goal in life, but suddenly, that wasn't as important to her as it used to be. Now, the thought of being married to that man for the rest of her life sent a chill down her spine that she couldn't shake.

Lottie climbed out of bed and pulled a comb through her curly brown hair. She needed to start breakfast. Now that Ella was gone, Lady Anna made Lottie prepare breakfast every morning. Hopefully, they would be able to hire more help soon, but so far, no one was willing. Word had gotten around that Lottie and her mother were not the most pleasant people to work for.

She sighed. Once she married the duke, she would have servants. Was a world of luxury worth spending her life with that man? Lottie stepped into her house shoes. Did she even need to try anymore? If she was fated to marry the duke, that meant she didn't need to impress anyone, and dressing up seemed like a colossal waste of time.

Lottie slunk down the long, red-carpeted stairs and made her way to the kitchen. She grabbed a few eggs and cracked them into a bowl. She didn't know why her mother couldn't take a turn cooking breakfast now and then. It seemed like the fair thing to do, and her mother never did anything important.

As Lottie mixed the eggs, she thought back to her most recent dream. She dreamed she was in a strange world. A world where there weren't horses and carriages. A place where there were machines with wheels that you got inside of and pushed a pedal, and it moved without the help of an animal. It was so strange, and at the same time, it felt familiar. The dreams were making Lottie feel uncomfortable.

In the dream, there were people walking around in strange clothing, greeting her and smiling as they passed. The women were wearing britches, just like the men. Some people looked familiar, and some didn't. They used strange words, and they seemed a lot more relaxed than people around here.

"You don't need to beat the eggs to death," Lady Anna scolded when she came into the room.

"I'm just thinking," Lottie said, setting the bowl of eggs down.

"Well, I hope you're thinking about ways to push up your wedding. I can't keep living with the gossip. It was one thing to lose Ella to the prince. It's a whole other thing to have Mara in love with a stablehand. Your marriage will make people respect us again."

Lottie had grown tired of this conversation. Her mother seemed to bring it up every day.

"It's disgraceful to have your younger sister marry before you. I've worried that the duke might decide against you once Mara made that poor decision. If you marry before she does, it will be beneficial to all."

Lottie turned to her mother. "I'm not so sure I want to marry the duke." There. She said it.

Lady Anna's head jerked up. "What? How could you even say that? If you don't marry the duke, we will continue to be the laughing stock of the county."

Lottie took the eggs over to the counter and slammed them down. "Mother, have you ever cared once what me or Mara wanted?"

"Of course I care what you want, but I know what you need."

Lady Anna flickered. That was the only word Lottie could use to describe it. She could see right through her. Lottie sat down hard in a chair.

"What is it now?" Lady Anna asked.

Lottie fanned her face with her hand. "I don't think I'm well."

"I should think not," said Lady Anna. "Talking about not marrying the duke. That would be disastrous."

Lottie swallowed hard. "No, Mother. Something's really wrong with me."

Lady Anna sighed. "Well, I suppose we can take you to the doctor tomorrow. I don't have time to take you today. If you want to go now, you can take yourself."

Lottie decided she would do just that. She forgot about breakfast and ran back up the stairs to get dressed. She wasn't going into town looking like a disaster, no matter what she'd thought earlier.

Now that Stephen no longer ran the stables, they didn't have anyone to help harness the horses, and she had no idea how to do that. Taking the carriage was out of the question. She had never walked to town, but she could do it.

When Lottie got to town, she felt exhausted. She wasn't used to walking those kinds of distances, and her feet were throbbing. The town had a small cozy feel to it, with only one road going through the center. Shops and businesses lined the dusty road. Normally, Lottie loved to come to town and eat at the inn or shop for dresses. Today, Lottie glanced around the town in horror. People were flickering in and out, like her mother had.

Panic rushed through her as she scurried toward the doctor's office. The ground seemed to roll, but no one else appeared to be affected. Perhaps something was wrong with her brain. She had heard of people with brain diseases. Everything started spinning, and Lottie covered her face. The next thing she knew, she was falling.

Lottie shoveled mashed potatoes in her mouth without thought. She didn't even try to pay attention to what the duke was saying. He liked to talk about his vast estate. Lottie was positive there was no way she could marry this man. Her idea of a good match did not involve neglected teeth and horrid body odor. Lady Anna glared at her, and she realized she was pushing the food into her mouth in an unlady-like manner.

Lottie sighed and sat back. Her hands still hurt from her collapse the other day. She wasn't sure if her mother had been concerned with her health or concerned that people had seen her fall. Lady Anna had been upset ever since. The duke asked Lottie a question, and she realized she wasn't listening.

"What was that?"

He steepled his fingers together and smiled. "I said I was thinking that I might buy a boat. What do you think about that?"

Lottie tilted her head and glanced at the large crystal chandelier hanging over the table. "Oh, I don't know." This room was too big to be comfortable. The table could seat at least twelve, and the duke was the only one who lived here. Did one person need this much space? It was a foreign thought, and Lottie was surprised it popped into her head. She'd always liked to have bigger and better things to show off.

Lady Anna smiled. "A boat would be a wonderful thing to have."

"I agree," said the duke, pushing his greasy hair back over his large forehead.

The duke flicked, like Lady Anna had. Lottie turned to her mother. Lady Anna was also blinking in and out. Lottie's stomach tightened, and she tried to push the fear away.

"Excuse me for a moment," she said, blotting her mouth and putting her napkin on the table.

The duke smiled. "Of course, my dear."

Lottie rushed from the room. Something was terribly wrong with her, and she had to figure out what it was. The doctor said she was fine, but he was obviously wrong. She rushed down the hallway and out the front door.

She hurried down the path and then turned and stared at the large manor in front of her. It stood four stories high with large balconies and beautiful foliage surrounding it. All this would be hers... and she didn't want it. This came as a tremendous shock. All of Lottie's life, all she had wanted was money and attention. What was wrong with her?

The ground shifted unsteadily beneath her feet, and sweat ran down her back. If she went down the road, it wouldn't be long before her mother found her. She wasn't in the mood to talk to her right now. If she walked through the forest, she was bound to come out and meet the road later on. Lottie dashed through the trees, ignoring the unstable ground.

Carson sank into a large, comfortable chair in front of the fireplace. He tossed his boots aside and stared into the flames. Everything was wrong. He laughed bitterly to himself. That wasn't a new revelation. Ever since he had come to this horrible place, things had been wrong. But now, things were wrong even for this world.

The door creaked open, and a large monkey entered, carrying a serving tray loaded with food. Carson was ready. He caught the tray when the monkey threw it to him. It only spilled a little. Carson growled, and the monkey jumped and scurried away.

"I don't understand why you need to scare him every time," a middle-aged man with brown hair and a fuzzy beard said, entering the room.

Carson ground his teeth as he glared at the short muscular man. "Yeah, and I don't understand why he throws it at me every meal."

The man regarded him thoughtfully and rubbed his chin. "He is a monkey, after all. If you want good servants, you might want to reconsider that."

Carson pounded his fist onto the chair's arm. "I already told you, Jurry. I didn't choose any of this. I didn't choose to look like this, have monkeys as servants, or to live in this dark, rundown castle."

Jurry pulled a footstool next to the fire and sat down. He leaned forward and rested his elbows on his knees. "None of us choose exactly what happens to us."

"Yes, but at least you aren't a monster." Carson looked down at his claws and scowled. "Do you know what it's like to keep fur clean? I used to be attractive."

Jurry chuckled. "I'll take your word for it."

"It wouldn't be so bad if things weren't so messed up. Where is the girl? She should be here by now."

Jurry frowned. "What girl? I still don't understand you most of the time. I never know when you are talking to me or muttering to yourself."

Carson's nostrils flared. "If I told you about my life, you wouldn't believe it."

"You might be surprised. I've seen some strange things as of late."

In all his years in this world, Carson had only tried to tell a few people what had happened to him. None of them believed him. Jurry might be different. Jurry and his brother Earl had gotten lost in the forest, and Carson had allowed them to stay in his castle. He had been a little wary of them at first, but it was nice to have someone to talk to.

Carson studied the man. "I'm from a different world."

"Ah," said Jurry, shifting on his seat. "We should get Earl for this."

"For what?" Earl asked, coming into the room. Carson was always surprised to see the two brothers together. They were both short and strong, but that was where any resemblance ended. Earl's hair was the reddest Carson had ever seen, and he was clean shaven. Jurry's beard looked like a small animal might be living inside.

Jurry glanced at his brother. "Carson says he's from a different world."

Earl nodded and pushed his red hair from his eyes. "I suspected something like that."

Carson's brows came together. "You believe me?"

"Sure," Earl said, sitting on the floor next to his brother. "Our friend Snow was from another world."

"Her name was Olivia," Jurry corrected his brother. "Snow was only her name in our story."

"Yeah, well, I'm still calling her Snow."

Carson leaned forward. "You know about the stories?"

"From what we learned, there are a lot of people stuck here," Jurry said. "We aren't even sure if we're real or just part of the fairy godmother's mixed up world."

"Fairy godmother?"

Jurry nodded. "Our friend Olivia had issues about love. I won't go deep into it, but a fairy godmother brought her here and made her act out a bunch of fairy tales. Every time she messed up, she had to do the day over. When she finally fell in love, she returned to her world."

Carson rubbed his furry chin. Could it be that easy? "That's the answer? I have to fall in love to get out of this place?"

Earl shrugged. "Tell us your story, and we'll try to help you."

Carson's heart was pounding. He had hope for the first time in years. It would have been nice to know earlier that he was supposed to be working toward something. "I was feeling down one day after a bad date. I decided I was done with dating. The subway was late, and I was in a bad mood. An old lady sat by me and started grilling me about my life. I tried to ignore her, but she wouldn't leave me alone. She wanted to know why I was so angry."

Earl rubbed his chin. "That must have been Nancy."

"I don't know if she told me her name. It was a long time ago. I finally told her that love was a waste of time. She got all teary-eyed and told me she would help fix me. I got off at the next stop to get away from her. When I stepped out, my vision blurred, and I woke up here. Well, not here, but in this world."

Jurry nodded. "That sounds similar to what Olivia told us."

Carson itched his furry arm. "I ended up in a fairy tale, and every time I didn't follow the story, the day started over. If I follow it, everything is fine."

Earl's eyes sparkled. "Then, you kiss the girl and poof. You're in a new story."

Carson blinked twice. "Exactly. I never wanted to kiss them, but they usually kissed me. If I'm supposed to be falling in love, I guess I've been doing it wrong."

Earl grinned. "I bet no girl is gonna want to kiss you now. Girls ain't into beasts."

Carson shrugged. "I don't care about that, but I want to get out of here. Something is wrong, though."

Jurry leaned forward. "What?"

"No girl has come this time. Everything seems off. If I'm going to be stuck here, I don't want it to be as a beast."

Earl tilted his head. "Things have been messed up. There's a man that hated the fairy godmother. His name is Terry. She brought him here, and he learned to do magic. He could flip through stories at will. Whatever he did messed up the stories, and everything got wonky."

Jurry frowned. "The world became unstable. Some of our brothers started blinking in and out. We aren't for sure, but we think that means they aren't real."

"I can't get stuck in this story. It might be tolerable if I looked like myself, even in this ruin of a castle, but being a beast is uncomfortable in so many ways." Carson glanced around the gloomy room. The gray stone was dull, and cobwebs filled all the corners. He'd thought about getting rid of them, but they were too high.

Earl grinned. "We can help you find a girl."

Carson shook his head. He was glad to see at least someone was amused at this horrible situation. "I don't think I can make myself fall in love."

"Have you ever been in love?" Earl asked.

Jurry glared at his brother. "Don't ask personal questions."

"It ain't personal."

"You're just saying that because you've never been in love."

"It's fine," Carson said quickly before the brothers got into a big fight. He didn't have siblings, and he wondered if it was normal for brothers to fight as much as these two did. They appeared to be in their late thirties. You would think they were old enough to be past childhood spats.

"Alright, Carson. Let's hear your heartbreak story," Earl said, leaning over and grabbing a handful of carrots from Carson's plate.

Carson sighed. He didn't want to tell his story, but if Jurry and Earl could offer him any insight into getting out of here, it would be worth it. It wasn't easy to speak with his large teeth getting in the way, and he hated his deep, gravelly voice.

"Growing up, I was best friends with a girl that lived next door to me," Carson remembered. "We had so much fun together. During high school, she became a cheerleader. All the cheerleaders dated people on the football team. I was on the track team."

Earl nodded. "I don't have any idea what half of those words mean, but I get the gist."

"I wanted to ask her to a dance, and I knew she loved attention. I set up an elaborate way to ask her during a track meet she was cheering at. Everyone's attention was on us. She laughed in my face and said no."

Earl frowned. "She laughed? Even though she was your friend?"

"Yeah," Carson said, hating the memory. "She tried to apologize later and thought I was being unreasonable to not forgive her. Maybe if she'd apologized in front of the entire school... It didn't make sense. I was popular and well liked. I just wasn't on the football team. She usually wasn't like that. I was surprised she would treat me that way after everything we'd been through together."

"So, you became a crusty old beast?" Jurry asked.

Carson rolled his eyes. "The beast thing only happened a few months ago, and I'm not old."

"Didn't deny being crusty, though, did he?" Earl said with a grin.

"I was eighteen when I came here. I don't know how long it's been."

"How many stories have you been in?" Jurry asked.

"I don't know. Six or seven. I was in the first one for a long time."

"So, what is this story?" Earl asked.

"I was sure it was *Beauty and the Beast* when I woke up looking like this. Now, I'm not so sure."

"How does that one go?"

"There is a spoiled prince that gets turned into a beast. He can't turn back until he gets someone to love him despite his appearance. I don't know the actual story, only the movie and play I saw. The movie was a lot more fun than this place."

Jurry rubbed his beard. "So, we gotta find someone to fall in love with you so you can change stories?"

"Something like that."

Earl studied him. "That might be hard. When we first met you, I darn near soiled myself. You're a little hard on the eyes."

Carson ignored that. "In the play, the girl's dad comes to the castle and steals a rose. The beast gets angry and demands he send his daughter. In all the time I've been in this story, you are the only people I've seen. I ran around the forest and never found a village or anything."

"Did the monkeys come with the castle?" Earl asked. "I like monkeys."

"Yeah. They clean up and cook. They won't leave, even though they're all scared of me."

"They don't clean very well," Jurry said, glancing around the dusty room.

"I've lived in some nice castles since I came here. It figures I might end up in this dump forever." Carson leaned back and sighed. He hoped this wasn't the place he would spend the rest of his life.

"We don't know if we've been in different stories," Jurry said. "I only remember one life. It's a bit depressing to think we might not be real."

"I betcha we're real," Earl said, sitting next to Jurry. "We aren't flickering like some of our brothers."

"Are there seven of you?" Carson asked. "You said Snow. Are you part of the seven dwarfs?"

Jurry glared at him. "Dwarfs? Just because we're a little shorter than the average man doesn't mean you can go calling us dwarfs."

Carson held his hands out in defense. "Sorry. There's a story called *Snow White and the Seven Dwarfs.*"

Earl shook his head. "Well, don't that beat all."

"What do you do for your jobs? Do you work in a mine?" Carson asked.

"Yeah," Jurry growled. "We're pretty good at it, too. Well, except our brother Roco. He's as lazy as anything. You don't get muscles like these from being idle."

"I think we need to leave this place as much as Carson does," Earl said. "It's strange not knowing anything. I dunno how I feel about being a part of someone else's story."

Chapter 2

Lottie woke up in the forest, covered in a light sprinkling of snow. She had never found the road, and after walking most of the night, she had fallen asleep. Hopping to her feet, she brushed the snow from her dress and folded her arms for warmth. Her sleeves were long but thin, not offering much heat. She didn't know which way she had come from, but with luck, her mother had sent out a search party.

She frowned and trudged through the trees. If she didn't know which way to go, this way was as good as any. It was so cold, and her stomach was complaining. Something fell onto Lottie's head, and she screamed. She pulled it off and threw it to the ground and stomped on it. She breathed deeply as she looked down at a pile of red cloth.

"Jumping at everything," she muttered, as she picked up the cloth. It was a cloak, and it was warm and dry. She gazed up into the trees, but there was nothing to be seen. She quickly pulled the cloak on, snuggling into the warmth. An owl flew by overhead and hooted. Had the owl dropped the cloak? Something nudged her leg, and she glanced down to see a red fox.

She gasped and backed up. "Good fox," she said, taking another step back. The fox had a branch with berries in his mouth. He came closer and dropped it at her feet. Lottie held a hand to her racing heart and bent down to scoop up the branch. "Thank you," she said, keeping a close eye on the animal. He scurried away into the bushes.

Lottie ate the berries as she walked. Everything in this forest felt peaceful. Nothing was spinning, and there were no people to flash in and out of existence. If it wasn't for the cold, she might be content to stay here a while. Her mother was going to be furious when she was found.

"Hey, lady," a man said, stepping into her path. Lottie startled, but composed herself. He didn't appear threatening. He was shorter than she was by a few inches and a little scrawny. The man studied her closely. "You lost?"

"Yes," Lottie said. She normally wouldn't admit that to a stranger, but she had few options. "Can you point me to the village?"

"I wish," the man said. "I'm lost myself."

"Oh," Lottie said, trying not to let her disappointment show.

"My brothers disappeared a while back, and I'm trying to find them. Mind if we travel together?"

Lottie was not a trusting person, but this man seemed harmless. "I suppose."

"I'm Roco."

"Lottie."

He tapped his lip with one finger. "Lottie, Lottie. Why does that name sound familiar?"

"My family is very affluent in the village," Lottie bragged. "My mother is Lady Anna. Perhaps you've heard of her?"

"It sounds familiar," Roco said. He smiled and snapped. "That's it! You are Olivia's wicked stepsister!"

Lottie wrinkled her nose. "Excuse me? I am not wicked, and I don't know anyone named Olivia."

"She told us all about you. I guess her name wasn't Olivia when she lived with you. You had a stepsister, right?"

"Yes, but her name was Ella."

"Right, she did say that. And you called her Cinderella."

Lottie's mouth formed a tight line. Ella was spreading stories. Sure, they hadn't treated her well, but—but what? She couldn't remember. Lottie tried to picture Ella, but her memory was acting up. First, Ella had blonde hair, then brown. Her face was even changing in Lottie's memory. She put a fist to her head. "I need to get home."

"Of course. Let's walk." Roco ambled through the trees, and Lottie hurried to catch up.

Lottie glanced sideways at the man. "How did you know Ella?"

"She wasn't really Ella," Roco explained. "Her name was Olivia, and a fairy brought her here from a different world. She went back, though."

Lottie snorted. "Back to the other world?"

"Yes."

This man was crazy. Still, she would rather travel with a crazy man than by herself. The red fox ran out from the trees and dropped another branch of berries at her feet.

"You know this fellow?" Roco asked, bending down and patting the fox's head. The fox rubbed against Roco's hand.

"He brought me some berries a few minutes ago."

Roco rubbed the fox's ears. "What should we call him?"

"I don't know," Lottie said, picking up the branch.

"I'll call him Max."

Lottie nodded and kept walking. The snow was coming down harder. "I think an owl dropped this cloak to me."

He nodded. "The animals in these woods are very accommodating."

Lottie's headache pulsed. "It appears so."

They walked in silence, and Lottie tried to sort the strange dreams she'd had the night before. In one, she had been in a crowded hallway with a bunch of people her age. It felt so familiar. It was chaotic with people going every direction, talking and yelling to one another. She'd been pushed around a few times. It felt so much more real than a dream. It felt like a memory.

"Is that the owl you saw?" Roco asked, pointing into the sky. The white owl flew overhead.

"I think so."

"She's pretty. Strange, she's out during the day. I'll call her Aspen. Hey, Aspen!" he called. "Come down here!"

Lottie rolled her eyes. "If you just named her, she won't recognize the name."

The owl flew down and landed in the tree to the side of them.

"Sure, she does," Roco said. "Hi, Aspen. Lottie wants to thank you for the cloak." The owl looked at Lottie and cocked its head. Did she actually understand what Roco was saying?

"Yes, um, thank you," Lottie stuttered.

The fox grabbed the hem of Lottie's dress in his teeth and pulled forward. Lottie let him lead her. They walked around a large tree and Lottie gasped as a castle appeared in the distance.

"Wow," Roco said, coming up beside her. "That castle looks old."

"I'm surprised it's here," Lottie said, squinting through the snow. "I've never heard of a castle in this area."

"Yes, well, everything has been wrong lately. I wouldn't be surprised if it disappeared before our eyes."

Lottie put a hand to her middle. "What do you mean, wrong?"

"People blinking in and out, the ground rumbling. That kind of thing."

"I thought it was only me," Lottie said with a surge of relief. "I feared I was dying or something."

Roco shook his head. "No, there is definitely something wrong."

Lottie shivered. "I'm terrified, but relieved it's not only me."

"Should we go to the castle?"

"Do you think anyone lives there? It doesn't appear well cared for."

"I don't know. It's at least out of the snow."

"Did you hear that?" Jurry asked.

Carson looked up from the checkerboard. "What?"

"It sounded like a knock."

Carson's heart sped up. Could it finally be the girl? Or even her father? He wasn't going to be picky. Anything to get this story moving would be nice. He jumped from his seat, knocking the checkerboard to the floor, and dashed across the castle. It didn't matter what the girl was like. He was going to try his hardest to fall in love with her. He needed to leave this world.

Throwing open the two large wooden doors, he found two people. The man's eyes widened, and the girl screamed and turned to flee. He was such a fool. He'd forgotten he was an enormous, ugly beast.

"Stop!" Carson roared. He grabbed the girl's arm, and she turned to him, her eyes full of fear. He stared with unbelief into her familiar eyes.

"Let me go!" she demanded, pulling backwards.

"Charlotte?"

"Let her go!" the man said, finally finding his voice.

"I'm not a monster," Carson said in a low voice. He didn't want to scare them more than he already had. "I'm a person. A fairy changed me." It sounded lame, but Charlotte seemed to relax a little.

"Roco? What are you doing here?" Jurry asked, pounding the visitor on the back.

Roco crossed his arms. "I've been searching all over for you guys. Why'd you leave? Is Earl here?"

"Yes, let me take you to him."

Roco side-eyed Carson. "What about the monster?"

Jurry grinned. "He's harmless. His name's Carson." The two men pushed past him and disappeared into the castle.

Charlotte was still breathing deeply and watching him suspiciously. He released her arm and moved backwards so she could come in. She hesitated but entered. A small red fox followed her inside. He shrugged. It wasn't like it could damage anything.

"Follow me. I have a fire going." He felt awkward.

It had been a long time since he'd seen Charlotte, and she was as beautiful as he remembered. He tried to push back the bitterness of their last meeting. She followed behind him, and he tried to decide the best way to tell her who he was.

"Here we are," he said. She rushed to the fireplace and kneeled before it, holding her hands close to the orange flames. "Monkey, bring something warm to eat!" he yelled, startling Charlotte. He wasn't sure where the monkeys hung out when they weren't in front of him, but yelling commands usually worked. "How did you get here?" he asked her.

She peered up at him, her eyes still showing fear. "I–I got lost in the forest."

He rolled his eyes. "I mean, how did you get to this world?"

Her eyebrows came together, and she frowned. "I don't understand. I've always been in this world."

Carson ran a paw over his face. Maybe she didn't know she'd switched worlds. It was possible she had just gotten here.

"I'm Carson."

"Lottie."

"I mean, I'm Carson. Carson Johnson. From next door."

Charlotte raised her eyebrow. "I don't understand."

He sighed. He didn't know how to be more clear than that. "Come on, Charlotte. We lived next door to each other our entire lives."

"I think you have me confused with someone. My name isn't Charlotte. It's just Lottie."

"That's impossible. I would know you anywhere. We went to school together?"

Her eyes narrowed. "I don't think so."

"Maybe she just looks like someone," Jurry said, entering the room with Earl and the other man close on his heels. "This is our brother Roco." Carson's eyes raised in surprise. Jurry and Earl were muscular and fit. Roco was thin and didn't look like he had ever seen a day of work in his life.

"I know this is Charlotte," Carson said. "I've known her my whole life."

"Can we go somewhere else?" Charlotte asked Roco. "I'm not comfortable here."

"There isn't anywhere to go," Carson assured her. "I've been all around this area, and I couldn't find any other people."

The red fox curled up next to her, and she patted it awkwardly.

"Charlotte, you have to remember me. Of course, I didn't look like this."

Her eyes opened wide. "My name is Lottie, and I don't know you."

"Then, where are you from?"

She hesitated. "The village."

"Which one?"

Her eyebrow arched, and she crossed her arms. The fear was gone from her eyes, and she appeared annoyed. "This is ridiculous. I hope my mother sends a search party for me soon."

"Who is your mother?"

"Lady Anna."

He raised his eyebrows. "Your mother's name is Susan."

Her glare deepened. "I think I know my mother's name."

"Stop bothering her," Roco said. "She doesn't have to tell you anything."

"Carson is trapped in this story like Olivia was," Earl told his brother. "We need to help get him out of here."

Roco shrugged. "What does that have to do with Lottie?"

"Maybe she's forgotten her real life. Or she's going crazy like Terry."

"I'm not crazy," she pouted.

Carson studied her. Was it possible to forget who you were? Perhaps she'd been here too long.

"She is one of Olivia's evil stepsisters," Roco said. "She don't seem too evil, though."

"I'm not evil," Lottie protested.

He shrugged. "Maybe not, but you weren't nice to Olivia."

Lottie's bottom jaw moved back and forth, and Carson knew they were all going to get a tongue lashing if things didn't calm down soon. He remembered that look.

A monkey entered the room with a serving tray. It had two cups of hot chocolate and some rolls. The monkey took the tray to Lottie and handed it to her. She placed it on the floor and thanked the monkey. It jumped up and down and then ran from the room.

"Why didn't he throw it at her?" Carson wondered.

"Because she ain't a scary beast," Jurry said, grinning.

Lottie picked up a mug and took a sip.

"The only way I know of to get out of this place is if we kiss," Carson said, watching her closely.

Lottie choked on the hot chocolate and wiped her mouth. "Kiss? I don't think so."

"I'm not really a beast. If we kiss, we will leave this story and go to a different one." He had given up on his idea of falling in love with whatever girl came. Charlotte had made it clear she wasn't willing to go to one dance with him. She definitely wasn't going to fall in love with him.

She grabbed a roll and ripped it in half. "I don't know what you mean. I just need to get home."

Lottie sat on a large, fluffy bed and cried. Max was curled up on her lap, sleeping. The room was large and dimly lit and almost echoed from its lack of furnishings. It had a nice wardrobe made of oak, and one small bookcase full of ancient books. She should be happy this room was so nice compared to the rest of the castle, but all she could think about was how confusing everything was. Why did the name Carson Johnson feel so familiar? She knew he didn't live next to her. They didn't have any houses close by.

The fireplace in the corner flickered, and she watched it with blurry eyes. At least she didn't have to spend another night out in the forest with all the wild animals and the spiders. Though, she probably didn't have to worry about bugs in this weather.

A knock sounded at her door, and she froze. She hoped it was a monkey. She had never seen animals act the way the ones in this forest did. Max seemed tame, and so did the monkeys.

She wiped her eyes. "Come in."

Carson poked his enormous head in the door, and she looked down. He was unnerving with his fangs and enormous claws. "I thought of a way to prove I know you," he said.

"Oh?"

"You have a scar on the bottom of your foot. You cut it on some glass when we were playing in a field when we were ten."

Lottie's eyes locked on him. How did he know about her scar? She couldn't remember how she got it, but it had always been there.

"This world isn't real," he told her. "We need to get out of here."

Panic filled Lottie's middle, and a tear ran down her face. She wasn't used to crying. She usually got whatever she wanted, so she'd had no reason. Normally, she would dismiss Carson's claim, but something told her he was telling the truth.

"Don't cry," he said gruffly. "We'll figure it out."

"Things have been strange since my stepsister got married," she admitted. "My mother and some villagers have been flickering in and out. Sometimes they disappear for a few seconds at a time. I keep getting headaches and having strange dreams."

"Jurry and Earl told me about a fairy godmother. They said she brings people to this world and has them act out stories. It sounds like things got messed up. The stories aren't progressing right."

"So, you're saying my whole life is a story?"

"Possibly. It sounds like you've been stuck in *Cinderella*."

Lottie flinched. That was what she used to call Ella. Strange that he should know that. She listened while he told her the story of *Cinderella*. The more he told, the more she frowned.

"So, Ella got what she wanted, and I'm the villain."

"It's not your fault. The fairy godmother manipulates the story, it seems."

"All I ever wanted was to make a beneficial match and have people admire me. I know it's a horrible way to be, but I can't seem to help it. Was I like that in your world?"

The beast tilted his head. "You did like people to admire you, but you weren't heartless. At least, not most of the time."

Lottie bit her lip. She'd been hoping he would say she was a better person. Sometimes she felt like doing better, but her vanity always won in the end.

"Are you alright?" he asked.

Lottie nodded. "I need time to think."

He nodded and closed the door. Lottie climbed onto the bed and curled up in a ball. If Carson was right, not only had she been stuck in a story, but she wasn't even the main character. She was a distasteful side character. Max rolled up near her head, and she rubbed his back. At least he seemed to like her.

Chapter 3

Carson sat in his chair and yawned. He spent too much time sitting. If he wasn't careful, the chair would have his shape permanently carved into it. Still, he couldn't motivate himself to get up. It was still early, and the castle was quiet.

The door burst open, and he turned to see Lottie. Her brown hair was tangled, and she was wearing the same rumpled red dress from the day before. What had he expected? He hadn't found her anything else to wear.

"Carson!" she said, rushing toward him. "Did you have blond hair and a blue shirt?"

He held back a tired grin. "Yes, on the hair. I'm sure I've owned a blue shirt or two over the years."

"I had a dream that I was talking to someone over a white fence. I called him Carson."

"We used to talk over the fence all the time." This was progress. She must believe him.

"So, we were good friends?"

"We were," he said, grinding his teeth.

She smiled. "I've never had friends."

He took a deep breath through his snout and let it out slowly. He'd been angry with her for so long, but now didn't seem the time to tell her that. "You had a lot of friends. You were popular."

She rubbed her upper arms. "I feel so conflicted. It's like I'm two people. One of them is lost, and I'm losing the other."

Pink smoke rose in front of the fireplace, and an older woman in a long pink dress appeared. Lottie screamed and jumped back. Carson hardly flinched. He'd been in this world long enough to not get ruffled by something unexpected.

The woman pushed her long silver hair over her shoulder and frowned. "You are lost, indeed," she said, glaring at Lottie. "How did you get here? You are in the wrong story."

"You must be the fairy godmother," Carson said.

"Of course. I'm Nancy. Don't you remember me?" she asked, placing her hands on her hips.

Carson nodded. She was the woman he'd talked to in the subway.

"Hey, Nancy," Roco said, entering the room with a handful of raw peas. He popped a few into his mouth. "I'd like to say it's nice to see you again, but there must be a problem if you're here."

Her forehead creased. "Roco. What are you doing here?"

He shrugged. "Don't know. Jurry and Earl are here, too."

"Move," Nancy commanded, pointing at Carson. He got off his chair, and she sank into it. "How can this be?" she muttered. She sat tall and studied them.

"You sent me here," Carson accused. "Send me home."

"But you haven't made any progress," Nancy said. "I brought you here to help you find purpose in your life. It's my calling in life to help people find their happy ever after."

Carson growled. "I haven't been happy since I came here."

She gazed up at the ceiling. "That's because you haven't tried."

"So, I have to fall in love before you'll send me home?"

She smiled. "That's how it works."

"What about me?" Lottie asked.

The smile slid from Nancy's face. "You are beyond fixing."

Lottie raised her brow. "Excuse me?"

"I'll return you to your story shortly. You too, Roco."

"Everything is messed up," Roco said. "Ever since Olivia left, nothing has been stable."

Nancy put a hand to her head. "I was afraid of that. Terry messed the world up. I thought it would slowly fix itself, but it appears it hasn't."

"Send us all home," Carson growled. "We don't need you meddling in our lives."

She shook her head. "Lottie and Roco don't even remember their old lives. There is no reason to send them."

Lottie's eyes hadn't left the woman. "I'm starting to remember a different life."

Nancy frowned. "That shouldn't be possible."

"My mother keeps flickering out, and everything is confusing."

"Why can't Charlotte remember her life?" Carson asked. "She only barely remembers me."

Nancy's forehead furrowed. "Remembers you? Why would she remember you? You were never in the same story."

"We grew up next door to each other."

"Oh," Nancy said, tapping her lip. "Wait. Lottie is the girl? The one who broke your heart?"

Carson growled. He didn't want Lottie knowing that. Lottie's eyebrows knit together, and she frowned.

Nancy's face lit up with a smile. "Maybe hope isn't lost for the two of you. What are the odds you two would both end up being selected by me? It must be fate!"

"Why did you say I was beyond fixing?" Lottie demanded.

"When I brought you here, you were as stubborn as anything. You wouldn't finish a single story. I prodded and pushed for months, and you would not cooperate. When people are that uncooperative, they eventually become a side character in a story and forget who they are."

"I thought you were trying to make people's lives better," Roco said.

"I am. Releasing people like that back into the world isn't in the best interest of the rest of the world."

"So, you just left me here?" Lottie asked.

Nancy beamed. "Yes, and you've played the part nicely, for seven different Cinderellas."

"What about me?" Roco asked.

"Pretty much the same. You and Jurry and Earl. All stubborn."

"So, we have another life somewhere?"

"You did. I think you are happier here. You've met a lot of nice Snow Whites."

Roco crossed his arms. "But Jurry fell in love with Meena, and you never let him leave."

"Jurry? And Meena?" Nancy frowned. "How did I miss that? I've never had people I'd given up on fall in love. This is giving me a lot to think about. Perhaps I'll send them home."

"You need to be stopped," Carson said. "It isn't your job to mold people into who you think they should be."

Her eyes narrowed. "How do you know what my job is? I don't have time to sit and argue with you. I was going to return you all to your stories, but I'll let you play this out. Hopefully, I'll have all the bugs ironed out soon and things will stop glitching."

"You can't leave us here," Carson grumbled.

"I've learned a lot this year," Nancy said. "You should be happy to benefit from it."

"What have you learned?"

"I used to believe it was enough to get people to believe in love. Things were messy because most of the characters in this world aren't real. When people fell in love, it was with the idea, not the person. Now I've realized putting two real people together makes for a better ending."

Carson narrowed his eyes. "It seems like that would be obvious."

"Yes, well, live and learn." She stood and smiled. "Try to get along." A poof of pink smoke appeared as she vanished.

Carson growled. "She is so infuriating."

Lottie raised an eyebrow. "What did she mean, I was the one who broke your heart?"

"Sounds pretty self-explanatory to me," Roco said.

Carson fought the urge to scream. "You didn't break my heart. I don't have a heart to break."

Roco grinned. "Poetic and dramatic."

"Then, what was she talking about?" Lottie asked.

Carson sighed. "That woman—"

"Nancy," Roco interrupted.

Carson rolled his eyes. "Nancy doesn't know what she's talking about. I met her once for about ten minutes, and in that small amount of time, she made a lot of assumptions."

"So, I didn't break your heart?"

"Not at all," Carson lied. "We grew up as friends. We drifted apart over time, and I guess Nancy took that to mean something it didn't. Friends grow apart all the time. It wasn't a big deal."

Lottie nodded. "I see."

The door banged open, and three monkeys entered, carrying breakfast. One handed a tray to Roco, one to Lottie, and the third one threw Carson's on his chair. He growled and scooped it up. He should probably work on his relationship with the monkeys. It would be nice to eat food that hadn't been thrown onto him or his chair every now and then.

Lottie slowly chewed her ham as she studied Carson. She wasn't sure what she thought about him. It was hard to see past his beastly appearance. His teeth alone were frightening, and his claws were so sharp. She wouldn't want to anger him. Still, he didn't act threatening.

From what Nancy said, Lottie assumed she wasn't a much better person in her real life than she was here. *Beyond fixing.* That was what Nancy had said. Was she really that bad? She thought back to the way she had treated Ella. She'd probably never been kind to her. Sometimes she thought about being nice, but the words seemed stuck in her throat.

If she understood correctly, the way she acted here wasn't her fault. It was nice to be able to blame your shortcomings on someone else, but if she had been unpleasant before she came here, that was all on her. She wished she could remember more. Carson said her mother's name was Susan. It didn't feel familiar.

"You alright, Lottie?" Roco asked through a mouthful of eggs.

"Yes, just thinking."

"I wonder what my life was before I came here," Roco said. "I wonder how much of our personality is who we actually are and how much has been manipulated. It seems wrong to mess with someone's thoughts."

"It is wrong," Carson said. "I guess I'm lucky I still remember who I am. I better figure a way out before I forget."

Lottie frowned. "I doubt you will forget. Nancy didn't say anything about you being beyond fixing."

Roco speared a piece of egg with his fork. "I hope I'm more productive in my real life."

"Doubtful," said Earl, as he entered the room. Roco quickly caught him up on what Nancy had told them.

"Hm. Well, I suppose that makes a lot more sense of what just happened," said Earl. "I was talking to Jurry and poof! He disappeared. I figured Nancy was behind it, so I wasn't too concerned."

"Now what?" Lottie asked. "If I'm in the wrong story, how will my mother find me?"

"She isn't your actual mother," said Carson. "You don't need to be found, you need to get out of this world all together."

Lottie took a deep breath and set her plate on the floor. Didn't this place have a kitchen? "I suppose I don't want to go back anyway. If I do, I'll have to marry Rodney."

Carson grabbed a handful of eggs. Lottie pursed her lips. Sure, he had claws, but that didn't mean he shouldn't try to use a fork. "Who is Rodney?"

"The Duke of Aldertown. He's quite wealthy." Lottie didn't know why she added the last part, and she hated the snobby sound of her voice.

"So, what's wrong with him?" Earl asked.

"He's disgusting. I can barely tolerate him. I thought I could because he has a large estate and an excellent position in society, but the more I'm around him, the more discontent I am."

Carson snorted. "Figures you were going to marry him for his position. A vast estate and a lot of money is probably even better than someone on the football team."

Lottie glared at him. She didn't know what a football team was, but she was sure she'd been insulted.

"Let's all be calm and decide what to do," Earl said. "It sounds like we all need to fall in love to get out of here. I suppose Lottie and Carson could try to fall in love, but that doesn't seem likely to me. Me and Roco need to find some women, or we will be stuck here forever."

"I don't know where we can find any people," Carson said. "I've searched all around and never even found a village. It would be better if we were in a different story."

"Why?" Lottie asked.

"Because I'm a beast. How am I going to find someone to fall in love with me when I look like this?" he asked, holding out his arms.

Lottie shrugged. He had a point. She didn't know what she wanted to do. She didn't feel desperate to get to her real life because she didn't remember it.

"I suppose you could kiss Lottie and change stories. That would leave me and Earl stuck here, though," said Roco.

Earl rolled his eyes. "They ain't in love."

"So? The story changes with a kiss. Not love. If it was love, the people would go home, not to another story."

"I suppose you're right," Earl said, scratching his head.

Lottie got to her feet. "I am not kissing a beast."

"Once again, not a surprise," said Carson.

Lottie's lips formed a tight line. What did Carson have against her? It was obvious there was something he wasn't telling her.

Roco's mouth turned down. "I guess we could set out in a direction and hope we come across some people. That sounds tiring."

"Everything sounds tiring to you," Earl said. "If you were any lazier, we would have to make sure you were breathing."

"You've been working in a mine for ages, and what do you have to show for it?" Roco asked.

Earl grinned. "A lot of money and muscle."

Roco shrugged. "I don't know what I'd do with muscle, and we share money, so I ain't hurting there."

"We might cut you off someday. Then, where will you be?"

"We should look for a village," Lottie said, hoping the brothers would stop fighting. She wondered if she'd sounded that bad when she fought with Mara. "I don't want to stay here forever."

"Not good enough for you?" Carson asked, crossing his arms.

Lottie scowled and put her hands on her hips. "No, it's not good enough for me. It's not good enough for anyone. It's about to fall apart over our heads."

"I guess we could try," Carson said. "We might have to travel pretty far." He might have been frowning, but with that mouth, who would really know?

"Perhaps Max can help," Lottie said. "The animals in the woods seem oddly helpful."

"We had a wolf helping us for a while," Earl said. "It might help to ask the fox."

"If we find a village, then what?" Carson asked. "All the people will be after me with their pitchforks."

"You don't have to come," Lottie said. She would be happy to leave him behind.

He glowered at her. "I'll come, but I don't understand why you can't kiss me. How would you feel if you were stuck like this?" He held out his arms so she could study him. "It's not like I'm asking you to marry me, just one little kiss."

Lottie swallowed hard. She would hate to be stuck like that, but kissing him was more than she could bear. She had been waiting a long time to get someone to kiss her, and a beast was not her idea of a nice first kiss. Still, was it fair to leave someone like that when she had the power to help? She imagined herself kissing Carson with his huge mouth and enormous sharp teeth and she shuddered.

"Whatever," Carson muttered. "We can leave tomorrow morning." He stomped across the room and left, slamming the door behind him.

Lottie sank into Carson's massive chair and covered her face with her hands.

"One kiss seems like a reasonable request, considering the circumstances," said Earl. "He might not be so ornery if he was a human again."

Lottie peeked over her fingers. "Did you know him when he was a human?"

"No," Earl said, pushing his red bangs from his eyes. "I only met him a week or so ago."

"I feel like there is a fight going on inside of me," Lottie said. "It's like I'm two people, and I can't pull the right one out."

"Nancy said we were other people, too," Roco said. "I'm not gonna bother trying to remember. If the memories come, they come. If not, I don't remember anyway, so there isn't anything to miss."

Lottie didn't understand his attitude. She wanted to know who she was, not remain a puppet.

Chapter 4

Charlotte jogged down the aisles of the store, searching for Carson. He was probably hiding somewhere she wouldn't want to look. Last time he'd done this to her, he'd hidden in the tire area because he knew she hated the rubbery smell. She'd already checked that area with no success. Carson might be her best friend, but she hated when he did this.

She slowed down and glanced over the children's clothing. He might be hiding in the middle of a display. She should probably stop looking for him when he does this. Or she should be the one to hide. Then, he would know how annoying it was. He might be trying to get her back for all the times she'd jumped out and scared him over the years.

"You seem lost," said a teenage girl in a blue vest with a name tag. "Can I help you?"

"I'm looking for my friend," she admitted. "I think he's hiding from me."

The girl rolled her eyes and pointed over her shoulder. "I saw some guy squatting down behind the strollers. I was going to call security, but if I called security for every person I saw hiding from their friends, I'd probably get fired for bothering them all the time."

"Thanks," Charlotte said, making her way toward the baby section. There were two ways to get to the strollers. You could come from the front or from behind. She smiled as she creeped up from the back. She could scare him, and he wouldn't see it coming.

When she got to the display, she bent down and peeked around the metal shelving. The space between the shelving and the strollers was empty. Charlotte frowned and stood up. He must have moved.

She spun around and smashed into someone. Jumping back, she glanced up to apologize only to see Carson standing there with a big smile on his blurry face. Why was his face blurry? He laughed, and she punched him in the shoulder.

He tilted his head and grinned. "What was that for?"

"You need to stop hiding from me every time we go any-where. It's annoying."

Carson laughed. "Not as annoying as when you get my mom to let you hide in my closet. You probably took ten years off my life last time you did that."

Charlotte smiled. She really had scared him that time. "That's different. I'm just keeping you on your toes."

Carson arched his brow. "On my toes? You scared me so bad, I tripped and fell over my laundry basket. I'd say you were keeping me on my head."

She giggled at the memory. "You shouldn't leave your laundry in the middle of the floor."

"Yeah, well, once you stop scaring me, I'll stop hiding from you."

"We better hurry and find the present for your mom," she said, rubbing her eyes. "I think I might have a migraine coming on."

"Uh oh. I can take you home and come back myself."

"I'm okay right now," she said, trying to get her vision to focus.

"Are you seeing spots?"

"Not yet. Everything is a little blurry."

Carson draped his arm over her shoulders. "Alright, I can hurry." He led them over to the pink and red Valentine's display and ran his eyes over the pink balloons filled with teddy bears.

"I always wonder how they get things in the balloons," she said, stepping away from him. She picked up a balloon with a small red bear inside. It was holding a heart.

"I dunno," Carson said, taking the balloon from her. "Should I get this one?"

"Does your mom want a teddy bear in a balloon? It seems a little... juvenile."

Carson shrugged. "I don't think it's so much what she wants as much as she wants to know I'm thinking about her. I know she's expecting something because she told me not to worry about getting her anything."

Charlotte picked up a silver heart locket and turned it around a few times. "And that means she wants something?"

"That's what I figure. I never would have thought about getting her a Valentine's present if she hadn't said anything. She was definitely hinting."

"Well, get her something she actually wants. I mean, I'd be happy to get a stuffed bear in a balloon, but that doesn't feel like your mom to me."

Carson placed the balloon back in its place. "My parents probably think my presents have gotten a lot better over the years. In sixth grade, I went to the dollar store and got my mom a plastic spatula and my dad a putty knife."

Charlotte smiled. "I'm sure they acted like it was the best thing in the world."

"Yeah. I was so proud of myself that I got them the same thing the next year."

"Look at that red sweater," Charlotte said, walking across the aisle. "This seems like something your mom would like."

Carson grabbed it from the rack and grinned. "Perfect. Thanks, Char."

"I'm going to go wait in the car while you pay," she said, rubbing her temples. "Maybe if I close my eyes for a minute, I won't get a headache."

She hurried out to Carson's car and got into the passenger's seat. Her head felt fine, but it never took long for a headache to creep up once her eyes started acting up. She closed her eyes and leaned against the seat. It was strange that nothing seemed blurry except Carson.

After a few minutes, Charlotte heard the trunk open and close, and Carson got into the driver's seat.

"Are you okay?"

"Yeah. I should probably get home and take something before it gets bad."

When they pulled into Carson's driveway, he hopped out and opened the door for her. Carson might be the class clown, but he was always helpful when she needed him. She walked across the Johnsons' lawn and up to her door.

"Hey, Lottie," Carson said, jogging up behind her. "I got you something." She turned around and frowned. No one had ever called her Lottie. Carson handed her a balloon with a bear in it and the locket she had been admiring earlier.

Charlotte's insides melted. Carson was giving her a Valentine's present? "What's this for?" she asked, her heart pounding in her chest.

"If I'm giving my mom a present for Valentine's Day, then I should give a present to my best friend."

"Right," she said, glancing down at her gifts. What had she been expecting?

"I mean, you don't deserve it or anything," Carson said.

Charlotte's eyes flew to him, and her heart dropped in her stomach. He crossed his arms and frowned. At least, she thought he frowned. He was pretty blurry.

"What do you mean?" she asked.

"Did you get me anything?" he asked. "No, you didn't. You won't even give me one kiss."

She swallowed and stepped back. Carson wanted her to kiss him?

"You're punishing me because I don't look exactly the way you want. What's wrong with a little fur?" Carson held out his arms, and he morphed into a beast.

Charlotte screamed and ran into the house.

Lady Anna walked around the corner and frowned. "What is with all the noise, Lottie?"

"You aren't my mother," she said. "T-this is a dream."

Lady Anna arched her eyebrow and left the room.

Charlotte looked down at the bear. "It's just a dream."

Carson watched Lottie pull her cloak more securely around herself. Perhaps it hadn't been wise to set out on a journey in the snow. It might be alright if they had a plan, or knew where they were going, but they were wandering without a destination. He wasn't cold, thanks to Nancy and his permanent fur coat.

They had set out early this morning, and if Carson was calculating correctly, it was getting close to noon. In the beginning, Roco and Earl kept everyone talking, but now they were quietly trudging through the snow. Max followed them, and an owl Roco called Aspen flew over about once every hour.

Lottie looked miserable. Carson had found her a warm dress and good boots, but she still shivered. Earl didn't seem bothered by the snow, but Roco suggested going back about every thirty minutes.

Talking to Lottie would probably help keep them both distracted, but Carson didn't have anything he wanted to say to her. He knew it wasn't nice of him, but he was still holding a grudge. It didn't seem fair to her since she didn't even remember embarrassing him in front of the entire school. Heck, she didn't remember him at all.

"What if we walk forever and never find anything?" Roco asked. "If this isn't a real world, who knows what it's like? Maybe we should go back."

Earl nudged his brother. "You just want to go back and sit by the fire and act lazy."

"Should we go back, Lottie?"

Lottie glanced over her shoulder. "I don't know."

Carson wanted to growl. They could end the story now if Lottie wasn't so stubborn. He understood not wanting to kiss a beast, but these weren't normal circumstances. The way he saw it, if they were to kiss, they would both be kissing a beast.

Lottie stopped and scanned the ground until her eyes fell on Max. "Max, do you know where we can find more people?"

The fox tilted his head, turned to the left, and scampered into a dense group of trees.

"Do we follow?" Earl asked.

"I'm going to," Lottie said, hurrying after the fox. Carson sighed and changed his direction. He might not want to spend his time with Lottie, but he would still feel guilty if she ended up lost and alone. That wasn't likely to happen, though. Roco and Earl would probably choose to follow her over him.

"I see smoke up ahead," Earl said.

Roco yawned. "I could use a rest by a fire."

"What if they aren't friendly?" Lottie asked.

"They won't be when they see Carson," said Earl. "You should stay back until we have a chance to explain your appearance."

"Good thing you thought of that," said Carson. "I forget I'm a monster sometimes."

"Lottie should probably stay back as well," said Roco. "We might be walking into anything."

"I'll go myself," Earl volunteered. "No sense in everyone walking into danger."

Earl vanished behind some trees, and the others waited. The snow was coming down harder. Carson couldn't believe he'd agreed to this plan. They should have waited for spring.

Max twisted around Lottie's legs until she picked him up. She rubbed his red fur and cuddled him against her.

"I thought you didn't like animals?" Carson said.

She shrugged. "As far as I know, I've been indifferent to them. I like Max, though."

"What about Aspen?" Roco asked.

"She's beautiful," Lottie said. "She makes me a little nervous, though. Her claws are a bit scary."

"Everything with claws is scary," Carson said, looking at his hands.

"Owls have talons, not claws," said Roco.

"It's the same to me. There's Earl," she said, pointing.

Earl came tromping through the snow. "They're friendly, come on." He led them toward a small group of men. Now Carson understood what the others had been talking about when they said people were flickering. Of the seven men sitting around the fire, six of them were blinking in and out.

All the men watched Carson with wary expressions. The one that wasn't fading in and out stood. He was tall with brown eyes and sandy brown hair that was almost as unruly as Earl's. "Sit by the fire and have some stew." Lottie, Roco, and Earl eagerly joined the men, but Carson hung back and sat a few feet away. He didn't want to give them reason to fear him.

"So, tell me who you are," the man said. "We've already met Earl."

"I'm Roco, and this here is Lottie. The fox is Max, and over there is Carson."

"Nice to meet you all," the man said. Carson didn't fail to notice the bow slung over the man's shoulder. "My name is Robin."

"Robin Hood, I assume?" Carson asked, as one of the men nervously handed him a bowl.

Robin smiled. "Ah. You've heard of me."

Carson just nodded.

"Well, perhaps you can tell us where we are? We seem to be a bit lost."

"Probably not any more lost than we are," Earl said, taking a bite of stew.

"Are you really Robin Hood?" Carson asked.

The man raised his brow. "What do you mean?"

"Are you Robin Hood, or are you someone Nancy sent here to play out her stupid stories?"

"Don't say stupid stories," Earl said. "Nancy won't ever let you leave with an attitude like that."

Robin stared at him and then looked up at the sky. "I don't know anyone named Nancy."

Carson gobbled down his stew. He hadn't realized how hungry he was.

Robin was shifting uncomfortably on the ground, and he kept studying Carson and the others. The men with him seemed content to eat their stew in silence.

"Maybe we should travel together," Roco said. "You know, safely in numbers."

"I'm not sure that would be a good idea," Carson said. "I doubt we're searching for the same thing."

"Can you tell me about this Nancy woman you mentioned?" Robin asked. "Does she have silver hair and ask a lot of personal questions?"

"That's her," Roco said through a mouthful of stew. "She's some type of fairy godmother. She likes to interfere with people's lives. She brings people here and makes them stay until they learn to believe in love."

"Interesting," Robin said, rubbing his chin. "That's the only way out?"

Roco nodded. "That's how it works."

"Do I know you?" Robin asked Lottie.

She sniffed. "I doubt we run in the same circles."

Carson shook his head. Didn't she know not to insult the person feeding her?

"Sorry," she muttered.

Robin smiled. "I recognize you. Stepsister number one."

"Excuse me?"

"You were the oldest stepsister in Cinderella. We danced once at the palace."

"I never danced with you," Lottie said, placing her bowl in the snow beside her.

Robin nodded. "You did. Cinderella was a long time ago, but I remember."

"I only danced with two people at the palace," Lottie said. "One was the prince, and one was Rodney."

"I was the prince."

"You don't look a thing like the prince."

Earl turned to Lottie. "Remember what Nancy said? She said you had been the stepsister to a bunch of Cinderellas."

Lottie sighed. "It's not fair that I don't get to remember things."

"How long have you been here?" Carson asked.

Robin smiled, but he looked tired. "I don't know. It's felt so long. It wasn't too bad until recently."

"That's because Nancy's world is falling apart," Roco said. He explained everything they knew to Robin. The men with him didn't seem interested. They just kept eating.

"I wondered what could be going on. My men follow me around, but they've stopped interacting for the most part. They keep blinking in and out of existence. One vanished for an entire minute yesterday."

"Come with us," Earl said. "We're trying to figure a way out of here."

"I've been trying to get out of this world for a long time. I didn't think it was possible until you all came." He stood and picked up a bag. He rummaged around in it and pulled out a book.

"What's that?" Earl asked.

"A diary. Is it yours?" he asked Lottie.

She stared at the book. "I've never seen it before."

"It belongs to someone named Charlotte Anne McLinn."

"That's you, Lottie," Carson said. "Or it was."

Lottie bit her lip. "I don't think so."

"I found it about a month ago, just sitting in the dirt. I've read it several times, as there is nothing else to do around here. The girl wrote things about a guy named Carson Johnson."

Carson stared at the book. He wished he could read it, but it might make him even more irritated toward Lottie than he already was.

"It's not mine," Lottie said.

"Can I read it?" Roco asked. "If it isn't yours, then it wouldn't matter, right?"

Lottie shrugged, but her brows knit together as she watched Robin hand the diary to Earl. Robin grinned, and Lottie's face turned a light shade of pink. Carson hoped she was blushing about the diary and not because Robin looked at her. He was a good-looking guy, even if he was a little rough around the edges. He shook his head. Why should he care who she thought was attractive?

"Wait," Carson growled. "Shouldn't I get to read it first? I am in it, after all."

"The Carson in that diary doesn't bear a lot of resemblance to you," Robin said with a grin.

"I haven't always looked like this."

"*Beauty and the Beast*?" Robin asked. Carson nodded. "That's unfortunate."

"Very."

"We should go," Lottie said, jumping to her feet. "We've wasted enough time."

"I'll take your ring first," Robin said. "As payment for the meal." Lottie looked at her ring.

"That's a steep payment for a meal," Carson protested.

"I am Robin Hood after all. Robbing the rich and everything."

"This is all I have," Lottie said, pulling it from her finger.

He smiled. "And I thank you for it. It will help me on my new quest."

"And what is that?" Carson asked.

"I'm going to fall in love with the first woman I see so I can get out of here. Then, I'm sure the girl will rip out my heart and jump on it, but at least I can be in my own house while I'm licking my wounds."

Earl chuckled. "I can see why Nancy brought you here."

Lottie pulled off her ring and threw it in the snow near Robin's feet. He bent and retrieved it.

"You could try to fall in love with Lottie," Roco suggested. "I don't see her and Carson coming to terms with one another."

"Nah," Robin said with a wink. He pointed at the diary. "I've read the book."

Lottie tossed her pack to the ground and sank down next to it. She couldn't believe she was hauling things around like a pack mule. Her legs ached, and her feet throbbed. She had never walked this far in her life. The snow had stopped abruptly about an hour ago, and this part of the woods was only slightly cold. Carson and Earl were searching for wood for a fire, and Roco sat down on a fallen log and pulled out the diary.

Lottie frowned as she watched his eyes scan the pages. She told herself it shouldn't matter. She didn't feel any connection to anyone named Charlotte, but it still made her nervous. Perhaps she should be reading it to see if it gave her any memories.

She thought about her dream from the night before and shook her head. Dreams didn't mean anything.

Carson dumped a pile of sticks in front of her and started making a fire. Earl wasn't far behind with his branches.

"Don't help or anything, Roco," Earl said. Roco didn't look up. He was focused on the diary. Max curled up near Lottie and yawned.

"You don't suppose the animals were once people, do you?" she asked. "Like, maybe Nancy thought they were beyond help."

Carson shuddered. "I hope not. It's bad enough to be a beast. It would be much worse to not be able to talk."

Roco laughed, and they all turned to him. "Never mind me. Just reading."

"I'm surprised Roco knows how to read," Earl said. "I wouldn't be shocked if it turned out he was faking it."

"Ain't faking it," Roco said. "See here, it says 'Carson is so funny.' It's said that at least five times since I started. Not very original, Lottie."

"Or accurate," she said. "I've never heard Carson say anything funny."

Carson either grimaced or smiled. Lottie couldn't tell which. It was hard to see past the large teeth. He focused on her. "You can't disagree with someone's diary, especially your own. I'm funny."

"Funny looking," Roco said with a smirk.

Aspen flew overhead and dropped something.

"What is it?" Lottie asked.

"A rabbit," said Earl. "Nice of her to bring us dinner." He picked it up and pulled out a knife.

A shiver ran down Lottie's spine. She wasn't opposed to eating rabbit, she just didn't want to see it before someone prepared it for her.

"Oh my," Roco muttered.

"Read it out loud," Earl said. Lottie couldn't make herself look to where Earl was working on the rabbit.

Roco nodded. "Some days, I want to tell Carson how I feel about him, but I don't want to ruin our friendship. I know I'll never have a claim on him, and sometimes it's more than I can stand. If you could see him, you would understand. He is the best looking guy in the universe. That isn't why I like him, though. Carson is funny and kind. Everyone likes him. I'm thinking of trying out to be a cheerleader to get it all off my mind."

Lottie jumped to her feet and tore the diary from Roco's hands. "You shouldn't be reading a person's diary." Her face was probably the same shade of red as her cloak.

"You said it wasn't yours," Roco said with mischief in his eyes.

"It isn't, but that doesn't mean you should read it." She shoved the book into her pack and avoided eye contact with Carson. "I'm going to sleep." She grabbed her bedroll and looked for a spot to spread it.

"You haven't had dinner," Earl protested.

"I'm too tired to eat."

"Don't get too far from the fire," Carson said. "It might get cold."

She tossed the bedroll to the ground and climbed inside. She turned her back on the others and squeezed her eyes shut. It was silly to claim she wasn't Charlotte. If only she could remember. It was ridiculous to picture herself in love with Carson. The diary said he was attractive, funny, and kind. She didn't see any of that.

She thought back to the dream. The feelings she'd had felt real. Lottie kept her eyes shut and tried to picture the Carson of her dream. He had been too blurry to make out too many details.

Lottie felt her face heat up again. She should have taken the diary when Robin first offered it. Now Carson knew that she, well, that Charlotte had been enamored with him. She had to admit he was better than the duke, but she could tell he despised her. The best thing to do would be to get out of this place.

She sat up and turned to Carson. He sat by the fire, glaring into the flames. "When you change stories, what happens?" she asked.

He kept his focus on the fire. "Everything spins, and you wake up in a different place. You have to figure out what story you're in."

Lottie swallowed and nodded. "We should change the story."

Carson's head jerked up, and he studied her. "Why?"

"I have a feeling we aren't getting anywhere walking aimlessly around."

"If you two disappear, that will leave me and Earl, and I ain't kissing him," said Roco.

Earl pushed his brother. "Let them go. We can travel faster with the two of us."

Carson stood. "Are you sure you want to do this? You could end up anywhere."

"I'm sure," Lottie said, even though her mind was telling her otherwise. She climbed to her feet and crossed her arms. Carson's mouth was as big as her head. How was she supposed to kiss him?

"You don't have to look so disgusted," he said. "If you would prefer, you can kiss Roco or Earl."

Earl laughed. "We're a might too old for her."

"I ain't nearly as old as you are," Roco said.

Lottie rolled her eyes. "Let's get this over with."

Carson took a step toward her, and she cringed. "Try not to eat me by accident," she said.

"I'll try," he said with a slight gleam in his eyes.

Lottie leaned in and closed her eyes tightly. She waited a few moments and then opened them. Carson was only a few inches from her. "Well, get on with it," she said.

Carson sighed. "I can't. I can't see past my own face. You're going to have to kiss me."

"What?"

Roco laughed. "This is great entertainment."

Earl shoved his brother. "Quiet."

Lottie took a resolved breath. She moved in closer. Carson's eyes were unnerving. "Stop looking at me."

Carson flashed her a frightening grin and closed his eyes.

"Stop smiling. I don't want to kiss your terrifying teeth."

Roco snorted.

"Go away, Roco," she said through clenched teeth.

"How long do I have to close my eyes?" Carson asked.

Lottie sighed and went onto her toes, kissing him quickly. She hoped she got his mouth, but with a head that size, who could really tell?

Carson's eyes opened, and his brows came together. "I feel weird."

Lottie tilted her head. "Shouldn't we disappear?"

Carson fell to his hands and knees and coughed a few times. "I think... I might puke." A bright light burst from around him, and Lottie covered her eyes. When she looked again, Carson was no longer a beast. He looked up, and Lottie sucked in a breath. He was handsome, even disheveled, and something about him stirred her memory. She thought about the blurry face in her dream. It was him.

He pushed himself back, so he was sitting on his heels, and he looked at his hands.

"If you tame that hair and shave, you might be passable," Earl said.

Lottie wanted to laugh. Even with messy hair and stubble, he was far better looking than just passable.

Carson ran a hand through the blond mess on his head and laughed. "Man, it's good to be me. I still feel like I might lose my dinner, though."

He had a nice voice. It was nowhere near as gruff as before. It felt familiar and warm. He looked up at her, and she took a step back. She tried to ignore his bright blue eyes.

"Why are we still here?" she asked, sitting back on her bedroll.

"I don't know. I'm just happy to lose the fur."

Lottie climbed back under her blanket. What had this accomplished? Sure, Carson was a man again, but now he was going to distract her. This wasn't what she wanted. She didn't know what she wanted, but this wasn't it.

Chapter 5

Charlotte watched Carson climb the jungle gym. When he got to the top, he stood and balanced. He looked down and grinned at her. She shook her head and put her hands on her hips. "Stop showing off," she said. "You're going to fall and crack your skull."

"Not me," he said, sitting on top. He grabbed the bars and swung down, dropping in front of her.

"One of these days, I'm gonna have to call your mom and tell her you're in the hospital. You know that, right?"

He flashed his white teeth. "Probably. Speaking of my mom, I should probably get home soon, or she's going to blow up on me. I have like seven assignments I need to catch up on."

They began walking away from the park at a leisurely pace. Charlotte side-eyed him. "It's annoying the way you let all of your school work build up and then at the last second you cram and get straight A's."

He shrugged. "That's the way I work. I have to have the stress of doing something last minute to push me. If the system works, why mess with it?"

"I do my homework every day, and I still have a hard time getting A's."

"But you do. Tell you what," he said, placing his arm over her shoulders. "I'll procrastinate one more day, and I'll help you with your math."

Charlotte wanted to take him up on his offer, but there were only three more days left of the term, and she didn't want him to fail. "My math is fine." She hated the way he always casually put his arm around her. Well, she loved it and hated it. She hated that he did it as a friendly gesture.

She'd finally given up hope on him falling for her. If he hadn't fallen in love with her in the last ten years, there wasn't a lot of chance of it happening now.

"Are you coming to my track meet?" he asked.

"Of course." She never missed them. They stopped when they got in front of Charlotte's house. She playfully tossed his arm off of her and started to her house. She threw a wave behind her. "See you tomorrow."

"I'll try to get all my stuff done tonight. If I do, we can go get pizza tomorrow to celebrate."

"Sounds good." She entered her house and closed the door. She leaned against it and sighed. There had to be a distraction to help her focus on something besides Carson. She needed to branch out and get some hobbies that didn't involve him. Someday, he would get a girlfriend, and she would be left with nothing to do.

Why did she have to fall in love with her best friend? It was ruining everything. She swallowed the lump in her throat and willed the tears to stay in. She didn't want her parents to see her and wonder what was wrong.

—— ℓℓℓ ——

Carson was physically and emotionally exhausted. It must have been after midnight, and his mind was racing. It was nice to not be covered in fur, but he'd had to make some adjustments to his clothing because they were much too big now.

The words from Charlotte's diary kept ringing in his ears. It didn't make sense. If Charlotte had really felt the way the diary said, she wouldn't have made a fool of him in front of everyone. Perhaps becoming a cheerleader had changed her. Carson had been surprised by her reaction when he asked her to the dance because she wasn't usually like that.

Sure, Charlotte liked the limelight, but she wasn't a mean person. It had been better before Roco read those words out loud. It had been easier to be angry with her. He wondered why Charlotte was here. Nancy seemed to bring people here who were angry about love. Charlotte had never seemed that way. And Nancy had said she was beyond fixing. What had happened to her?

Carson glanced over at Lottie's pack. It wouldn't be hard to slip the diary out and read it. It might be hard to see by the flickering firelight, but he was willing to try. Still, that would violate any trust they might have. Not that they had much. He had a feeling the answers might be in the book.

Lottie moaned and sat up, rubbing her eyes. Carson was glad he hadn't been rummaging through her pack.

"Are you alright?" he asked.

Lottie's head jerked toward him. He wasn't sure with only the firelight spilling over her, but it looked like her lip trembled.

"I'm fine," she said, lying back down.

He watched her as she stared up into the darkness. She looked troubled.

"I had a dream," she said. "It felt familiar. It might have been something that happened."

"Oh?"

"I was with you. Some of it didn't make sense. You were talking about needing to catch up on your schoolwork. And I was telling you it wasn't fair that you could save your work until the last second and still do well."

He leaned on his elbow and watched her. "We had a lot of conversations like that."

"What is a track meet?"

"Track is a sport where you race against other people."

"And you did that?"

"Yes."

"And I would watch?"

"You did at first. Then, you became a cheerleader, so you still came to the games, but I think you preferred cheering for the football team." Carson realized he sounded bitter, but he couldn't help it.

"What's a cheerleader?"

Carson sighed. "It's a person who jumps around and cheers. It's pretty much a waste of time. You should read your diary."

Lottie became quiet, and Carson wanted to kick himself. She rolled over so she wasn't facing him. He might look like himself, but he was still acting like a beast.

The next morning, Lottie skimmed through the diary as the others ate breakfast. Most of it was nonsense, and a lot of it was embarrassing. None of it caused her memories to return. She was feeling less like Lottie, the daughter of Lady Anna, but not more like Charlotte.

Her dream last night had felt real. Even upon waking, she had felt the pain of a sad heart, but no other memories had come. She shut the book and picked up the apple Earl had given her earlier.

"Where did you get that dress?" Roco asked. Lottie looked down and gasped. Her dress had changed, and it was stunning. What was even better was that it was clean. She stood and ran her hand over the smooth material. It was long and green and flowed past her feet.

"And you have a tiara. Did you rob someone?"

Lottie rolled her eyes. "Don't be ridiculous. You're wearing different clothing as well."

"Creepy," Roco said, studying his brown button-up shirt. "Do I look like a farmer?"

"We both look like farmers," Earl said, joining them. "Nancy's magic is strange."

Roco cringed. "I hope we don't have to farm. That's probably as bad as mining."

Carson came jogging over. "Look at my clothes. I'm definitely not a prince in this story."

Earl grinned. "I think we're farmers, and Lottie is a princess."

Carson sneered. "That figures. I hope you aren't expecting us to serve you."

Lottie ignored him. "How did our clothing change?"

He shrugged. "It happens when the stories change."

"But we didn't go anywhere."

"Yes, but everything has been weird."

Lottie placed the diary in her pack. "Are we going?"

"I'm ready," Carson said, slinging his pack over his shoulder.

"Did anyone feel that?" Earl asked.

Lottie nodded. The ground shook, but that had been common lately. This felt different somehow. The ground shook again, and a rumbling sound filled their ears.

Roco frowned. "Something big is coming this way."

"Run," said Carson. They all turned and ran from whatever was coming.

Lottie stumbled over her skirts but didn't fall. She grabbed the layers of dress and ran. She couldn't remember the last time she'd run, and she was sure she wouldn't be able to get very far.

She screamed as something grabbed her and scooped her into the air. She heard Carson yell something, but she couldn't make it out. Her hair hung in her face, and she kept screaming as the ground got further and further away. She pushed her hair from her eyes and looked into the terrifyingly large face of a man. Not a man. A giant.

The giant's large hand circled around her, and only her arms and head were free. Her pack was digging into her back. The giant had a large black beard and wide brown eyes.

He studied her for a moment, and then he laughed. "This is a better prize than I could have hoped for!"

Lottie covered her ears, his voice still bouncing around in her head. "Let me go!" she yelled. Carson and Earl were yelling at the giant from down below, but he wasn't paying them any attention. Lottie glanced down and swallowed. She didn't like heights.

"Let you go?" he bellowed. "Why would I let you go? Perhaps after your father gives me all of his gold, I will let you go. The king is stingy and needs to share his wealth."

Lottie pushed against the enormous hand. "I'm not a princess."

"Not a princess? I am not so easily fooled." He started walking, and Lottie tried to push away the panic from inside of her. There was no way Carson and the others could keep up with the large strides the giant was making.

"Stop!" she protested. She thought about biting his finger, but she didn't want him to drop her. There wasn't much she could do but wait until he put her down.

Carson pointed ahead. "A village!"

"Finally," Earl said, picking up his pace. "I still don't see how we lost a giant. That guy was massive! We should be able to see him from miles away."

Carson nodded and ran a tired hand over his eyes. The giant had scooped up Lottie and Roco and taken a few steps into the trees and then vanished. No trace was left of the giant, not even footprints to follow.

They hurried to the village, and Carson scanned the place. The village was small with tiny, thatched houses scattered all over the place. People walked the streets, too busy to stop and notice them. They were all flickering.

"Jack!" a middle-aged woman called, stomping toward him. She was wearing a worn brown dress and a dirty white apron. Her gray hair was falling from a messy bun, and she was pulling a sickly looking cow behind her. She flickered like everyone else in the place. "It's about time you showed up," she scolded, placing her hands firmly on her hips.

Carson looked at Earl, and the man shrugged. Carson opened his mouth to respond, but the woman held up a silencing hand.

"Don't give me your excuses," she said. "I know. You lost track of time. You lose track every time you go fishing, and you don't even have any fish. Lazy, that's what you are."

"Do we know you?" Earl asked.

The woman ignored him. She shoved the rope that was tied to the cow into Carson's hands. "Here. Take Milky-White and sell her. She's all we have left, and we need the money for food."

"Just eat the cow," Earl suggested.

"You need to choose your friends better, Jack," she said, glaring at Earl. "Now, go sell the cow. The butcher is still open if you hurry." She turned and disappeared the same way she'd come.

Earl scratched his head. "That was odd."

"It's *Jack and the Beanstalk.* It's another story."

"So, we find the butcher?"

"I can't remember. I know Jack sells the cow for some magic beans, and they grow a beanstalk that goes up to the sky and leads to the giant."

"Then, let's get on with it. We need to save Roco and Lottie."

Carson nodded and pulled on the rope. The cow didn't budge. "She doesn't want to come."

"Let me," Earl said, taking the rope. "Come on, girl," he said. The cow followed him.

"Why did she move for you?"

Earl glanced at him. "Cows can sense fear."

"They cannot."

"They can, and she knows you're scared. That makes her not respect you. She's not gonna move for someone she don't respect."

Carson rolled his eyes. "I'm not scared of a scrawny old cow." It was mostly true. He'd never been around a cow, so he wasn't sure what to expect from one.

Earl grinned. "You look scared."

"I do not."

"Hey, look at that man up there," Earl said, pointing. "He's not blinking in and out like the others."

Carson looked to where Earl was pointing and saw a young black man in a flashy blue and gold robe. He didn't fit in with the other townspeople, and he was standing in the middle of the road looking at his hand in confusion.

"Let's go talk to him," Carson said. They walked over, and the man looked up at them. He closed his fist and took a step back.

"Hey, man," Carson said, holding out his hand. "You look like you're in the wrong story."

The man's head bobbed up and down, and he shook Carson's hand. "I don't know what happened. I'm guessing you're real since you aren't fading."

"I'm Carson, and this is Earl."

"I'm Kirk. I don't know who I'm supposed to be here. One second, I was about to send Dorothy back to Kansas, and the next I'm standing here with a handful of beans. Everything has been messy lately, but I'm baffled by this one."

Carson nodded. "I didn't realize *The Wizard of Oz* counted as a fairy tale."

"I asked Nancy about that. I'm guessing you know Nancy?"

Earl chuckled. "Oh yes, we know Nancy."

"She said anything with a good story is a fairy tale in her eyes."

"How long have you been in this world?" Carson asked.

Kirk tapped his chin and looked thoughtfully at the sky. "Two years? That's my best guess. I've seen a lot of strange things, but I've never left a story before the end. There were a few other real people trapped in Oz. That's why I'm not surprised to run into the two of you. Nancy's losing her touch. And why am I holding beans?"

"This story is *Jack and the Beanstalk*. That's why we have a cow."

Kirk grinned. "Ah, that makes more sense. So, I'm supposed to give you the beans and take the cow? I don't want a cow, but you can take the beans," he said, dumping them into Carson's hand.

"Thanks. Do you want to come with us?" Earl asked. "We could use another person."

"Come with you to find the giant? If I were you two, I wouldn't do it. I don't think we have to follow the stories anymore. Things are too messed up."

"We have to go," Carson said. "The giant took some of our... people." He knew it sounded lame, but he didn't know what to call Lottie and Roco. It would sound weird to say he was looking for an ex-friend and a new acquaintance.

"I guess I have nothing better to do," Kirk said, patting the cow on the head. "Why is Nancy putting people in these stories anyway? I thought she was looking for love. Who are you supposed to kiss in this story?"

"I have no idea," Carson admitted, shoving the beans into his pocket. "Who were you supposed to kiss in *The Wizard of Oz*?"

Kirk laughed. "I don't know. My guess was a witch because they were the only ones that were close to humans. Dorothy was human, of course, but she was like ten or something."

"We should go plant the beans," Earl reminded them. "We have people to save."

"Right," Carson said, scanning the town. "The beans were supposed to grow overnight, correct?"

"Don't look at me," Earl said. "I only know my story."

Kirk's eyebrows came together. "What do you mean?"

"We found out that some characters in the stories are people Nancy gave up on," Carson explained. "She made them lose their memories and become a permanent character. Earl was in *Snow White*."

Kirk shuddered. "That seems low, even for Nancy. I hope that doesn't happen to me."

"It only happens to people that never progress. A person we are trying to find was stuck in *Cinderella*. She's getting some memories back."

Earl chuckled. "And some of her memories are of Carson. It's making life more interesting."

Kirk nodded. "You were in a story with her?"

"Their real-life story," Earl said with a grin. "I wish I knew what was in Lottie's diary."

"We were just friends," Carson said, not liking where this conversation was going. "Let's get moving. Since Nancy doesn't seem able to start our days over anymore when we do something wrong, I say we go plant the beans in the forest and spend the night there. I don't know where I'm supposed to live here, and the woman that's my mother doesn't seem pleasant."

"That's for sure," Earl agreed. "I'm up for sleeping in the forest."

"I've slept outside a lot since coming here," Kirk said. "It doesn't bother me."

Earl rubbed the cow's head. "What do we do about her?"

Carson glanced at the cow. "I guess we leave her here. A cow won't be able to climb a beanstalk."

"She might be good company for Max."

"I haven't seen Max since we ran after the giant."

Earl nodded and untied the cow. "I'm sure Max will find us again."

"Alright," Carson said, "Let's go." He headed toward the forest, and the others followed. The houses they passed were fading. Carson wondered what would happen if everything faded. Would they be stuck in an empty space? Hopefully, if it got that bad, Nancy would see the flaws in her plan and let them free.

Chapter 6

Charlotte ducked down in the backseat of Carson's car. He should be finished with his track practice any minute, and she had stayed after just for this. She was going to scare him good. She smiled as she imagined his reaction.

Both of the front doors opened, and Charlotte heard people getting inside. She frowned. It would be weird if she popped out and scared Carson *and* one of his track buddies. She would have to wait until Carson dropped him off and then she could scare him when they got to his house.

"I'm totally going to break the school record this year," Carson's friend Brandon said.

Carson chuckled and turned on the engine. "Sure you are. You know what the record is, right?"

"Of course I do. All I need to do is run the mile two minutes faster than my best time."

"Two minutes is a lot."

"I can do it."

Charlotte felt the car back up and then lunge forward.

"So, are you gonna ask Rachel to the dance?" Carson asked. Charlotte smiled. She hoped he would. Rachel had had a crush on Brandon for at least six months.

"I dunno, man," Brandon said. "I know she likes me, and I like her, but I'm so busy these days. If I ask her, she might expect us to become a couple or something, and I can't fit that in right now."

"Just tell her that," Carson said. "She might understand, and you can go as friends."

"Are you going to ask someone?"

Charlotte held her breath. She shouldn't be listening to this conversation.

"No."

"Why not?" Brandon prodded.

"There isn't anyone I want to take."

"Go with Charlotte."

Charlotte gasped and covered her mouth with her hands. She wasn't going to scare him now. That would make things awkward. She was going to have to stay hidden in the car until he left.

"I'm not going with Charlotte. She's my best friend."

"You told me to go with Rachel as friends," Brandon protested.

"That's different. Charlotte and I have been friends forever. You and Rachel are crushing on each other, but you don't even know each other that well."

"Still, taking Charlotte would be more fun than staying home and playing video games all night."

"Charlotte is a cheerleader now. I'm sure she'll be going to all the dances with football players. That's how cheerleaders are."

Charlotte frowned and tried to reposition her legs without giving herself away. What was Carson talking about? It was true most of the cheerleaders dated football players, but she wasn't shallow. She wouldn't turn someone down because they weren't part of the football team. She especially wouldn't turn Carson down. And why was he lumping her in with all the cheerleaders?

"You might be surprised if you ask," Brandon encouraged.

"I'll never ask Charlotte out. If I did, it would be as a joke."

The car stopped, and Charlotte wiped a tear from her eye. She didn't have to wonder anymore. Carson would never like her the way she liked him.

"Why don't you run in and I'll wait in the car?" Brandon said. Charlotte sucked in a breath. She'd hoped Carson was taking Brandon home, but they must be somewhere else.

"Alright," Carson said. "What do you want?"

"A water and some Cheetos."

"Only little kids eat Cheetos."

"That's only because adults don't want to have orange fingers. Deep down, everyone wants Cheetos."

Carson laughed. "Alright, I'll be right back."

The door slammed, and Charlotte bit her lip. Why hadn't Brandon gone in? Then, she could get off the cramped car floor and walk home.

"Don't take that the way it sounded, Char," Brandon said. "You know you're important to him."

Charlotte froze in horror.

"I know you're back there. I heard you gasp, and nobody else would hide in the back of Carson's car."

"This is so embarrassing," she muttered, climbing up onto the backseat.

"Don't be embarrassed. I'll never talk about it again," Brandon said, turning and looking at her. His deep brown eyes narrowed, and he frowned. "Don't cry. He didn't mean it the way he said it."

"I'm not crying on purpose," she said, wiping her hand angrily against her face. "It doesn't matter anyway. We've always been friends. I need to get out and walk home before he gets back. Please don't tell him I was here."

He ran a hand over his curly black hair. "I won't, but remember what I said. Don't hold it against him."

Charlotte nodded and hurried from the car. She dashed out of the store parking lot and scurried away before Carson had the chance to see her. Her tears dried up, and she frowned. What made her good enough to be Carson's best friend, but not good enough to go to a dance with? It was fine. She would find a football player and go to the dance. That was what Carson seemed to expect of her, so that was what she would do.

Lottie sat up and wiped the sleep from her eyes. She frowned at the dream and all the memories that came with it. She remembered being Charlotte. All of it. She remembered being so angry with Carson. She'd avoided him for the next three days and then had gotten the shock of her life when he asked her to the dance when she was cheering at his track meet.

She knew he was asking her because Brandon made him, or maybe as a joke, and she would not be the butt of his joke. She'd laughed in his face and told him no. He looked hurt, and then angry. She'd tried to talk to him later, but he was mad. Lottie had said some things that made her sound like a snob, and that had been it. A lifetime of friendship down the drain.

Lottie's heart didn't heal as quickly as she'd hoped. A year later, she was still upset, and that was when she met Nancy. She'd been stuck on an airplane, flying to meet her parents in Hawaii, and Nancy was sitting next to her. Nancy pried about Lottie's love life until her entire story had spilled out.

Nancy had asked Lottie what she was willing to do to mend her heart. Lottie had been confused but told the woman she would do anything. The next thing Lottie knew, she was waking up in one of Nancy's stories. She was confused for a long time, and eventually, Nancy had come and told her what she needed to do to progress in the magical world.

Lottie had demanded to be taken home, but Nancy told her she had said she would do anything to mend her heart. Nancy assured her this was the way to do it. Lottie was angry, and not in the mood to follow Nancy's plan, so she had refused to do anything. That must be why Nancy had deemed her unfixable.

She could remember all the Cinderellas she had bullied now. At first, she had gone through the motions of being an evil stepsister against her will. She did things and said things she couldn't control. Eventually, her old life had faded, and she had become the character.

"Are you alright?" Roco asked.

Lottie looked over to see Roco sitting on a bed across the room from her. She was sitting on a dirty old mattress with a tattered blanket covering her legs. The room was small and appeared to be made of stone. One small window with bars let in a stream of light.

"Where are we?" she asked.

"The giant's prison," Roco said. "You passed out before we got here. I was worried when you woke up and didn't respond. I said your name a few times."

"I didn't realize the giant took you." She climbed off the mattress and peered out the window. "How do we get out?" She could see a small lake and lots of trees. Even if they could remove the bars from the window, they were too high to get down.

Roco shrugged. "I don't know. I tried to break the door, but it's solid. We have to stay here, I suppose."

Lottie hurried to the door and ran her hand over the hardwood. "We have to try to get out."

He leaned against the wall. "It won't work. Might as well wait for Carson and Earl to find us."

She tilted her head as she studied him. How could he be content to sit and wait for help that might not come? "Shouldn't a giant's prison be bigger?"

"The castle is huge. When the giant put us in here, he bent over and opened a small door. Well, small for him. His hand barely fits in here."

"There has to be something we can do."

"I finished your diary," Roco said, holding up the book. "You can read it if you get bored."

Lottie scowled and ripped the book from his hand. "I told you not to read that!"

Roco shrugged. "Yeah, well, I needed something to do."

Lottie's face felt hot. She hoped she hadn't written about Carson breaking her heart. It was a farfetched hope. She wrote everything in there.

"I remember everything about who I was," Lottie said, running her hand over the book's cover.

"So, you remember being hopelessly in love with Carson and getting your heart broken?"

She rolled her eyes. "Yes, and thanks for bringing that up."

"I should start trying to remember things."

Lottie grabbed the tattered blanket and pulled it over her shoulders. She missed the red cloak. "I almost wish I didn't remember."

Roco laid back and stared at the ceiling. "I hope I have more motivation in my real life. I can't seem to find any here, no matter how hard I try."

"I'm not sitting around doing nothing." Lottie opened her pack and searched it until she found the knife Carson had given her before they left the beast's castle. She studied the hinges on the door and then looked at the doorknob. It had a straight slit for a key—could it be that easy?

Lottie stuck the knife in the slit and turned. The lock easily popped open.

"Wow!" Roco exclaimed. "How did you do that?"

"It wasn't hard," she said, placing the knife back in the pack and replacing the diary. "Let's go."

He sat up and frowned. "Go? But what if the giant finds us?"

"Let's hope he doesn't." Lottie was happy to be herself again. She felt braver when she knew her capabilities. She opened the door and stepped into a large stone hallway. The ceiling was so high up it made her feel dizzy to stare up at it.

Roco followed reluctantly behind her. "I still say we should wait for the others. They probably have a plan."

"We don't even know if they're coming. We have to get ourselves out of here. Come on."

Roco sighed, but followed. "Do you suppose that's the front door?" he asked, pointing to a large door. It was taller than any building she had ever seen.

"That would be convenient," she said, walking toward it. "I was worried we might be in a basement, and we would have to figure out a way to get up the steps." She realized that was a silly worry as soon as she said it. She'd seen out the window, and they definitely weren't in a basement.

Roco rubbed his stomach. "Wouldn't it be neat if someone left a giant sized piece of cake out? I've had dreams like that."

Lottie smiled. "I'd rather have a huge, warm cookie."

"Snow used to make us cookies. It was the only thing she could cook that tasted good."

"They were good, although they would have been better with raisins."

"How do you know about her cookies?"

"She was my stepsister, remember?"

Roco nodded. "Right—so, she made you cookies?"

"Yes," Lottie said, thinking back to the last Ella. "She was a terrible cook, but her cookies were amazing. I wish I could see her again and apologize for the way I treated her. I was ridiculous."

"It ain't your fault," Roco said. "It was all Nancy. Why would you want raisins in a cookie? That sounds like the worst idea I ever heard."

Lottie shrugged and stopped when they got to the door. The crack underneath was big enough to walk under without ducking. Roco pushed his pack under and then rolled out of sight. Lottie followed him. The early morning sun shone into her eyes. She grabbed her pack and slung it over her shoulder. She wished she wasn't wearing such a long puffy dress.

"There's the stairs you were worried about," Roco said. Lottie blew out a frustrated breath. There were several stairs they would somehow need to descend, and they were high.

There was no way they could get down without getting hurt.

"I don't see any way down," she said, peering over the edge of the first step.

"I do," Roco said, smiling. He pointed off in the distance.

Lottie's eyes widened as a wolf the size of a house bounded toward the castle. "Go back inside!" she squealed.

"No, no," he said, grabbing her elbow. "It's Finn. He's a good wolf."

"He's huge!" Lottie said, taking a step back.

"Yeah, that's new," Roco said with a shrug. "Still, I can tell it's him."

The wolf hurried up the steps and then lowered his massive head so his large amber eyes were level with them.

"Hello, Finn," Roco said to the black and gray wolf. "I hope you're here to help us."

The wolf moved his head in a motion Lottie figured was a nod.

Roco rubbed a spot on his nose. "Can we climb on?"

The wolf nodded again. He turned to the side and pushed himself against the step. Roco climbed on and sat on the wolf's back and held onto a handful of fur. Lottie took a deep breath and did the same. The wolf ran down the steps, and Lottie had to clench her teeth to keep from screaming. It was fast!

He didn't stop when he got down the stairs. He ran past the river and through a clump of trees. The trees were so tall, Lottie couldn't see to the tops.

"Can you help us find Earl?" Roco called. Finn didn't stop, he barreled through the forest. After a few minutes, he came to an abrupt stop, and Lottie had to hold on tight to not fall. Finn dropped down on his stomach and looked at them. Roco slid down the wolf's fur and landed in the tall grass. Lottie followed. If it hadn't been so high, it might have been fun.

Finn motioned forward with his snout. Lottie followed his gaze and saw the top of a large plant coming out of a hole. She walked cautiously forward and looked down when she came to it. Her stomach dropped. The ground around the beanstalk was missing. It was like someone had cut a perfect circle out of the earth. They were high. Really high. She could see clouds down below.

"*Jack and the Beanstalk,*" she muttered. "I should have known. Things made more sense now that she knew all the fairy tales again.

"Jack and the what now?"

"Beanstalk. It's a tale about a giant and a boy named Jack. We're going to need to climb down."

Roco looked down and shivered. "That's a long climb."

"We can do it." Lottie stepped over the hole and grabbed the stalk. She placed her foot on a large stem and sighed. This wasn't going to be easy.

"Now, that is a beanstalk!" Earl said, gazing up at the large green plant.

Carson had to admit it was impressive. It was as thick as a truck and went up until it disappeared into the clouds. The leaves were positioned in a way that would make it easy to climb the stems, if they could get on the first one. The lowest one was about five feet from the ground.

Kirk peered up into the sky. "That is going to take forever."

Earl walked around the plant. "Hey, look. There are people coming down."

Carson and Kirk hurried to the other side and looked up. Sure enough, two people were making their way down. It had to be Lottie and Roco. Carson's heart sped up. They were so high. One wrong move, and that would be the end.

Kirk ran a hand over his dark curls. "Should we climb up to them?"

Carson watched their steady descent. "No. They seem to be doing well, and I don't want to distract them and make them fall."

"I wonder how they escaped," Earl said. "Roco isn't the most imaginative person, and he ain't gonna try something he don't know is gonna work."

Carson's heart continued to pound in his chest. Lottie might not be his best friend anymore, but that didn't mean he wanted her to get hurt. If they fell from that distance, they would be more than hurt.

Earl and Kirk sat on the ground and chatted while they waited. Carson stayed standing. He couldn't take his eyes off them. After what seemed like an eternity, they were close enough for Lottie to spot them. She waved and kept climbing down. An imaginary clock was ticking in his head. They were coming slowly, but steadily.

Carson wiped his sweaty hands on his pants. They were almost down. Even if they fell now, they would be alright. Roco came to the lowest leaf and sat down, putting his hands around the stem. He dropped down so he was hanging by his hands and plopped to the ground.

"That was the most exhausting thing I've ever done in my entire life," he said, rubbing his hands together. "I'm gonna be sore for a week at least."

Lottie copied Roco and hung down from the large stem. Carson grabbed her around the waist, and she let go, putting her arms around his neck as he lowered her to the ground. Her brown curls were tangled, and she looked tired. Tired and beautiful. Carson shook his head. He shouldn't be having those thoughts. He didn't need to have a second heartbreak.

Lottie's brow furrowed, and her lips formed a tight line as he stared into her brown eyes. He wondered what was bothering her. Well, besides the fact that she'd just been captured by a giant and forced to climb down an extremely large plant. His mind flashed back to high school, and his heart felt heavy, remembering how important she'd been to him.

"You can let me go," Lottie said, pulling away from him. She took a few steps and sank to the earth.

"Are you alright?" he asked, offering her a hand.

She flinched and recoiled like he was a pit viper. "I need to sit for a minute."

His hand dropped. "Take your time."

Lottie nodded and glared up at him. "I remember everything."

"You remember being Charlotte?"

She nodded. "But you can still call me Lottie."

Carson was confused. "Why? You never went by Lottie."

"I do now."

Kirk pointed at the beanstalk. "Shouldn't we cut that down before the giant comes?"

Roco snorted. "Cut it down? It's huge!"

"Would cutting it down make a difference?" Earl asked. "The giant was down here before it grew, so he obviously has other ways to get here."

"True," Carson said. "Instead of wasting time cutting it down, we could just get out of here."

"Where do we go?" Kirk asked.

Carson had no idea. "I guess we could head into the trees. I don't know how safe that is. He found us in the forest the first time."

"How did you escape?" Earl asked.

"It wasn't easy," Roco said. "The giant was huge! He locked us in a dungeon with a fire-breathing dragon. A large and angry fire-breathing dragon."

Earl shook his head. "I don't want to run into a dragon."

"After the dragon, we ran into a sorcerer. He tried to trick us into following him to some unknown world, but we were too smart for that."

"So, Lottie outwitted him?" Earl asked. "I don't imagine you did."

"None of that happened," Lottie said, getting to her feet. "We popped the lock and escaped without even seeing the giant, let alone a dragon or sorcerer."

"Aw, come on, Lottie," Roco grinned. "You ain't any fun."

"We did get saved by a humongous wolf."

"It was Finn," said Roco. "You shoulda seen him, Earl. He was as big as a bus!"

Kirk shook his head. "I don't know that I want to see a wolf the size of a bus. We need to get out of here before the giant comes."

"Let's go then," Carson said, leading the group away from the beanstalk. He set a brisk pace, wanting to put as much distance as he could between them and the giant. "You said the wolf was as big as a bus," he said, glancing at Roco.

"It was," Roco said, walking up next to him. "I ain't exaggerating, right, Lottie?"

"I would say it was bigger than a bus," she agreed.

"How do you know what a bus is?" Carson asked.

Roco stopped and scratched his head. "I don't reckon I know. My brain has been a bit frazzled since the giant took us. I suppose he could've rattled some of my memories around."

"Can we discuss this later?" Lottie asked. "We need to put some serious miles between us and this place."

Chapter 7

Lottie yawned and rolled over on a soft mattress. When her eyes finally opened, she cringed. She had gone to sleep in the forest, and now she was in a large room, tucked under a cozy blanket. She sat up and studied the neat room. It was similar to her room at her house—at Lady Anna's house. Everything was neat and bright. Had she changed stories? Where were Carson and the others?

Across from the bed was a fireplace with a large painting hanging above it. The painting showed a king, queen, and... Lottie. In the painting, she was wearing a fancy purple dress and a tiara. She must be a princess, but how? Carson said the stories didn't change unless a kiss took place, and she was one hundred percent certain she hadn't kissed anyone.

Lottie hopped out of bed and wrapped herself in a robe that was flung over a chair near the bed. "Nancy?" she asked. Sure, she was upset at Carson, but that didn't mean she wanted to navigate this world on her own. When Nancy didn't appear, she bit her lip and sat back on the bed. What were the chances Carson, Roco, and Earl were in this story? She would even be happy to see Kirk, even though she only met him the day before.

The door opened, and the queen from the painting entered. Her eyes were red and swollen. She patted her dark brown hair and moved toward Lottie.

Lottie swallowed and remembered when she had first come to this world. She had refused to interact with anyone, and where had that gotten her? Perhaps she should try to follow the story so Nancy wouldn't turn her back into a puppet.

The queen sat next to her and squeezed her hand. She smiled at Lottie, but her mouth trembled. "Did you sleep well?"

Lottie shrugged. "I suppose so."

"I'm sure it was difficult. You realize all of this is for the best, though, do you not?"

"What is for the best?" Lottie asked.

"Your marriage to the young prince," the queen said, pulling a handkerchief from her pocket. She wiped at her nose. "The prince is a good man, as is his father. You will be happy."

"Of course," Lottie said, patting the woman's hand. She wondered if the prince would be Carson.

"You are taking this better than you did last night."

"Don't worry about me," Lottie said. "I'll be fine."

The queen smiled, and some of the worry left her eyes. "I'm sure you will be happy. Your father would have been so pleased to see you so grown up. Perhaps, if he had lived, things would be different. Aw, well... I suppose we hold our heads high and do our best."

Lottie nodded awkwardly.

"I won't make you travel alone. You may take Britta with you. She can serve you on your journey and after. I wish I could send you in a grand carriage, but there is none to be found. You may take Falada. He is the best horse."

"Thank you," Lottie said, forcing herself to keep her hands folded in her lap. The pounding of her heart echoed in her head. Was the uncertainty always so unsettling when the stories changed? And if this was a fairy tale, what was it?

"You must be on your way," the queen said, holding out a lock of hair. Lottie tried not to look disgusted as she took it. "Keep my hair close to you. It will protect you from evil. Now, hurry and dress."

Lottie nodded and watched the queen hurry from the room. She would keep the hair—not because she wanted to, but because it might be important later. She sighed and hoped Carson or Roco would find her soon.

Carson was going to puke. He leaned over the side of the ship and groaned. He'd always suffered from motion sickness, and he felt like the rocking of the ship was going to be his doom.

"Where are we off to today, Captain?" Roco asked, joining him at the railing.

"Don't talk to me," Carson moaned, closing his eyes so he couldn't see the rolling water beneath.

Roco laughed. "Captain of your very own pirate ship, and you can't even keep breakfast down."

Carson ignored him. Roco was the only person besides him that was real on the ship. Everyone else was flickering. He and Roco had woken up this morning on a pirate ship. Lottie, Earl, and Kirk were nowhere in sight. If that wasn't annoying enough, he had an inch of facial hair that itched like crazy. It was strange the things that Nancy could do.

"We need to make a plan," Roco said. "We need to find the others, and we aren't going to do that when we are in the middle of the ocean."

"Tell the crew to dock somewhere," he muttered. "Any-where."

"Alright," Roco said, whistling as he walked away.

Carson startled when a large white owl landed on the railing next to him. It was probably the same owl that had brought them food when they were in the forest. The owl studied him and cocked her head.

"Aspen, right?" he asked. The owl watched him. "Do you know Nancy? Can you tell her I want to talk to her?"

The owl took one last look at him and flew away.

"What's an owl doing out in the middle of the day?" a dirty pirate asked, peering up at Aspen.

Carson shrugged and tried to keep his breakfast where it belonged. He hadn't puked yet, but it was only a matter of time.

The pirate scratched his greasy head. "I don't like it. Don't like it at all. Owls shouldn't be out in broad daylight. Not unless it's up to something. It's a bad omen, indeed."

"It's fine," Carson said, moving a few steps away from the man. He smelled like spoiled milk that had been left out in the sun.

"Nah, it's a bad omen, I tell you. I bet Pan is behind it."

Carson swallowed, ignoring the unpleasant taste in his mouth. "What are you talking about?"

"Pan probably controls the owl the same way he controlled the crock that ate your hand."

Carson inspected his hands and sighed with relief when he found them both intact, then he grimaced. "Pan? Peter Pan? Are you saying I'm Captain Hook?"

The pirate frowned and took a few steps away from him. "I think I'll go check on the others."

Carson laughed as the pirate scurried away. He was Captain Hook. What was Nancy thinking? Who was he supposed to kiss to end this story? Wasn't this too modern for Nancy? She said she'd been messing with people for centuries and *Peter Pan* wasn't that old of a tale.

"You look a little crazy," Roco said, coming near him.

"I'm not crazy," he smiled. "Nancy is crazy." His smile slipped away as he turned and threw up over the railing.

Lottie tried to look at Britta, her maid, without the woman suspecting. Something seemed off about her. Something besides the fact that she was flickering. Lottie patted her horse Falada and kept riding. She was glad she had taken riding lessons when she was younger. She wasn't the best, but she could stay on the horse.

Britta pushed her blonde hair over her shoulder and kept her brown mare trotting forward. The woman couldn't be over twenty, and she seemed a little haughty for a chambermaid.

Lottie had tried making conversation with her in the beginning, but the woman only gave short answers and appeared annoyed. The two of them had been riding for hours, and Lottie's throat was getting dry. They'd been following a stream for most of the day, but they hadn't stopped.

"Let's take a break," Lottie said, as she stopped and dismounted. "I could use some water."

Britta sniffed. "Well, you can get it yourself! I refuse to do your bidding."

"I didn't ask you to," Lottie muttered while walking to the stream. Why had she been forced to travel with this woman? Weren't maids supposed to be more obedient? Lottie kneeled next to the stream and cupped her hands. She dipped her hands into the water and hesitated for a moment. She'd never drunk from a stream before and worried about disease. Her dry throat won, and she drank the water.

Lottie squealed and jumped to her feet. Something had moved in her pocket. She reached in and grabbed the lock of hair the queen had given her. Had it moved? That would be impossible.

"Oh, how your mother would weep if she knew how that woman treated you," said the hair. Lottie dropped it to the ground. Hair couldn't talk—but it had. She put a hand over her pounding heart and looked at Britta. Britta appeared to have missed it. She sat on her horse, staring at nothing.

Lottie retrieved the hair and put it back in her pocket. She couldn't guess what this fairy tale might be. So far, it was unfamiliar. She climbed back on the horse, and the two women rode in silence.

"So, Britta," Lottie said, determined to not ride in awkward silence. "Where are you from?" Britta didn't answer. She flickered a few times, and Lottie shuddered. Was there any point in trying to befriend someone who wasn't real?

It wasn't long before Lottie's throat was dry again. She didn't want to stop, but it was getting painful to swallow. "I need to stop for more water," she said.

Britta turned and frowned so hard Lottie worried her mouth might get stuck like that. "Get your own water. I will not serve you. You do not deserve my help."

Lottie narrowed her eyes and dismounted. "I never asked for your help. Why don't you return to the castle?"

She stared blankly at Lottie. "I must do my duty."

"What is your duty?"

"To take you to the prince and be your servant."

Lottie raised a brow. "Shouldn't a servant serve?"

"I will not do your bidding. Get your own water."

Lottie pinched her lips together and walked to the stream. As she drank the water, she heard a sound from her pocket. It must be the talking hair. She rolled her eyes and ignored it as she drank. The hair kept talking, so she pulled it from her pocket.

"Oh, how the queen would weep," the hair said. Lottie dropped it into the stream and watched it float away. Important or not, she wasn't keeping talking hair. Something about it left her with an unsettling feeling.

"That is unfortunate," Britta said, coming up beside her. She flashed her white teeth, and her eyes were now filled with life. "What will keep you safe now?"

Lottie stood and took a step back.

Britta smirked and came closer. "Trade me dresses."

Lottie crossed her arms and stepped back. "No. Why would I do that?"

"Because you no longer have your mother's hair to keep you safe."

Lottie moved swiftly toward Falada. "I'm not trading you clothing."

"She's rotten that one," Falada said.

Lottie screamed and stepped away from the talking horse. "What is wrong with this place?" Lottie asked. "Talking hair and now a talking horse!" Britta was coming slowly toward her with a strange grin on her face. Lottie was taller than Britta and, from the looks of her, stronger, but there was something terrifying about her.

"You will trade me dresses and give me your horse," Britta demanded.

"Don't let her ride me," Falada said. "Evil surrounds her."

"I need to get out of here," Lottie muttered. She turned and ran away from Britta and the talking horse. A rock tripped her, and she slipped and yelled out as she fell. She put out her hands, expecting to hit the dirt, but felt herself falling much longer than she should've. She closed her eyes, and when she opened them, she was sitting on Britta's old horse, following behind Falada and Britta.

Lottie took a deep breath and shivered. Britta was wearing her nice green dress, and Lottie was wearing Britta's worn brown one. Nancy had to be stopped, but how? If she couldn't even leave, what good could she do? She thought about riding away, but the story might just pull her right back to where she was. Why had she tossed the hair?

Carson stood on the beach and took a deep breath through his nose. It felt good to be on land. It would take a lot to get him back on the ship.

"Yer lookin' a lot less green," Roco said, dumping sand from his boot. "Now that you can think better, have you come up with a plan?"

"Why do I have to be the one with a plan?"

"Dunno," Roco said. "It seems like that's the way it should be."

Carson shook his head. He didn't have the faintest idea what to do. Roco was putting too much faith in him. *Peter Pan* wasn't a romantic tale, so why was it even here? Still, he hoped Lottie and the others were around somewhere.

Roco kicked at the sand. "What kind of story is this any-way?"

"Not one you are supposed to be in," Nancy said, marching up to them. "How did you get here?" She was wearing a blue blazer and skirt with high heels. The shoes quickly disappeared beneath the sand. In a different situation Carson might have smiled when Nancy scowled at her feet.

"How should we know how we got here?" he asked. "One second, we were sleeping in the woods, and the next, we woke up on a ship."

"This is all such a mess," Nancy said, putting her hands on her hips. "No one is where they are supposed to be, and things are not progressing at all."

"Why are you mad at us?" Roco asked. "You're the one with the magic wand."

"Yes, and a whole lot of help it is these days. I don't understand how any of this is happening. This is *my* world. Things like this should be impossible."

"Just send everyone home," Carson said. "You say you're trying to help people, but what good is any of this? If you can't control this place, then there's no one who can."

Nancy pulled her wand from her pocket and stared at it for a few seconds. "I would, but I can't."

"Can't or won't?" Roco asked.

"Can't," Nancy admitted. "I tried to send Jurry home. Jurry and Meena. It didn't work at all. They ended up in a swamp somewhere. I haven't dared to try anything like it since."

Roco snorted. "Jurry's in a swamp? That'll make him angry for sure. Wish I could see it."

Nancy tapped her wand against her leg. "I hate to admit this, but I don't know what to do. When I created this world, it was a place of love and happiness. I never would have believed something like this could happen."

"How did you make it?" Carson asked.

"Oh, it was easy. The place I'm from is full of magic. Anyone can make a world similar to this one. They are more like a shadow of a world than a real world. I was so proud of this one until it fell apart."

"And it's all your fault," Carson said. "You never should have put people here to begin with."

"It's not my fault," Nancy said, glaring at him. "I will get it all straightened out, and then I will consider sending everyone home and starting over."

"Even the people you believed can't be helped?" Roco asked.

Nancy nodded. "Yes. I've been all over, and there are several people who are getting their memories back. Have you?"

Roco shook his head. "Nah, I remember what a bus is, though. Can you maybe tell me who I am?"

Nancy studied him for a moment. "I suppose it wouldn't hurt. Your name is Roco St. James, and you are from Tampa, Florida. You taught high school English."

Roco blinked twice, and Carson grinned. "That don't seem right. I taught English?"

"Yes."

"Like I was a teacher at a school?"

Carson clapped him on the shoulder. "Maybe you aren't lazy in your real life. You must have made it through college."

"I'm not sure I believe that." Roco rubbed his chin. "I'm guessin' I wasn't married if you dragged me here."

"No, you weren't," Nancy confirmed. "Now, I really need to go."

"Wait, can you tell us where the others are?" Carson asked.

Nancy looked around the beach. "What others?"

"Lottie, Earl, and Kirk."

Nancy put a hand over her heart. "Kirk was with you? Thank goodness. I lost him a while back and I was worried. I don't know where they are. People are moving around without my guidance. It's stressing me out, to be honest."

"It should be," Carson said. "I thought about trying to gather up all the real people, but if we can just get torn away and thrown into a different story, I'm not sure it would do much good."

"I will figure this out," Nancy promised. "I hope I can do it without going to my father. That would be a last resort."

"You have a father?" Roco asked. "And he's still alive?"

"Are you saying I'm too old to have a father?" Nancy grinned and suddenly looked sixty years younger. Her silver hair turned red and her wrinkles faded. Carson's eyes widened.

"Wow," Roco muttered.

"This is what I actually look like." Her voice was higher and more melodious. "Where I come from, people are immortal. I can look whatever age I want. I choose to look older because that calms people down. Older people are easier for some people to connect with. No one wants advice from someone who looks like this."

"I dunno," Roco said. "I think you should keep lookin' like that."

Carson hid a grin.

Nancy gave Roco a pointed glance. "Yes, and that is why I don't. If I appear this way to people, the men all try to flirt, and the women are all intimidated. I am a fairy, after all, and it's hard to find a mortal that is as beautiful as a fairy."

Carson wasn't going to give her the satisfaction of agreeing with her, even though it was probably true. She was stunning.

"Why is *Peter Pan* a thing?" he asked. "There isn't a love interest."

Nancy drew in a deep breath through her nose. "Yes, well, there are times I try to make a story, and it fails."

"Oh?"

Nancy stared out at the water. "Most of the stories here came from my world. My world is a magical place. There are fairies and witches. There are mortals there as well. I tried my hand at matchmaking there before my father let me make this place. I tried to help the mortals."

"And you failed?" Roco asked.

Nancy crossed her arms and glared at him. "I didn't fail. I was quite good at what I did, and I used those experiences to help shape this place. I've tried to add more stories over the years, but they don't work the way they used to."

Carson motioned to the island. "And *Peter Pan* is one of the mistakes?"

Nancy frowned. "Yes. I was on Earth, and I found Peter. He was an unhappy baby, and his mother was neglectful. I thought if I took him to one of the magical worlds, he would do better. He would grow up happy and then I would help him fall in love. Something about Neverland is messy. It's not as bad as Wonderland, but it comes close sometimes. Once Peter reached a certain age, he stopped aging. I have no idea why. I probably shouldn't have transferred any of the story here, but what's done is done."

"Is that the same for *Alice in Wonderland* and *The Wizard of Oz*?" Carson asked. "Kirk said he wasn't sure who he was supposed to kiss in *The Wizard of Oz*."

Nancy ran a hand through her perfect hair. "More or less. Every time I've tried to do anything new in the last two hundred years, it's failed. I still made spots for them here because they took effort, but I never sent people to them. People only started entering them recently with all the problems. They are good stories, if nothing else. I also found people to write them that did a satisfactory job. Not like the earlier ones."

"So, now what?" Roco asked.

"Now I need to leave. I shouldn't have stayed chatting while things are so uncertain," Nancy said. "Try not to mess anything up more than it is." There was a puff of pink smoke, and she was gone.

Carson shook his head. "This is all so strange."

"Wowee," Roco said. "Who would have believed Nancy looked like that?"

Carson grinned. "It's more unbelievable to know you were an English teacher."

"I'm still not sure I believe it. Wait till I tell Earl. He'll get a laugh out of that for sure."

"We should have asked her about Earl's life," Carson said. He glanced out at the ocean and watched the pirate ship sail away. He'd told the other pirates to come back for them in a week. By then, he hoped they would be out of this story. He wasn't getting on a boat again.

Chapter 8

Carson's legs were getting tired. He and Roco had been walking around the island for a while, and all they had found was a bunch of sand and trees. There was no sign of people and no food they could see. It might have been hasty to send the ship away.

He could hear running water, so he turned in that direction. They stepped through a clump of trees, and a beautiful waterfall came into view. It came from a large rocky mass and fell into a crystal clear lake.

"Do you suppose it's safe to drink?" Roco asked. "I'm really thirsty."

"Probably," Carson said, hurrying over to the water's edge. He was thirsty and more than a little hungry. He kneeled down and cupped some water in his hands and smelled it.

"What does it smell like?" Roco asked, squatting beside him.

"Nothing." Carson took a sip and shrugged. "Tastes fine."

"Good," Roco said, lying on his stomach. He leaned over the water and slurped it up.

Water splashed into Carson's face, and he sat back on his knees, wiping it from his eyes.

"Watch it," Carson said.

"Stay out of our lake!" a feminine voice commanded.

Roco jumped up, and Carson's eyes bounced around until he saw a mermaid sitting on a rock in the water. She was wringing out her long black hair with both hands.

"We were just getting a drink," Carson said, standing next to Roco.

A thin mermaid with shoulder-length brown hair popped out of the water near the first one. "Unlikely."

"We don't let pirates touch this water," the first one said, pointing an accusing finger. "Leave now before we call for Peter."

"Yes," said the other. "You don't want to lose your other hand."

Carson held up both hands. "I still have two hands."

The first one tossed her hair over her shoulder. "So you say."

"Yes, I do say." He shook his head. Was there really any reason to argue with a pretend mermaid?

A golden-haired mermaid splashed up from the water and pulled out an orangish pink seashell and blew into it. A loud blare came from the fist sized shell and caused Carson and Roco to cover their ears. It was loud and sounded like a dying cow.

"What was that?" Roco said. "That was an awful sound."

The mermaids giggled.

"Now Peter is going to come teach you a lesson," the mermaid on the rock said with a smirk.

"I hope so," said the one with golden hair. "It's been boring around here."

The thin one grinned. "So boring. I won't even mind if he gets blood on our shore."

Carson rolled his eyes. They needed to get out of here. He didn't have time to mess with Peter Pan. *Peter Pan* was one of his least favorite stories. Who wanted to hear about a bratty kid that could fly? Not him.

"Hey, look," Roco said, pointing into the trees. Carson turned and saw a girl clothed in what looked like a dress made of leaves. He thought she was Lottie for a moment, but she was shorter with darker hair. She stood up straight and walked cautiously toward them. She held a small dagger, and her hand was shaking.

"She seems scared," Roco whispered. Carson nodded.

She stopped ten feet away and studied them carefully. "Are you Captain Hook?"

"I seem to be," Carson said. "Who are you?"

She laughed and then frowned. "Peter Pan."

Carson raised his eyebrow. "You? You're Peter Pan?"

She glanced down at her dagger. "Yes, I know. It's all rather ridiculous."

"Come on, Peter!" called one mermaid. "Teach these pirates a lesson!"

"She isn't blinking out," Roco said. "She must be real."

The girl's frown deepened. "I am real. I assume you aren't actually Captain Hook? You know about this mess and Nancy?"

"Yes. My name is Carson, and this is Roco. We're trying to get out of here and find our friends."

"I'm looking for my sister, Lottie, and my... friend Stephen."

"Are you Mara?"

She took a step back. "How did you know?"

"We were with Lottie until recently. We woke up in different places."

Mara sighed. "I need to find her. Lottie doesn't know how to do anything, so she might be in danger. Does she remember her life before she came here?"

"Yes. She's not as helpless as she was before she got her memory back. Do you remember your life before you came here?"

Mara's lip trembled, and she nodded. "Unfortunately, I am as helpless as I was before I remembered who I am. Well, not helpless, but clumsy. Can I come with you? I hate being by myself, and all the lost boys I've met on this island are flickering in and out of existence, and they are as rude as anything. It makes me uneasy."

"Of course ya can," Roco said. "We can't guarantee we won't disappear, though. With Nancy losing control, there's no telling what might happen."

"Stop talking to the pirates and fight!" said the golden-haired mermaid. "We haven't had anything exciting happen in so long."

"Yes, Peter," said the one on the rock. "You've been so dull lately."

"They are so obnoxious," Mara whispered. "They blow that stupid horn all day long and expect me to come running. If

I don't, they keep blowing it, and it can be heard all over the island."

"We can hear you, you know," one said. "If you keep insulting us, we might not help you anymore."

Mara rolled her eyes. "When have you helped me?"

A fourth mermaid sprang from the water and grabbed Roco's arm, pulling him in with her. The others laughed and shared amused grins.

"Roco!" Carson yelled, leaning over the water.

"Stay back, it's deep!" Mara yelled. She dropped her dagger and dove into the water.

Carson was in a panic. Now he was going to have to save both of them, and he wasn't the best swimmer. He could get himself across a pool, but he'd never had to save anyone.

Before he could react, Mara popped out of the water and pulled Roco to the surface. "Get him."

He reached for Roco's hand and pulled the coughing man onto the shore. Roco rolled to his hands and knees as coughs continued to rack his body.

The mermaids were laughing like it was the funniest thing they had ever seen. Mara gave the mermaids a dirty look and swam to the rock where the first mermaid sat. She pulled herself to the top and pushed the mermaid into the water.

The mermaid surfaced next to her friends. "What's the big deal, Peter?"

Mara stood on the rock and held her head high. "What did I tell you about trying to drown people, Azra?"

Azra frowned. "Not to."

Mara placed her hands on her hips. "So, what are you doing?"

"We didn't think you would care about pirates." Azra sniffed. "We thought you only cared about those silly little boys that follow you."

"Yes, Peter," the golden-haired mermaid pouted. "You used to care about us more than those boys. Now you neglect us to a fault."

"That's because you are rude and dangerous. No more attacking people. If you do, I'll be upset. Do you understand?"

"What are we supposed to do, then?" she huffed.

"I don't know. Not drowning anyone would be nice."

"Fine, but we aren't calling for you again for at least a day. We're angry." The mermaids all disappeared beneath the surface.

Mara let out a shaky breath. She leaped into the air and flew the short distance to shore. Carson's eyes widened. Nothing here should surprise him. Mara's foot touched the ground, then the other one. She shrieked as she tumbled to the dirt.

"Are you alright?" he asked, holding out a hand. She grabbed it and let him pull her up.

"Fine. That's actually one of my better landings."

"Thanks for saving me," Roco said, getting to his feet.

Mara nodded. "I'm a strong swimmer. It's a good thing, too. I've had to pull out at least three lost boys since I came here. Those mermaids are horrid creatures."

Carson's eyes drifted over the trees. "Are there any fruit trees or anything around here?" he asked. "We missed breakfast."

Mara picked up the dagger and turned it around nervously in her hands. "I suppose I could take you to the hideout. There is plenty of food there, but you will have to deal with the lost boys."

Carson's stomach growled. "We can deal with that."

"Alright," Mara said. "But don't say I didn't warn you."

Lottie wasn't sure what to do about Britta. The woman was riding Falada like she was the queen of the world. Every time Lottie tried to protest, the woman cut her off, and she found it difficult to speak. She didn't know what kind of power Britta was using, but it was frustrating.

Trying to turn the horse in the other direction had proved futile. The horse kept moving forward and wouldn't stop so she could get off. She thought about jumping, but breaking something would only slow her down. She had no clue where she was, and she didn't want to be hurt and alone with no one to help.

"You smell foul," Falada said to Britta. "I'd prefer to carry the princess."

Britta smacked him on the side. "Shut up, horse. You will carry me, and you will call me the princess."

Falada whinnied. "Calling you something does not make it so."

"Falada, can't you throw her?" Lottie asked.

"Throw her? Indeed not," Falada said with a neigh. "I would like nothing better, but I cannot."

"Can you do anything?" Lottie asked.

"Sorry," he said, dropping his head. "All I can do is tell the king and the prince when we arrive."

"Oh, no one will believe you," Britta said with a manic laugh. "You will probably end up losing your head if you speak. No one wants to hear from a horse."

Lottie wished she knew the story. If she did, she might be able to predict what was in store for her.

She sat back and tried to relax. Riding this far was uncomfortable. With luck, the king would believe the horse. Believe the horse. She snorted. Who believed a horse? Although, most horses didn't talk, so people might be shocked into listening. It would definitely get everyone's attention.

She thought about Carson and hoped with everything in her that he was the prince. If he was, things would be smooth. If not, who knew what would become of her?

Carson was stunned by the chaos. Mara had led them to an underground hideout and given them some oatmeal. Not exactly what Carson was hoping for, but it was better than nothing. He had never seen anything like the lost boys. They must be the reason the phrase bouncing off the walls had been invented.

The hideout was cluttered with clothing, homemade toys, and garbage. Mara had to kick a path through the mess just so they could all sit down. Before they had been there a minute, he had been bitten, kicked, and tripped. It had gone no better for Roco.

He hurried and shoveled his oatmeal into his mouth. He didn't want to be here any longer than he needed to.

A boy with messy long hair dumped a cup of water on Roco and then ran around the room laughing. Mara stood in the corner looking like a scared mouse. She gripped her dagger and frowned.

"THAT'S ENOUGH!" Roco yelled, getting to his feet. The boys all paused and watched him. "Sit. All of you."

The ten boys all sat down, their eyes wide.

Roco pointed his finger at them. "Has no one ever told you how to behave?"

A boy with a scar running down one cheek crossed his arms defiantly. "This coming from a dirty old pirate?"

"Why'd you bring a pirate, anyhow?" said the biter. "That seems like going against your own code, Peter."

Mara frowned. "They aren't real pirates."

The boys laughed.

"That's Captain Hook, you got there," said a small redheaded boy. "You can't fool us, Peter. Is this some kinda trick?"

"That's it," said a boy with black hair and eyes. "This is a test, right?"

"It's not a test, it's a trick," said the redhead.

"No, it's a test."

"No way!" The boy jumped from his seat and took down the other boy. They started slugging each other, and some of the other boys joined in.

"Please get me out of here!" Mara called over the noise. "I can't take it anymore. They've been like this since I came."

Carson shoved the rest of the food in his mouth and stood. There wasn't any reason to stick around.

"STOP!" Roco yelled.

The boys all kept fighting, and Roco started pulling them off each other. "I said stop!" he commanded. "Fighting is not the answer."

Carson watched in shock. He couldn't believe the small man was getting them all separated. Once he pulled them off, they all sat silently watching him. Carson didn't fail to notice they were all blinking in and out. None of them were real.

Once Roco had them separated, he started on a lecture. "Fighting is a show of weakness."

"We ain't weak," one protested.

"It's weak, I tell ya. Strong people deal with their problems in different manners. They talk things out. Anyone can take a swing at someone. It takes a person with discipline to control their temper and act with honor."

"Sometimes fighting is the only way," the redhead said. "Right, Peter?"

All heads turned to Mara. She fiddled with the dagger. "I suppose it is sometimes. Not just because of a disagreement."

"I think Peter bonked his head," said the boy with dark hair. "He's been acting funny for a while."

"Let's go," Carson said. "They aren't real, so lecturing them is a waste of time."

Roco nodded. "It is the first time Nancy's claim that I'm a teacher felt right."

Mara stepped over a pile of papers on her way to the trapdoor they'd come in through. "Galvin, you're in charge," she said to a tall boy with sandy hair. "I won't be back."

Carson and Roco followed her out. Behind them, Carson could hear the arguing pick up again. Roco's lecture hadn't stayed with them.

Chapter 9

Lottie wanted to scream, but she kept it in. Britta was in more control of this story than Lottie was comfortable with, and she wasn't even real. She didn't blink out a lot, but enough to make it obvious. They had arrived at a castle the night before, and Britta had announced herself as the princess. She told them Lottie was her servant, and everyone believed it. She hadn't seen Britta or the prince since.

Lottie needed to get out of here and find Carson. She might be angry about the memories she had of their last few meetings, but he was the closest thing to home. She rushed through the halls, trying to find the way out.

This castle was like a maze. Lottie wondered if that was to keep her in. The halls were all painted a shimmering white and paintings of royalty and picturesque scenery popped up every five feet. None of the paintings stood out more than the others, so it was hard to know if she was passing the same ones and going in circles.

"There you are, my dear," the robust king said, rushing to her. He ran a hand over his gray beard. "I've been talking to the princess, and she wants to keep you on as staff. I've the perfect task for you."

"Oh?" Lottie asked through gritted teeth. She tried to look passive so she wouldn't offend the man.

"I need an able-bodied person to help care for the geese. There is a younger boy who has been good with them, but he could use some help."

"I don't know how to care for geese," Lottie admitted. She regretted saying it as soon as it came out of her mouth. If she could go outside, she could leave.

"Oh, that's not a problem. Young Conrad will help you. He loves the geese and knows quite a bit about them."

"Wonderful," Lottie said, bowing her head.

"And you need not worry about the horse the princess rode in on. She has commanded the dangerous beast to be beheaded."

Lottie's head shot up. "Beheaded? But why?"

The king patted her shoulder. "The princess said the creature is possessed, and that it cannot be trusted. Nothing for you to worry about."

Lottie sighed. Now she was going to have to go save Falada. Every time the horse spoke, it shook her to her core, but that didn't mean he deserved to lose his head. Britta had probably only demanded it because Falada could tell her secret.

"Wait here, and I'll have someone come take you to the goose pasture."

Lottie nodded and watched the king waddle down the hallway. She wanted to hurry to the stables and free Falada, but she would probably end up more lost than she already was. Footsteps sounded behind her, and she spun around.

"Lottie?" a man said.

Lottie smiled and ran toward him. "Stephen! I am so happy to see you!" The man's eyes widened as Lottie crushed him in a hug. He patted her awkwardly on the back and coughed. Lottie wasn't surprised. When she was playing the wicked stepsister, Stephen had been their hired hand. She had never treated him well. No one had until Mara fell in love with him.

"I'm surprised to see you here," he said when she released him and stepped back.

"I have to get out of here," Lottie said. "This castle is impossible to navigate. Can you help me?"

"The king wants me to take you to the goose pasture. You can follow me," he said, leading her down the long hall. "Seeing you is probably the most shocking thing that's happened to me lately, and that is saying something."

"I can't tell you how happy I am to see you. I need you to take me to the stable. There is a horse I need to save."

"Falada? I heard the princess's horse was going to be put to death."

"Yes, and I need you to help me save him."

"*You* want to save a horse? How did you get here?" he asked, turning and beginning down a long stone staircase.

She tried not to feel insulted. Her character in *Cinderella* couldn't have cared less about a horse. "It's a long story. I'm sorry for how I always treated you. I didn't mean to. Something was controlling me and making me into someone else."

Stephen glanced at her. "Did you remember a different life?"

"Yes, and I'm appalled at the way I've been treating everyone."

He opened a door at the bottom of the stairs, and sunlight steamed onto their faces. Lottie walked outside and glanced around. They must be in the back of the castle. Perhaps it was a servant's entrance.

"We didn't have a lot of control over what we did in that story. The stables are this way. Do you know where Mara is?"

Lottie frowned. "No. I was going to ask you the same thing. I haven't seen her since the day after Ella left."

"We were planning on getting married—well, our characters were. Then, one day, I woke up here. Nancy came and told me everything. I assume you know Nancy?"

"Yes."

"Now I remember my real life, but I still can't get Mara out of my mind."

"Let's leave. We can take the horse and look for Mara and Carson."

Stephen tipped his head to the side. "Who is Carson?"

Lottie looked at her hands. "He's my... neighbor."

Stephen looked at her from the corner of his eye. "Neighbor?"

"Yes. From the real world. He was here, stuck in *Beauty and the Beast*. We were traveling with some other people and then one day I woke up in this story. I don't even know what it is."

Stephen pushed open the door to the stable. "It's *The Goose Girl*."

"I don't know that one."

"It doesn't end well for the horse."

"Never does," Falada called from inside.

Lottie hurried to the horse stall and fumbled with the latch. She opened it, and the horse nuzzled her face.

"If we are going to go, let's be quick," Stephen said.

The horse shook his head. "Nancy doesn't like it when people change the story. It's already too different this time. There is a silly little fox that won't leave me in peace."

"Where is he?" Lottie asked, glancing around the immaculate stable.

Falada motioned to the stall. "Curled up in the straw."

"Max?" she asked, poking her foot around the straw. Max popped out, and Lottie smiled. She picked him up and cradled him in her arms.

Stephen shook his head. "I never would have thought I would see you cuddling an animal."

"I'm not that Lottie," she said. "I swear I'm nowhere near as horrid."

Stephen laughed. "You were pretty awful. I know it wasn't your fault, though." He led another horse from the stall and mounted it. "I'm guessing this isn't really stealing a horse, since this is all fake."

Lottie placed Max on Falada's back and climbed on behind him. "It's strange that something can seem so real and not be." Falada followed Stephen's horse out of the stable, and they galloped toward the dirt road. Lottie stayed even with him so they could talk.

"I'm glad I already knew how to ride when I came here," she told him. "My character never rode a horse. I was always in a carriage."

"So, tell me about this Carson you are looking for. He was your neighbor? Old, young?"

"My age," Lottie said, staring ahead. "We went to school together and stuff."

"And stuff?"

Lottie was sure he was raising his eyebrow, even though she wasn't looking at him. She could hear it in his voice.

"We were best friends for a long time."

"Just friends?"

Lottie could feel her cheeks heat. "Yes."

"Hm."

"He's the reason Nancy brought me here," she admitted.

"Ah," Stephen said. "One of those kinds of friendships."

Lottie blew a strand of hair from her face. She didn't know why she felt like telling Stephen. He probably hated her for how many times she'd been rude to him. She'd been unkind over and over with each Cinderella, and Stephen had never reacted unkindly. Maybe that was just his character, but she had a feeling he was a nice guy.

"I was in love with him for so long," she said, patting Max on the head. "He didn't know. I overheard him tell his friend he would never ask me out. It's a long dumb story."

"So, why is he here?"

"I don't know. We got into a fight, and I didn't see him for over a year after high school, and then I came here."

"He must have had some problem with love," Stephen said, following a curve in the road. "From what Nancy told me the other day, she only brings people with love trouble."

"What happened to you? Why are you here?"

Stephen rubbed the back of his neck. "My fiancée left me at the altar—well, not at the altar, but might as well have. The day we were supposed to get married, she called me. Called me on the phone. She couldn't even tell me in person. She said she'd changed her mind, and she never wanted to see me again."

"I'm sorry. That's terrible." Lottie couldn't even imagine how hard that would be.

"Yeah, I still don't know what happened. I was angry. I met Nancy the next day. She sent me here without even giving me enough time to recover. I would have sorted it all out in time, but here I am. I refused to cooperate with the stories. Nancy begged me to try, but I wouldn't."

Lottie nodded. "That sounds familiar."

Stephen sighed. "I eventually became the character. I guess that's the same with a lot of people here."

"It sounds like it. So, did Mara help you get over your fiancée?"

"Mara was my fiancée."

Lottie's eyes widened. "Did you talk about it?"

He patted the horse. "No. I didn't remember until after we were separated."

Lottie tilted her head as she glanced at him. "And you still want to find her?"

"More than ever. We had something special. Something must have happened that she didn't tell me about."

The trail ended, and they led the horses into the trees.

"I'm surprised Nancy put you two near each other," Lottie said. "Maybe she wanted you to fall in love again?"

"Of course she did," said Falada. "When Nancy finds hopeless cases, she often puts them near one another. She's giving them a chance to fall in love again without remembering their past heartaches. Of course, it never amounts to anything."

Lottie's mouth turned down. "Why would a horse know all of this?"

Falada neighed. "I'm stubborn. In my story, my head gets chopped off. I will not keep doing that over and over without an explanation. Of course, she never actually told me she puts hopeless cases near each other, I'm guessing. It seems like something she would do."

Stephen shook his head. "I have to pry any information I can out of Nancy and she tells a horse?"

"I'm more than a horse," Falada claimed. "I'm Nancy's friend. She tells me about all of you."

"Do you know where our friends are?" Lottie asked.

"Not even Nancy knows that these days. She's only finding people by accident."

"What's that up ahead?" Stephen asked. Lottie looked up and saw a thin tower.

Falada sped up. "It's Rapunzel's tower, of course. I've always wanted to see it."

The tower was tall and made of dull gray stones. There was no door that Lottie could see, and only one window near the top. They stopped when they got closer and dismounted.

"How are we going to get up there?" Stephen asked.

Lottie looked up. "Do we need to get up there? I doubt anyone we are looking for is here."

Stephen cupped his hands and held them to his mouth. "Is anyone up there?" he called. No one answered.

Lottie put a hand to her head. She felt dizzy. She closed her eyes, and when she opened them, she was looking out the window of the tower. How had she gotten clear up here? She grabbed the window ledge and looked down. Stephen and the horses stared up at her from way down below.

"Now what?" she called down.

"Did your hair grow?" Stephen called back.

Lottie grabbed a handful of hair and pulled on it. It kept coming. "Yes!"

"Then, throw it down, and I'll try to climb up."

"That sounds painful!" Lottie looked around the small circular room. There was a narrow bed with fluffy blue pillows and a closet. Next to the closet was a narrow spiral staircase. She turned back to Stephen. "There's a staircase! Let me see if there's another way in."

Lottie turned to hurry to the stairs and tripped on her hair. She fell and smacked her knees and palms against the ground. She stood back up and grabbed her long brown hair, wrapping it around her hands. It was surprising how heavy hair could be. Once it was all twisted around her hands, she walked carefully down the stairs. It was hard to see past the wad of hair.

At the bottom of the stairs was a stone wall. Lottie pushed her weight against it and a hidden door opened, flooding the space with natural light.

Lottie waved to Stephen. "Over here!"

Stephen walked over with Max tucked safely in his arms. "Impressive hair."

"It's not as manageable as some popular movies would make me think," Lottie said, gazing down at the knots. She'd rolled it into a nice mess. "I wonder if we can cut it."

"Is there anything inside we can use?"

"I'm not sure. Where are the horses?"

"They disappeared when you were coming down."

Lottie sighed. "Walking will take so much longer."

"Why don't we stay here?" Stephen asked. "Where would we walk to? With everything in chaos, I don't see any reason to wander around aimlessly. It might be best to stay in one place and hope Nancy gets things under control."

"If we're staying in one place, I need to cut this hair. I already tripped on it." Lottie could still feel a throbbing pain in her knees.

"Let's go check inside," Stephen suggested. Max jumped from his arms and ran into the tower. Lottie followed. She didn't have a better idea.

"We need to get back to the boat," Roco said, pointing at the pirate ship. The pirates had come back the next day instead of following Carson's instructions to come back in a week. Carson watched with resignation as the dinghy came closer. Two pirates sat inside, rowing toward to them.

"We're going with pirates?" Mara asked. "Is that safe?"

Carson rubbed his short beard. "I don't see any other options. We've been trying to find a way out of here since yesterday, and we aren't coming up with any good ideas."

"What good will the ship do?" she asked. "Can we sail out of Neverland?"

"Normally, I would say no, but things have been so weird, it might work."

Roco angled his head to the side. "What about fairy dust? I'm having a memory about fairy dust making a ship fly."

Mara cringed. "I can call for Tinkerbell if you want me to, but she is not a nice fairy."

Carson ran his tongue over his teeth as he weighed their options. He wished he had a toothbrush. If he didn't brush his teeth soon, he was really going to look like a pirate. When he changed stories, things like that always fixed themselves. He would worry about that later.

"Hey, Captain!" one pirate called from the small boat. "You sure you want us to be gone for a week?" The man flickered and so did his companion.

"No, we're coming." Carson motioned with his head toward the dinghy, and Mara and Roco followed him into the ocean. The water was warm, and the sand was soft. Something poked his foot, and he bent down and picked up a pretty pink shell. He tossed it and watched it get swallowed up by the ocean. If they were anywhere else, he would have kept it. It was pointless to keep anything here. It would disappear.

"What are you doing with Pan?" a pirate with an eyepatch and a scruffy chin asked. "Is he your prisoner?"

"No, he's coming with us."

"But, Captain..."

"No. Don't question me," Carson said. He put on his best scowl, and the pirate bowed his head.

Mara put one leg over the small boat and immediately fell into the water. He'd learned in the last eighteen hours that Mara had been right. She was extremely clumsy.

She popped back up before he could react. "I'm fine!" she said, pushing wet hair from her face.

Carson picked her up and set her down in the boat. Roco climbed in while Carson held it steady and then Carson climbed in. The dinghy rocked dangerously from side to side but didn't tip.

The pirates rowed to the ship in silence. Mara was shivering, and Roco looked tired. Roco had changed in the last while. He wasn't complaining about everything any more.

Carson sighed as they came closer to the ship. He wasn't thrilled about being back. Hopefully, his stomach would do better than before. If Nancy could control so many things, she could at least have the decency to not let him get seasick.

***

"Hey, I see a tower," Roco said, gesturing ahead.

Carson sighed with relief. They'd been walking for days, seeing nothing but trees. "Good. I hope that means something is going to happen." He didn't know what they would have done without Aspen dropping food to them every day. They had gone to sleep on the pirate ship and woken in a forest. Thankfully, they were still together.

"It's so strange the way our clothing changed," Mara said, glancing down at her blue tunic and tan pants. Mara hadn't said a lot. She didn't complain. She just walked, tripped on everything, and looked somber.

"It shows how broken the world is," Carson said. Only part of his clothing had changed. He still had his pirate hat and boots, but his shirt had changed into a regular gray tunic. The beard was still there, but it didn't seem to grow. He wished he could shave. It reminded him too much of being the beast.

They approached the tower and looked up. It was as high as a three story building. Roco went up to the stone structure and started pushing on it with his hands. Nothing happened. Carson joined him, looking for any way in. His finger slipped around one stone, and he pulled on it. A heavy stone door creaked open.

"Should we go in?" Roco asked.

Mara bit her lip. "What if someone is inside?"

"I guess we'll see," Carson said. If no one was there, they could stay until Nancy fixed this mess. Or until they got torn away and thrown in some other random place. It would be nice to have shelter. The sky was gray and threatened rain.

Carson could tell Roco and Mara were nervous, so he went first. There was a narrow spiral staircase going up. He walked up cautiously, listening for any sign of occupants. When he got to the top, the first thing he saw was Lottie sleeping in a small bed.

"Lottie," Mara whispered. "Thank goodness!"

Carson's heart pounded against his chest. Was everything alright? Lottie was lying on her back with her hands folded against her stomach. It looked... scripted. Her hair was draped across the pillow and looked like she had hacked it with a knife. Max was sleeping at the foot of the bed, rolled into a ball.

"Is she okay?" Roco asked. "She looks a little like Snow did when she was magically dead."

Mara's eyes widened. "Magically dead? What does that mean?"

"It means she can only come back to life with love's kiss or something like that."

Roco and Mara both looked at Carson. He swallowed and glanced away. Was this *Sleeping Beauty*? If so, could he wake her? Deep down, Carson knew he was still in love with Charlotte, but she wasn't in love with him. She'd made that more than clear.

"We were only friends," Carson choked.

"I dunno," Roco said. "I saw the way you watched her and tried not to watch her before. It was a look you don't give a friend. Might as well try anyhow. What do you got to lose?"

Carson took a deep breath and stepped toward Lottie. Roco was right. If it didn't work, they wouldn't be any worse off. He sat on the bed and leaned toward her and paused. He'd wanted to kiss Lottie for years. She had kissed him when he was the beast, but he'd been too hairy to even feel it. Now, she was asleep. Magically asleep, if Roco knew what he was talking about. That wasn't how his daydreams went.

"Why are you taking so long?" Roco asked.

He rubbed his hand over his beard and glanced at Roco. "What if she gets mad?"

Roco rolled his eyes. "She won't get mad. It ain't like she can give you permission if she's magically dead."

"Please try," Mara pleaded.

Carson leaned forward and lightly pressed his lips to hers. Lottie jerked up, hitting her head into his. He stumbled back and grabbed his head.

Lottie held her head and glared at him. "What are you doing?"

"He was kissing you," Roco said, as if it was the most obvious thing in the world.

She frowned. "Kissing me? Why?"

"Because you were magically dead. True love's kiss and all."

"I was not magically dead. I—Mara!" Lottie hopped off the bed and caught Mara up in a hug. "Are you alright?"

Mara wiped a tear from her eye and laughed. "I'm fine. I was scared I'd never find you."

"I was so worried when you disappeared. I know we aren't actually sisters, and I was awful to you so many times. Sorry about that. We've been through so much together, and I was terrified you weren't real."

"I'm real. I had the same worry about you."

"I knew you were real when I ran into Stephen. He told me about... things."

Mara looked at the floor. "He told you?"

"Some of it."

"Do you know where he is?"

"He's out hunting. I couldn't sleep last night, so I was taking a nap."

Mara peered up at her. "So, he's going to be back?"

Carson could see the worry in her eyes.

"I hope so," Lottie said. "It's hard to know what's going to happen around here."

"Where's Earl?" Roco asked. "And Kirk?"

"They aren't with you?"

"Naw. We hoped they were with you. Perhaps they're in the swamp with Jurry and Meena. This is a fine mess Nancy's put us all in."

Carson gazed around the small room. It was going to be crowded with all of them here, but it would be better than sleeping outside in the rain.

"What happened to your hair?" he asked Lottie, reaching out and touching the jagged edges. It was longer than before, but uneven.

"It was too long. We found a knife, and Stephen cut it. It didn't go very well, but it was better than carrying around miles of hair."

"*Rapunzel*?"

"Yes, but so far, no scary witch."

"Mara?" Stephen said from the top of the stairs. He dropped the apples he was carrying and rushed toward her.

"Hi," she said in a whisper. He wrapped her in a hug, and Mara started sobbing as she clung to him. "I'm sorry," she said. "I'm sorry for what I did. Can you ever forgive me?"

Stephen rubbed a hand over her hair and kissed her forehead. "Yes, but I want to know why."

Roco looked as confused as Carson felt.

Mara sniffled. "My father didn't want us to be together. I let him bully me."

Lottie grabbed Carson and Roco by the hands and pulled them down the stairs. She pushed against the wall and pulled them through the secret doorway. Carson closed it behind them.

"It's gonna rain," Roco said, glancing at the dark clouds.

"They need a minute," Lottie said. "Stephen and Mara were engaged before Nancy brought them here."

Carson nodded. He could handle a little rain.

"I ain't gonna stay out here," Roco said, pulling the door open. "Don't worry, I'll stay at the bottom. I'm not gonna get rained on if I don't have to."

Lottie walked away from the tower, and Carson followed. Aspen flew overhead, and Lottie stopped to watch. Carson studied her as she gazed at the majestic bird. Her mouth turned down, and she seemed tired. Then, the rain began.

Carson ignored the drops as they ran down his face and arms. He wondered if Lottie was aware of the rain. She kept her focus on Aspen. Carson swallowed a lump in his throat. It didn't matter what Charlotte had done. He was always going to care. No matter how much he wished he could forget her, he never had. He never would.

Shaking his head, he realized Lottie was staring at him with her eyebrow raised. He hoped he didn't look like a lovesick idiot. He put his hands in his pockets and walked away. It would be better if he could keep the image of her laughing in his face at the forefront of his mind. Picturing her any other way would only cause more pain.

Chapter 10

Lottie sat under a tree and ignored the rain running down her face. The tree sheltered her from the worst of the storm. Aspen sat on a branch nearby, her head tucked into her back feathers.

"Hey, Lottie," Roco said, sitting beside her. "I was going to sit at the bottom of the stairs and wait for your sister to finish talking, but it was cramped at the bottom, so I went up a bit further."

"You eavesdropped on them?" Lottie asked, smiling at her friend.

Roco shrugged unapologetically. "A little. They worked things out between them."

"So, we can go back in?"

"Yeah. I peeked around the corner and saw the two of them kiss. They disappeared right before my eyes."

Lottie frowned. "I'm glad for them, but I was hoping to talk to Mara. We spent most of our time here fighting, but we had some good times. It felt like she *was* my sister. I don't have any siblings back home. I didn't even ask her what her real name is and where I can find her if I ever get out of here."

"Nancy's magic must still work to some extent or they wouldn't have gone back home."

Lottie nodded. "I hope they did go home and didn't end up in the swamp like your brother."

Roco's mouth turned up in a mischievous grin. "You and Carson should try it."

"Try ending up in the swamp?"

Roco rolled his eyes. "No. Try kissing and getting sent back home."

Lottie looked down at her wet hands. "We would have to be in love for that to happen."

"I read your diary, you know."

Lottie looked up at him and pushed a stray lock of hair from her forehead. "Then, you know he doesn't love me."

"Garbage," Roco said. "If you're worried about that conversation you heard in the back of his car, then you're being ridiculous."

Lottie laughed bitterly. "He said he would only ask me out as a joke."

"Perhaps you took it wrong. Or maybe he thought about it later and decided he did want to go to the dance with you. Since you were friends, it might have seemed weird to him at first."

She pulled her knees to her chest and hugged them. "I don't want to think about it."

"Give him a chance."

"He doesn't want a chance. I was the one who wanted a chance."

"If he wasn't heartbroken over you, then why is he here?"

Lottie rested her chin on her knees and sighed. "After our fight, I didn't talk to him for a year. Anything could have happened in that time. He could have fallen in love and had his heart broken by someone else." She wanted to cry, but she wouldn't.

Roco stared ahead for a moment and appeared to be in a daze. "I was only an English teacher part time. The rest of the time, I was a guidance counselor."

"You remember?"

"Yes, and I'm horrified at the grammar I've been using. I'm also embarrassed that I read your diary. Sorry about that."

Lottie raised her head. "So, why did Nancy send you here?"

Roco shook his head. "Nope. We are talking about you. You and Carson had a misunderstanding, and you need to have a talk. Get it all out in the open."

"No, I can't. I don't want him to know he broke my heart. He never knew that I loved him."

"Do you still love him?"

Lottie grimaced. "I don't want to talk about it."

"I think you do."

She swallowed hard. "I'm not going to talk to Carson. It won't do any good."

"What won't?" Carson asked, coming toward them.

Lottie felt her neck turn at least three shades of red. Had he heard them? Probably not, or he wouldn't have asked.

"The rain stopped," Lottie observed, looking anywhere but at Carson.

"Mara and that man disappeared," Roco said. "I was telling Lottie the two of you should kiss and see if you get sent home, but Lottie doesn't think it will work."

Carson narrowed his eyes. "Of course it won't work. Even if everything wasn't messed up, I'm pretty sure the people kissing have to be in love."

Lottie's mouth formed a hard line, and she tried to swallow the lump that had formed in her throat. Carson couldn't be any more clear than that. She stood and tried to brush the mud off her wet dress. She wasn't going to stand here and let Carson break her heart again.

"I don't see why you can't try," Roco said, joining them on his feet. "What if it worked? It would be silly to be stuck here if you didn't have to be."

"There's something different about you," Carson said. "I can't quite place it."

"I remembered my old life," Roco said, a far off look in his eyes. "It all came spilling into my mind. At the high school, I spent a lot of time counseling teenagers, and I think you should take my advice."

"And you counseled them to kiss each other?" Carson asked.

"Of course not," Roco said. "There was way too much of that going on in the high school already. Now that I remember who I am, I'm going to go back to the tower to think for a while. You two should stay here and talk about the past. You aren't going to get past it if you don't."

Lottie and Carson watched Roco walk away.

"That was so weird," Carson said. "He looks the same, but he feels like a different person."

"He is," Lottie said. "I wasn't a thing like the character I was supposed to be."

Carson folded his arms across his chest. "So, anything you want to talk about?"

"Not really." There was no way Lottie was going to spill her feelings to him. She didn't need his rejection or his sympathy.

"Kissing probably wouldn't do any good. We already kissed when I was the beast and when I thought you were magically dead."

Lottie wasn't sure if either one of those kisses would have counted, even if they were both in love. The first time she had kissed him and it was like kissing a furry animal. The second time she hadn't even realized Carson had kissed her until someone had pointed it out. She'd wanted to kiss Carson since she was twelve, and now she had, and it still felt like she hadn't.

Carson cleared his throat, and Lottie realized she was staring at his lips. Her eyes darted away, and she had the sudden urge to stomp on his toe and run away. That would only make her look guilty, though.

"Like I was saying, I don't think it would work, but what if it did?"

Lottie's eyes widened. What was he saying?

He took a step toward her. "It would be stupid to not try if there is even the smallest possibility of it working."

She crossed her arms and bit her nail. She couldn't make anything come out of her mouth.

"Come on, Char. It's just one kiss. What's it going to hurt?"

Lottie could feel tears threatening to burst forth, and she shook her head. It could hurt a lot. She'd daydreamed about it for years. How many times could a heart break? She was sure that was what would happen if he kissed her.

"Still not good enough for you?" he growled. "Fine, we can stay here forever." He turned and started back in the direction of the tower.

Lottie bit her lip. What if he was right? What if there was the possibility of getting out of this horrid place? "Carson, wait!" Lottie said, running after him. He turned his head and looked at her, but kept walking. "What if we try and end up in the swamp?"

Carson stopped. "At least we'll know."

Lottie's heart pounded in her chest. "Know what?"

"That it wouldn't work. We won't have to wonder."

Lottie nodded. "Alright."

Carson elevated an eyebrow. "You want to do it?"

"Yes," Lottie said with a confidence she didn't feel.

He took a step toward her and paused. He looked unsure of himself. Lottie would have smiled if she wasn't so nervous. He still made her stomach fill with butterflies when he looked at her.

She cocked her head and studied him. He wasn't going to do it. He had an expression Lottie couldn't decipher, but he didn't look like a man who was about to kiss anyone. Before she could turn and run away to the forest, Carson placed his hands on her upper arms. Goosebumps broke out across her them, and she tried not to appear nervous.

Carson's eyes searched hers, and she reminded herself to breathe. If he didn't do it soon, she was going to pass out or break into a hysterical fit of laughter. Nothing about this was healthy, she was certain.

"Just do it," she finally said.

The corners of Carson's mouth twitched upward. "Strange, I never thought you would beg me to kiss you."

"Beg? I didn't beg. I just want to get it over with."

His eyes sparkled. "Uh huh."

"It's true."

He winked. "You don't have to deny it."

Lottie glared at him. "Please. I think you're stalling because you don't know how."

Carson grinned, and Lottie's eyes narrowed. She broke free of his grasp and put her arms around his neck. He wrapped his arms around her and leaned down. When his lips met hers, everything inside of her felt warm, and if circumstances were different, she would be elated.

Lottie felt dizzy. She wasn't sure if that meant she was about to change stories or if finally kissing Carson was causing it. She had waited for this moment for so long. After a moment, she realized she wasn't fading to a different story, and she wasn't going home. She should pull away, but she couldn't make herself.

This was better than any daydream she had ever made up, and soon, she was going to have to pretend indifference. She didn't even mind Carson's scruffy facial hair. If she could stay in this moment forever, she would do it.

Carson needed to get a hold of himself. The longer he kissed Charlotte, the worse it was going to be. It felt so right to be here with her. He could almost forget their fight and the way she had trampled his heart. He held her closer and then she broke away.

"I guess it didn't work," she squeaked. "I'm going to go find Roco." She turned and rushed toward the tower. Carson stood rooted to the spot and watched her. He shivered and put his hands into his pants pockets. It was cold, but he didn't want to follow her.

He took a deep breath through his nose and let it out slowly. After all this time, he'd finally kissed Charlotte, and it was better than he'd ever imagined. Better, until she walked away. Now, he felt empty and tired.

"That was pathetic," a voice said from behind him. He jumped and spun around to see Earl walking toward him. He was covered in mud and a black and gray wolf followed behind him.

Carson frowned. "Where have you been?"

"Swamp. It seems to be the place most lost folks end up around here."

"Is Kirk with you?"

"Nah. He said he'd rather strike out on his own. Now let's talk about that kiss."

"I'd rather not," Carson said, running a hand over his face.

"I'm no expert, but you let her run off pretty easy."

Carson shrugged. "We tried something, and it failed. There's nothing else to it. We're still here. Not that it's surprising. We aren't in love or anything."

Earl snorted. "Sure you aren't."

"We were trying to go home."

"Just because you didn't get sent home doesn't mean Lottie's not in love with you. Everything's messed up."

"Lottie's not in love with me." It was painful to hear himself say it, even though he'd always known it. "Where did you get the wolf?"

"This is Finn. He shows up now and then when someone needs help. Without him, I never would have found you. Is Roco here?"

"Yes," Carson said, happy to have the subject changed. "He's in that tower over there. He got his memories back."

"So did I."

"Oh?"

Earl sighed. "Nothing exciting. I was a personal trainer at a local gym."

Carson could believe it. Earl and Jurry looked like bodybuilders. "So, why did Nancy send you here?"

"I'm not sure it's worth telling."

"You keep butting into my personal life."

Earl scratched his head. "Yeah, but that's different."

"How?"

"I don't know. Just is. Are we going to sit out here freezing or go inside and warm up?"

Carson laughed. "We can go inside, but I still want to hear the story. I guess you can tell me in front of Roco and Lottie." They walked through the mud in silence.

When they got to the tower, the door burst open, and Roco peered out. "Earl! Where have you been? You look awful. It's too bad this place doesn't have a shower. I can hardly tell you have red hair. Did you roll in the mud?"

Earl ran his hand through his hair. "I was in the swamp. It's not the most pleasant place to be."

"Earl was about to tell me about his life before he came here," Carson said, as Earl scowled. "Let's go up and talk."

They climbed the spiral staircase and entered the room. Lottie was stirring something over the fire. She spun around when they got to the top, and her cheeks were a nice shade of pink. Carson pretended not to notice.

"Earl's going to tell us about his life before he got here," Roco told her.

"I'm glad you found us," Lottie said, ladling hot cider into tin cups. She handed one to Earl and one to Roco. When she handed Carson his, their hands touched, and her face changed from pink to fiery red.

"Where did this come from?" he asked, taking a sip. It was good.

"Roco found it in that cupboard," she muttered. She took her own cup and sat on the bed.

Carson glanced at Earl. "So, are you going to tell us?"

Earl gulped down his cider and then placed his cup near the fire. "I was a personal trainer. I worked a lot of hours to make up for the low pay. It didn't give me time for much of a social life. I met a lot of women, but none of them were interested in me. Sometimes being short is a curse."

Roco nodded. "You've got that right."

"Well, one day, a woman came into the gym. She bought a membership and a session with me. Her name was Izla. She was as nosy as anything, but she had the brightest smile and the prettiest green eyes. She started coming in regularly, and I thought we were hitting it off pretty well."

"So, what happened?" Carson asked.

"I asked her out. I thought she would agree, but she didn't. It made me a little angry, and I told her off. I told her I knew she would go with me if I was taller. She got defensive, and I got defensive. That's about all there was to it."

"Then, you complained to Nancy, and she sent you here."

"No. I don't know what happened. Next morning, I woke up, and I was in this place. I didn't meet Nancy until I was here. She showed up and tried to boss me around when I didn't catch on to the story thing. We exchanged some rather choice words, and I refused to cooperate. I guess that's why I ended up stuck in *Snow White*."

"Nancy's not fair," Lottie said. "She's looking for reasons to bring people here."

"Agreed," Roco said. "I didn't even have anything against love or happiness like some people. I wasn't interested in it at that point in my life."

Earl tilted his head. "Who were you in your real life?"

"An English teacher, slash guidance counselor."

Earl broke into laughter. "That's the funniest thing I've heard in a while. Now really, who were you?"

Roco smiled. "I'm not joking."

"His grammar has improved since he remembered," Carson said, grinning.

Earl laughed again. "That's hilarious. I thought you were a delinquent college student or something. I found Jurry and Meena when I was in the swamp. They had their memories back as well. Jurry was a truck driver. With that beard, it makes sense. But you? A teacher? I'm surprised you made it through college."

"I wasn't lazy in that life," Roco said. "I had a master's degree, and I was working on my doctorate."

Carson clenched his fists. Nancy talked about helping people, and in reality, she was the bad guy. Well, bad person. She might believe she had good intentions, but she had interrupted a lot of innocent people's lives. It was worse for people like Charlotte, Roco, and Earl. They had almost lost themselves completely.

"We need to do something," Lottie said. "Is there a way we can help fix things? Nancy said something about a person messing things up. Jerry, maybe?"

"Terry," Earl and Roco said at the same time.

"So, can we find him?" Carson asked. "What did he do?"

Earl and Roco shared a look.

"Terry could do magic. Nancy couldn't figure out how he was learning it," Earl said. "He started manipulating the stories. He chose which ones he wanted to be in, and he messed them up. For some reason, he started following Olivia and bothering her."

"Can he fix things?" Carson asked.

"Don't know. He's not exactly... useful at the moment. Nancy did something that made him fall into a deep sleep. We put him in Snow White's glass coffin and left him in a tower similar to this one."

Lottie shifted on the bed. "Can we wake him?"

"I doubt it," Roco said. "It has to be someone who is in love with him. It can't just be a kiss. Nancy wanted to make sure he wouldn't wake up."

"Is anyone in love with him?" Lottie asked.

Roco shrugged. "Not that we know of."

"We wouldn't want to wake him up anyway," Earl assured them. "He wasn't very stable, and he was dangerous."

"We can't stay here forever," Carson said. "If Terry can fix this, then we should try to wake him."

Earl shook his head. "Terry wanted revenge on Nancy. He planned to take over, not return home."

"But if everything is messed up forever, he may be the only one who can help."

Lottie frowned. "If he wanted to take over, I doubt he would help us."

"He might if he realized how messed up this place is." Carson knew he was grasping at straws, but he didn't want to spend the rest of his life in a place where he might wake up anywhere at any moment.

"It's a bad idea," Roco said. "Terry was unsettling. One minute, he was playing a part, and the next, he was making threats. Still, it might be our only option."

Lottie placed her cup on the floor. "How is he an option? If he can't wake up without a true love's kiss, and no one is in love with him, then finding him won't help."

"There is also the problem of us not knowing where he is," Earl said. "The tower was somewhere in *Alice in Wonderland,* and we don't know how to change stories."

"Perhaps the animals can help us," Roco said, glancing at Max. "They've led us places before."

Lottie crossed her arms. "I'm not sure I want to run into someone like him. Even if we were to find him, how would we wake him up? And if we did wake him up, what would we say to get him to agree to help us?"

Carson didn't miss the fear in Lottie's eyes. Still, he couldn't help thinking this might be the only way. He'd wasted enough of his life in this place, and it was time to go back home.

"I'm going to look for him," he said. "Any of you are welcome to come with me."

"It's too dangerous," Lottie protested.

"You don't have to come." Carson wouldn't make any of them come. He would go on his own if he had to. "I can't wait around, hoping we figure something out. I need to be doing something."

"I'll come," Earl said. "It's not like I have anything better to do."

"So will I," Roco added. "If you manage to find Terry and wake him up, you're going to need help."

They all looked at Lottie, and the corners of her mouth turned down. "I'll come. It doesn't sound smart, but I don't want to be left alone here."

Carson nodded. "Great. Let's get a goodnight's sleep, and we can start tomorrow."

Chapter 11

"I can't keep going at this pace," Lottie said, as she jogged behind Carson and Earl. Roco was a few paces behind them, and Finn and Max were in the lead. She hoped the wolf and fox knew where they were going. As soon as Carson had asked the animals to take them to Terry, the two animals had taken off into the forest, leaving them little choice but to follow.

Carson turned around and grinned at her. "Are you getting soft? Not enough cheer practices since you got here?"

Lottie scowled. "Cheerleaders don't run that much, Mr. Track Team. Ask the animals to slow down."

Finn and Max came to a stop, and Carson had to jump over Max to avoid running over him.

Roco stopped and leaned over, resting his hands on his knees. "I—think—I'm gonna puke."

Earl laughed. "That sounds about right."

"Hey," Roco protested. "Not all of us were personal trainers."

"Or track stars," Lottie panted. She rubbed the stitch in her side. "Any chance we can get where we are going without running?"

Max tilted his head and glanced up at Finn. Finn was a lot less scary when he was the size of a normal wolf.

The scenery started going out of focus, and Lottie squeezed her eyes shut and opened them again. Everything was moving in waves, and she worried Roco might not be the only one that was going to lose his breakfast.

"What's going on?" Earl asked, stumbling to the side. Lottie closed her eyes again and felt herself fall. When she opened her eyes, she was sitting on the ground.

Carson was getting to his feet. "Are you alright?" he asked, holding out a hand. Lottie grabbed it and let him pull her to her feet.

"Fine," she said, brushing off the back of her dress and looking around. Where were they? The trees were checkered with purple and yellow, and the dirt beneath their feet was a dull blue. The rocks weren't even the right colors. What was even worse was that Finn, Earl, and Roco were nowhere to be seen.

"I wonder where the others are," Carson said, scanning the landscape. Max grabbed Lottie's dress and pulled. "He wants us to go that way. We aren't back in *Beauty and the Beast*, are we? Your dress reminds me of the cartoon."

Lottie looked down at her blue dress and apron. "The thing that disturbs me the most about this place is that our clothes change." The front of the dress came to her knees, and the back went to her ankles. She was wearing one black slip-on shoe and one knee high boot. Carson was wearing jeans and a white t-shirt. It reminded her of high school.

"I'm glad the beard is gone," Carson said, running a hand over his smooth chin. "I won't miss that. Are you going to have trouble walking with different shoes?"

She glared at her feet. "I hope not. It feels weird, though."

They followed Max, who was setting a more leisurely pace now that they were here. She watched Carson from the corner of her eyes. Beard or not, Carson was attractive. Lottie blushed and looked away when he caught her staring at him.

"Can we have a truce?" Carson asked.

"A truce?" Lottie choked.

"I've missed you, Char. We were good friends for so long. Can things go back to the way they were?"

Lottie's mouth turned down, and she kept her eyes on the red fox. Could things go back to the way they were? She doubted it. Did she even want it to? She couldn't remember when she'd first fallen in love with Carson, but she could remember the pain in her heart when she'd heard him tell Brandon he didn't want to take her to the dance. Still, he had been more important to her than almost anything in her life.

"Does your silence mean no?" he asked, not looking at her.

"I'm just thinking," Lottie said. She wasn't sure she could be friends with him again. Not after her broken heart, and not after that kiss yesterday. If they went back to trying to be friends, she would feel awkward. Not having him in her life seemed equally painful.

"I won't ever hold the way you acted against you," he said. "It was a long time ago, after all."

Lottie's head whipped toward him, and her eyes narrowed. "The way *I* acted?"

He arched an eyebrow. "You can't believe I was partially to blame. I mean, sure, I should have forgiven you, but you embarrassed me in front of so many people."

Lottie stopped and put her hands on her hips. "I embarrassed you? And what were you trying to do to me?"

"Ask you to the dance? I didn't think that would embarrass you. I thought you would like the attention."

"But you were planning on telling me it was a joke. You didn't want to take me to the dance." Lottie could feel herself trembling with rage—or perhaps sadness. It was hard to separate the emotions. Max curled up on the ground and watched them.

"What are you talking about?" Carson asked, crossing his arms. "Why would I ask you if I didn't want to take you?"

"I-I heard you tell Brandon you would never ask me out unless it was a joke." A rebellious tear slid down her face, and she wiped it away.

"What are you talking about?"

Lottie sighed and looked up at the grayish purple sky as she tried to hold in any more tears. She'd already started, she might as well finish. "I snuck into your car. I was going to scare you," she admitted. "When you got in the car, Brandon was with you. I didn't want him to know I was there, so I stayed quiet."

Carson raised his brow. "Okay... and?"

"Brandon told you to ask me to the dance, and you said you would never ask me out unless it was a joke."

Carson stuck his hands in his pockets and sighed. "I don't remember saying that."

"Well, you did. Then, you stopped at the store, and Brandon stayed behind because he knew I was there. He told me not to take it the way it sounded. He promised not to tell you, and I walked home. A few days later, you asked me to the dance."

His frown deepened. "And you laughed in my face and said no."

"Because I knew it was a joke." Lottie sniffed and wiped another tear. Why were these tears betraying her?

Carson ran his hands through his hair and let out a slow breath. "I don't remember saying anything about a joke, but if I did, it was because I didn't want Brandon teasing me. I asked you to the dance because neither one of us was going, and I thought we would have fun."

Lottie clenched her teeth and nodded. Maybe she had over reacted back then. Hindsight was so—well, just stupid. There was no reason to dwell on it now. He still had only asked her because he had no one else to go with.

Carson peered into her eyes. "Why did Nancy send you here?"

Lottie flinched, then opened her mouth. She didn't know what to say. If she told him the truth, she would be embarrassed, and if she told him something else, he would know she was lying. He always did.

"I'm sorry I upset you," he said, using his thumb to wipe a tear from her cheek.

She took a step back. "I can't remember when I first fell in love with you." Carson's eyes widened, and Lottie took another step back. She didn't know why she was telling him. "I joined the cheerleading squad to get you off my mind, but it didn't work. When I overheard you in the car... it broke my heart. For some dumb reason, I spilled the entire story to Nancy."

"Char, I—"

"No," she interrupted. "Don't say anything." She couldn't take the sympathetic look on Carson's face. He was probably trying to think of a nice way to tell her it never would have worked. She turned and started walking. Max hopped up and ran in front of her to lead the way.

Carson stared after Lottie. Nothing in the world could have prepared him for what she just said. She'd been in love with him. He could kick himself for not realizing it earlier. Now she must despise him. He thought about her tears and wondered if it was possible she still had feelings for him.

After a moment, he came out of his daze and hurried to catch up to Lottie and Max. It wouldn't do any good if he lost them. He could tell Lottie knew he was walking behind her because she became stiff as she followed the fox. Carson opened his mouth to talk a couple of times and then shut it. He couldn't think of anything to say that wouldn't sound forced and ridiculous.

Staying quiet could be as bad as talking. Perhaps worse. Lottie was probably wondering what he was thinking, and the longer he didn't talk, the more she could be stewing over what he thought.

The ground wasn't stable, and Carson had to concentrate on it to not fall over. Small ripples were running along the dirt, making it hard to walk naturally. A larger ripple was coming toward them, and Lottie fell back into Carson when it reached her. He steadied her, and she mumbled something he couldn't understand.

Carson gently turned her to face him. "Char?"

"Hm?" Her eyes flickered toward him and then away.

"I know you don't want me to talk, but I can't walk in silence with my thoughts. It's going to drive me crazy."

She shrugged and let her gaze follow Max. He was pacing back and forth, probably wondering why he had to keep stopping for them.

"I wanted to ask you to the dance. I wanted to ask you to every dance. When I was thirteen, I remember hoping you would fall in love with me someday."

Lottie's lip trembled, and she rubbed her hands over her arms.

Carson struggled to make his thoughts clear. "I've been in love with you for so long. You showed no sign of wanting anything more than friendship from me, so I tried to keep it to myself. Nancy was right. When you wouldn't go to the dance with me, I was devastated. After that, I was mad. I've spent more time than I want to admit being angry at you."

Lottie nodded. "I understand that. I shouldn't have reacted the way I did. You have to understand, I honestly thought you were going to make it into a joke."

"Even though I was mad, I still loved you. I still love you."

Lottie's eyes widened, and she covered her mouth with her hand, and more tears ran down her face. She turned away from him as her shoulders shook. Carson's heart was beating so hard he wondered if she could hear it. He wished he knew what was going on in her mind.

He needed to know what she was thinking. They couldn't go on having more misunderstandings. Carson reached out and touched her shoulder. "Char?"

Lottie turned and buried her face in his shoulder. He wrapped his arms around her and let her cry. He rested his head on hers and swallowed a lump in his throat. Crying wasn't something he did normally, and he didn't want to start now.

"I'm sorry I laughed at you," she said, her face still pressed against his shoulder.

He ran his hand over her hair. "I'm just sorry the entire thing happened. We were good friends. We should have talked it out instead of going our separate ways."

"So, we're good now?" she asked, pulling back and searching his eyes.

"More than good." He leaned down and pressed his lips to hers. Her arms reached around his neck as she kissed him back.

Max made a yipping sound, and they pulled apart.

"I guess Max is ready to go," Lottie said.

"I think you're right." Carson couldn't blame the fox. He was doing them a favor, and they kept slowing him down. Still, it would have been nice if he'd given them another minute.

"There's a house up ahead," Lottie said, pointing. "Should we see if anyone lives there?"

Carson squeezed her hand. "Sure. Maybe they'll give us some food."

That was what Lottie had been hoping for. It was getting dark, and they had been walking for hours. Her feet hurt, and her stomach kept growling. Even being hungry and uncomfortable, she was still happier than she'd been in a long time. Carson loved her.

The house was smaller than Lady Anna's house had been but was still a good size. It had wooden beams making an archway around the door and large windows with matching wooden shutters. The dirt walkway leading to the house was overgrown and neglected.

"It doesn't look like anyone has walked this way in a while," she observed.

Carson scanned the area. "Yeah, I bet no lives here." When they got to the large wooden door, Carson pounded on it. They waited but didn't get a response. "We could go in and see if there's any food."

"We can't just go into someone's house," Lottie protested.

"Since everything here is all part of Nancy's story, I don't see why it would matter. It seems abandoned anyway."

"I don't know. It still feels wrong."

"We have to eat, and this is the only house we've seen since we came here."

Lottie shook her head. "If we go in, we will get caught by someone, and it will cause us more trouble than we already have. What if this is the three bears or something? We could go in and then get eaten by talking bears."

Carson laughed. "The bears didn't eat people. They ate porridge. Come on. No one's going to catch us. Whoever Nancy had stationed here is obviously gone."

"You said no one would catch us that time in middle school when you wanted to sneak into Mr. Garrett's classroom to toilet paper it for April Fool's Day. I still can't believe I went with you. We were lucky we didn't get suspended."

Carson grinned. "Good times, good times. Mr. Garrett wasn't even mad. He knew it was all in fun. That's why I chose him."

"You also said no one would catch us when we snuck into your mom's pantry to get the Oreos. And there was the time—"

"Okay, so we've been caught a few times. Look at this path, though. No one has walked down it for a while." Carson grabbed the doorknob and turned it. The door creaked open.

Lottie shivered. "I'm not going in."

"You've seen too many movies. Where's your sense of adventure?"

Lottie sighed. She'd gotten into trouble a bunch of times over the years because of Carson. None of it had been serious, but things here were different. With magic, anything could happen.

"Come on," Carson said, entering the dark house. This was more like the Carson she knew. Carson had always been up for an adventure, and he was usually smiling. He must be feeling more like himself.

"It's too dark," Lottie said, holding on to his arm. He led her through the shadowy hallway. Lottie tried to breathe normally, but she hated things like this. She expected someone or something to jump out at any moment.

"Where is Max?" she whispered, glancing behind her.

"He must have stayed outside."

Lottie had never been one to sit around listening to ghost stories, and she never watched scary movies. She couldn't handle them. This felt like something out of a scary movie. Chills ran down her spine, and she gripped Carson's arm tighter than was necessary.

"We found the kitchen," Carson said, as they entered the shadow filled room. "Try to find a lamp or something."

"I'm not letting go of you," she said. "I don't think I can if I try."

Carson chuckled. "Are you afraid the boogeyman might be hiding in here?"

Lottie frowned. "I know I'm ridiculous, but I am seriously freaked out right now."

"There has to be some type of light somewhere. In most stories I've been in, there is a lantern or something by all the doors."

"I don't see anything," Lottie said, squinting as she looked at the silhouettes of different kitchen objects. Any of them could be a monster. She knew she was exaggerating, but she didn't know this place.

"Right there," he said, guiding her forward. She kept her hands locked around his arm and hoped he wouldn't end up with a bruise. "There are always matches by the lanterns. It's nice Nancy is consistent in some ways." Carson grabbed something, and soon, the room was flooded with light—well, flooded was a generous word, but it was bright compared to what it had been.

Carson blew out a match, sat the lantern on a large wooden table and glanced around. Lottie forced herself to release him and started checking the cupboards. Everything had a layer of dust on it. There were canisters full of an assortment of things, but she wasn't sure what they were.

"I wonder how old this stuff is," she said. "Do you think it's safe to eat?"

"I'm sure it's fine."

Lottie frowned into a canister of what might be flour. "How do you know? There aren't any expiration dates."

Carson opened a drawer and scanned its contents. "I eat stuff past the expiration date all the time, and I'm fine. The dust isn't that thick—Did you hear something?"

"No, what?" Lottie asked, a chill running down her spine. She sat the canister down and hurried toward him. She strained her ears and fought back a feeling of panic. When she got to Carson, she wrapped her arms around his middle. "What did you hear?"

He put a hand on her back. "It sounded like someone yelling outside. We should go check."

There was a door in the kitchen that probably led to the backyard. Lottie didn't want to go see what it was. Why was she such a wimp? She was startled when she heard a man yelling something behind the closed door. "I don't think we should go," she whispered.

"What if someone needs help?"

"I don't know. They sounded angry."

"You can wait here, and I'll check."

"That would be worse. I'll come." Lottie forced herself to let go of Carson, and they walked to the door. Carson opened the door a crack and peeked outside.

"What are you doing in my house?" an angry voice called. Carson stepped outside, and Lottie grudgingly followed. Her eyes widened in surprise. The backyard was lit with colorful hanging lanterns, and there was a large rectangular table covered in more pastries than Lottie had ever seen. A man with wild gray hair sat at the head of the table, and at his side was a man with the head of a rabbit.

"Sorry, friends," Carson said. "We knocked and nobody answered."

"Well, we couldn't very well answer," the gray-haired man said. "And just because someone doesn't answer when you knock, does not give you permission to enter their house un-invited."

"It's rude, indeed," said the rabbit. Lottie tried not to stare at him. He had the body of a man and the head of a rabbit. It was unsettling to see him talk. Max was on top of the table, lapping something from a bowl. Next to him was a small mouse in a suit.

"We've been walking all day, and we are hungry," Carson said, approaching the table. "The house looked abandoned and so we thought we would look for food."

"Well, I'll forgive you this once," the man said. "Just make sure you don't do it again. Now, why don't you sit down and have some tea?"

"Thank you," Carson said, pulling out a chair for Lottie. There were at least twelve chairs going around the table. Lottie sat down and looked longingly at a cinnamon roll. Carson sat beside her.

"Eat," the man said.

Lottie picked up a roll and bit into it. She tried to eat it slowly so they wouldn't think she was rude. Carson grabbed one as well. Lottie was never one to pass on a desert, but she wished there was something more nutritious. Too much sugar on her empty stomach might end poorly.

Lottie's eyes jumped to the rabbit. He was flickering. She frowned. It made sense that he wasn't real. He was a talking rabbit, after all.

"Did you see that?" the man asked. "You saw him flicker?"

Lottie nodded.

"Oh, good. I thought I was losing my mind. He keeps doing that, but he doesn't believe me when I tell him."

"You think I'm flickering because you are mad," the rabbit said.

"I'm the Hatter," the man said, keeping his eyes on his companion. "This is the March Hare, and that is the Dormouse. Both of them started flickering some time ago, and I can't understand why."

"It's because they aren't real," Carson said.

The Hatter's face clouded up. "I thought it might be something like that." The hare shrugged and drank from his cup. "Things have been strange around here, and that is saying something."

"You aren't flickering," Lottie said. "That means you're real."

He scratched his head. "Of course I'm real. But what does all of this mean?"

"This world isn't real. Do you know Nancy?"

The Hatter nodded. "Who doesn't? She pops in every now and again for a cup of tea. Of course, she hasn't been here for a while, but she'll be back. She always is."

"And she's as mad as anyone," the hare said. "She might be worse than the lot of us."

Carson swallowed a bite of his roll. "Nancy made this world. She took people out of the real world and placed them here."

"Makes as much sense as anything," the hare said. He took a sip of tea. "I don't see how it affects us, though."

The Hatter buttered a piece of bread. "I keep having memories of being a baker named Herman. I'm sure it was a lovely life, but it can't compare to this one. All we do here is have tea parties."

"Not that we have a choice," the hare said, sticking his finger in some cupcake frosting. He licked it off and smiled. "Let me tell you. If you ever see Time, avoid him at all costs. We wronged him, and he cursed us to have eternal tea parties."

"We don't know that time is a he," the Hatter said. "It could be a she."

The hare snorted. "I'm positive it was a he."

"How can you be positive?"

Lottie and Carson shared a look. Lottie started eating faster. This was obviously *Alice in Wonderland,* which meant they weren't going to get much help here. She might as well eat fast so they could leave.

"How would Time be a woman?" the hare asked. "It doesn't make any sense."

The Hatter pointed his butter knife at his friend. "I'm only saying we shouldn't rule it out. There is no way to know for sure. The voice was inconclusive, to say the least."

"Can we stay in your house for the night?" Carson interrupted.

The Hatter sighed. "I suppose so. It's not like I'm using it at the moment. There are several rooms upstairs. Make yourself at home."

"Thank you," Carson said, standing. Lottie gulped down some water and joined him.

A drumming sounded in the distance, and Lottie froze. "What was that?"

"Oh dear," the hare said.

"Oh dear, indeed," the Hatter whispered.

Carson glanced toward the sound. "What?"

"The queen's guards," the Hatter said. "You always hear the drums before they appear."

"Annoying woman," the hare said, taking another sip of tea.

"I would hide if I were you," the Hatter said. "Of course I'm not, so I won't."

"Why? We didn't do anything," Lottie said.

The hare laughed. "Didn't do anything? I'm sure that isn't true. Anyone up for a song?"

"A song would be lovely," the Hatter said.

"Yes, it would. Pity we don't know any."

"Maybe this young lady can favor us with one?"

The drumming was getting louder. "Not right now," Lottie said, gazing up at Carson. "What should we do?"

"You should leave," the hare said. "If you think you can come in here and eat our food and not even give us a song, then you are not welcome here."

"Not welcome at all," said the Hatter.

Carson rolled his eyes. "I think we will leave."

The Hatter pouted. "Oh, must you? I suppose you should. If the queen's guards find you, you will likely lose your heads."

"This is ridiculous," Carson said, grabbing Lottie's hand and pulling her toward the side of the house. On the other side, a line of playing cards the size of humans came into view. They had heads, arms, and legs.

"There they are!" the hare called, pointing at them. "Hurry and catch them!"

Carson glanced at her. "Run."

Chapter 12

The woods were dark, but they had outrun the cards. Aspen had dropped a red cloak to Lottie and was perched in a nearby tree. Carson sat down against the tree and yawned. It must be pretty late. The only light was coming from the moon shining through the trees.

Lottie was standing, staring up at Aspen. She held the cape around herself and shivered. It wasn't terribly cold, but cold enough to be uncomfortable. Max had found them and was curled up in a ball at Carson's side.

"Come here, Char," Carson said, patting the dirt next to him. Lottie looked down at him and nodded. She came near and sank to the ground. He put his arm around her and pulled her close.

"I hate sleeping outside," she said, resting her head against him. "There are probably bugs and snakes all over."

"It's too cold for most things to be out."

Max got lazily to his feet and walked on Carson to get to Lottie. He sat on her lap and she ran a hand over his fur. The fox must know Lottie needed to be comforted.

Carson put his head against hers. "We should try to get some sleep. Who knows what time it is?"

"I've been having a hard time sleeping since I got my memories back," she admitted. "I keep wondering how my parents are doing. They're probably so worried."

Carson's mouth turned down. "I know what you mean. I try not to think about it or it makes me crazy. How did you get here?"

"I was meeting my parents in Hawaii. I was seated by Nancy on the plane."

"Were my parents with them?"

"Yes. They all traveled a few days before me."

Carson nodded. It wasn't odd for the Johnsons and the McLinns to vacation together. After Carson and Lottie's falling out, their parents still went on trips together.

"So, they invited you and not me?" He shouldn't care, but he did.

"I didn't want to go if you were going to be there. My mom said you were busy and couldn't get time off, so I went."

"Right," he said, remembering. That was right before finals. "They asked me to pick them up from the airport. I never did, though. I ended up here instead. It feels like so long ago."

"Does that mean we both came here at about the same time?"

"We must have. If we hadn't, one of us would have heard that the other one was missing. My mom brought you up all the time. It really irked her when we stopped being friends. She thought you were a calming influence on me.”

Lottie laughed softly. “I tried. I don’t know if I succeeded very often. It bugged my mom, too. She would bring you into every conversation.”

“Oh?”

“She was like, ‘Have some lemonade, Charlotte. It’s Carson’s favorite. Wear your red shirt, Carson likes red.’ We got into a few fights about it. She tried to get me to call you at least once a week.”

“It’s strange the way we both ended up here, and Nancy didn’t even realize we knew each other. What are the chances she found both of us? It seems impossible.”

A man stepped out of the trees. “Not impossible, but very improbable, without help.”

Carson and Lottie jumped to their feet, and Max yelped as he slid off Lottie’s lap. The man was tall with dark hair and a neatly trimmed goatee. He had broad shoulders and appeared to be around thirty. He looked cynically at them. In his hand was a ball of light. It was bright enough to light up the entire area. He was wearing a blue ornate robe and a gold crown.

“Who are you?” Carson asked. He knew the story had a king, but this man didn’t fit the little he knew about the book.

“You may address me as King Henan. I’ve come to inspect the mess that my daughter made in this place. I cannot seem to find her.”

Carson swallowed. “Who is your daughter?”

He tilted his head. “I believe you know her as Nancy.”

Carson glanced at Lottie. “We know Nancy.”

"Everyone does," the king said. He pointed downward and an orange stream of light shot from his finger and burst into fire on the earth. Lottie squeaked and jumped back, and Carson tried to ignore his pounding heart.

The king studied them and frowned. "Sorry. I forget humans get spooked by magic. Please, sit by the fire." He waved his hand and three padded chairs appeared. Carson and Lottie cautiously sat, as did the king.

King Henan sat tall and watched them both. "So, Nancy brought you here?"

"Yes, and we would appreciate it if she took us back," Lottie said. "Our parents are probably crazy with worry."

The king rubbed his chin. "I wouldn't worry about that. Nancy may be impulsive and somewhat careless in some aspects of her life, but she does a good job of covering for herself."

Carson shifted in his chair. "What do you mean?"

"Nancy finds people she wants to 'help' and she comes up with ways to make sure no one realizes they are missing. Sometimes she puts them into comas. Other times she takes them back to the same time she took them from. If it's a person with no family or friends, she makes it look like they've relocated. She has an endless number of tricks up her sleeve."

"Well, she's lost control of everything," Carson said. "She can't send any of us back, and the stories are malfunctioning."

"I guessed as much," the king said, glancing at an orange and blue tree. "I've let her go too far. I thought allowing her to create a world would be good for her. Her ideas for the world weren't sound, but she was determined. I could see some problems with her plans, but I wanted to allow her to experiment and work things out for herself."

"It isn't right to pull people from their lives the way she does," Lottie muttered.

The king nodded. "It isn't. After a while, I began interfering without her knowing, but I should have stopped her. That is why you both ended up here. I could see her plan wasn't working the way she thought it was. When she chose Carson, I learned of your story, and I guided her to Charlotte without her knowledge. I knew there was more hope for you if you found one another."

Lottie frowned. "We were here a long time before we found each other."

"Yes. I didn't want to interfere too heavily. I have been influencing things for the last few years. She's been at this for hundreds of years, and I assumed she would get better at it. If anything, she is getting worse."

"Falada said Nancy puts hopeless people near each other to give them another chance."

"Who's Falada?" Carson asked.

The king chuckled under his breath. "Falada is a horse that happens to be good friends with Nancy. She believes everything Nancy does is perfect and gives her credit where none is due. Nancy never thought to put people together once she gave up on them."

"Can you send us back?" Lottie asked.

The king sighed. "I could, but it would complicate things. Only Nancy knows how to take you back without causing problems. If I took you back, you might miss months or even years of your lives. Since humans have such short life spans, I don't think you would like that."

Carson rolled his eyes. "So, why are you here?"

"This world needs to be fixed, but I need to help without Nancy's knowledge. The key is Terry."

"We're looking for him."

The king leaned forward. "And what will you do when you find him?"

"We don't know," Carson admitted.

"There are things about Terry that Nancy doesn't know. It's unfortunate she chose him. If I would have been keeping a closer watch, I would have stopped that."

"Can you take him out of here?" Carson asked. "If he's the reason everything is messed up, that might help."

"It's complicated."

Carson scowled. "Of course it is."

"On Earth, Terry is in a coma. In this world, he is in a magical sleep. I can't wake him up on Earth because his consciousness is still here. If I tried, he would be unresponsive."

"Can you wake him here first?" Lottie asked.

"I can't. Nancy's spell put him into a sleep that can only be broken by love's kiss, or by Nancy. Nancy isn't admitting this to anyone, but she can only do limited magic right now. I don't believe she can wake him."

Carson frowned. "What's wrong with her magic?"

"When fairies from our world feel a tremendous amount of guilt, they start to lose their magic."

Carson's brow rose. "Are you saying she feels guilty about what she's done to everyone?"

The king shifted in his chair. "Yes. The last people Nancy helped were named Olivia and Jerron."

"We've heard of them," Lottie muttered. Carson wondered if she still felt guilty for bullying Olivia in *Cinderella.*

"They were the first people to be put into a story together. Much to Nancy's delight, they fell in love and returned home happy. They told Nancy to go check on all the other people she thought she had helped over the years to see if they were happy. She did, and it turned out she hadn't helped anyone. Nancy believed the people would learn about happiness here and go home and look for it. Since they hadn't fallen in love with real people, most of them felt like she had given them happiness and ripped it away."

Max jumped on Lottie's lap, and she rubbed his head. "That's exactly what she did."

"Yes," the king said, running a hand over his chin. "And I think after all these years, she has finally seen the error of her ways, but she's stubborn."

"Why are you telling us all of this?" Carson asked.

"I would like to solicit your help."

"Why us?"

"Because word has reached me that you are already searching for Terry."

Carson nodded. "How do you know that?"

"It doesn't matter. From what Nancy has told me, Terry fell in love here. He fell in love with a real person. It was an accident on Nancy's part." He glanced at Lottie. "He fell in love with someone she had deemed beyond help."

"Shouldn't that make her happy?" Carson asked. "She thought Lottie was beyond help, and she seemed happy to realize she was wrong."

"It had never happened before, and she panicked. She split them apart, and Terry became angry."

Carson couldn't blame the man. He would be angry, too. "I heard he can do magic. Has that happened before?"

The king shook his head. "Humans can't do magic."

"But he can."

"Terry is a special case. I can't get into it all right now. Nancy told me the story, but she didn't tell me who Terry fell in love with. She still believes he is too much of a danger to let run free. She wants to fix everything by herself, with her minimal magic."

"What good can Terry do?"

"My hope is that he can release any hold his magic has had in this place. He must have put some spells into place that aren't going away while he is asleep."

Carson snapped his fingers. "You want us to figure out who Terry was in love with and have her wake him?"

The king stared into his eyes. "That is exactly what I want you to do."

"Are you going to sleep all day?" a voice asked, ripping Lottie from her peaceful sleep. She jumped from the hard ground and looked at the guards surrounding them.

Carson stood and yawned. "Don't worry," he whispered near Lottie's ear. "They are just big playing cards. What are they going to do?"

Lottie stepped closer to him, trying not to panic. The red and black cards had formed a tight circle around them, but Carson was right. They could probably run into them and cause them to fall over. Still, their human heads were unsettling.

"What do you want?" Carson demanded.

A guard with a thick black mustache stepped forward. Another card moved into his place. "The Queen of Hearts does not like unknown visitors. You are under arrest for loitering where you should not. You will stand trial and most likely lose your heads."

"I don't think we will," Carson said, rushing the guard. Before he could reach him, the man pulled out a sword and pointed it at him. Carson skidded to a stop, and Lottie covered her mouth.

"That's what I thought," the card said. "You will follow us to the palace and stand trial. You may address me as Captain Card. Now, walk."

Lottie grabbed Carson's hand and smiled weakly. There had to be a way out of this. Captain Card was the only guard with a sword. If there was a chance to run, they could probably outrun them again. Cards would have to deal with the wind catching on their large fronts.

Half of the cards filed in front of them and started marching. The other half stayed behind them. Captain Card poked Carson with his sword, and Carson mumbled something Lottie couldn't understand. There was nothing to do but follow.

"It might not be bad to talk to the queen," Lottie said. "She might listen to us and be of some help."

Max ran around Carson and Lottie's ankles, making it hard to walk as fast as the others. If he was trying to be helpful, he was failing.

"I think I could take them if I try," Carson said.

Lottie squeezed his hand. "Don't. I don't want you to get hurt."

Carson smirked. "So, your opinion of me has changed since we met up here?"

Lottie bumped her shoulder playfully into his. "You can't hold that against me. I didn't know who you were, and you looked terrifying."

"I'm glad that's over. You can't believe how uncomfortable it is to be covered in fur. Maybe the queen will know something about Terry. She might let us go if she knows we're trying to help—ouch!" Carson exclaimed, letting go of Lottie and spinning around. "Watch it with the sword!"

Captain Card kept his sword pointed at Carson. "What do you know about Terry?"

Carson rubbed a spot on his back and glared at the card. "Not a lot. Just take us to the queen."

"I will, and I will tell her you mentioned Terry. That could save you or cause you to lose your head. Think hard on how you want to approach the queen about it."

"About Terry?"

"Yes. I don't like to see people lose their heads, so you best prepare something eloquent to say."

Carson crossed his arms. "How can I decide what to say if I don't know what the queen's opinion of him is?"

"Sure is a nice day," Captain Card said, glancing into the trees. "Let's get moving, shall we?"

Lottie pulled her cape close to her as they started back toward the castle. She wondered if they could get the captain to say more. They needed to know if the queen was for or against Terry.

"How long have you been the captain?" she asked, glancing over her shoulder.

Captain Card puffed out his flat chest. "As long as I remember."

"The queen must really trust you," Lottie said. Carson shot her a questioning look. She kept focused on the guard.

"Of course she does. I haven't lost my head yet, and she sure likes to chop them."

"She's sure to be pleased when you bring us in. And more pleased when she finds out we know about Terry."

The captain grinned and fiddled with his mustache. "She will, indeed."

"How is she feeling about Terry these days?"

"Upset, of course. What else could she be? If we don't find him soon, we will all lose our heads."

"Because she's angry he's messed up the world?" Lottie wondered.

The captain sucked in a breath and coughed. "I wouldn't say that to her if I were you. No more speaking."

Lottie turned and walked in silence. Perhaps the queen was one of Terry's allies. She glanced around at all the cards. None of them were flickering. Did that mean they were real people? Lottie shuddered at the thought. She hoped not.

The path turned, and as they rounded the bend, a castle came into sight. It would only take a few minutes to reach it. It was a lot different from the castle she had found Carson in. Where Carson's was a ruin, this one was immaculate. It looked like something from a children's book. Neatly trimmed green grass filled the grounds, and there were several rose bushes making a hedge next to the pathway leading to the large door.

"Hurry, men!" Captain Card commanded. "The labyrinth isn't in front today! We might be able to get there without the confounded thing giving us trouble."

They all picked up speed, and Lottie and Carson had little choice but to match their pace.

"Faster!" the captain said, as the ground rumbled. "Run, run!"

Lottie didn't question, she just ran after the cards. When they reached the front, the door swung open, and the guards began throwing themselves through the entrance. When Lottie ran past the front door, she was pushed and shoved by the cards from behind.

"Careful," Carson said, helping her get stable. They both looked out the door, and Lottie's mouth fell open. A hedge filled the area they had vacated.

"Where did that come from?" she asked, catching her breath.

Captain Card raised his eyebrow. "It comes from where every hedge comes from. The dirt."

Carson studied the thick foliage. "But how did it grow that fast?"

"It appears you are both as mad as everyone else around this place."

A white rabbit came running in on two legs and bounced toward them. "You're late!" he yelled, pointing at a gold pocket watch. "Captain Card! The queen will see you now."

Captain Card gulped and rubbed his neck.

"Don't act so dramatic," the rabbit said, rubbing his furry chin. "Hurry in. The trial is about to start."

"What trial?" Carson asked.

"Yours, of course," the rabbit said.

"But you didn't know we were coming."

The rabbit frowned, and Captain Card shrugged. "I know. They are both as mad as the Hatter."

The rabbit's eyes bulged from his head. "Really? As mad as the Hatter? That's a hard feat to accomplish in my humble opinion."

"They haven't made a lick of sense since we captured them. I'm not sure they are even capable of standing trial."

"Well, follow me," the rabbit said, scurrying down the hall. "It's not like we haven't had mad people around here before."

Chapter 13

Carson watched Lottie as she fidgeted on the stand. The rabbit had led them to a courtroom that was loaded to the brim with strange creatures. They were all squawking and conversing with one another. Carson had been placed with the audience, and Lottie had been led to the front. A turtle occupied the seat next to him. He tried not to stare at all the animals wearing clothing. He'd let his gaze linger on an owl in a raincoat, and it had screeched in his face. Not all owls were as pleasant as Aspen.

The door opened, and the room fell silent. Carson hadn't realized how chaotic it had been until the silence. He turned and watched as a woman decked in red entered the room. Her long dress trailed gracefully to the floor. She wore a delicate gold tiara, and when she walked, she appeared to float. Around her neck was a gold heart-shaped locket.

Carson tried not to stare. The Queen of Hearts was nothing like the movie he had seen. She had a long, graceful neck and a slender waist. Her long black hair fell in soft curls past her shoulders. She was beautiful. Carson glanced at Lottie and frowned. She was glaring at him. He winked at her, and she blushed.

The queen walked gracefully toward the front, and her eyes narrowed as they fell on Lottie. She turned and faced the spectators.

"It would be nice if you all stood when I entered the room," she said in a smooth, even tone. Everyone scurried to their feet, including Carson. "Thank you." Her eyes scanned the occupants, and she paused when her gaze fell on Carson. Her brow arched, and she turned around, glaring at Captain Card, who stood next to Lottie.

He cleared his throat. "Announcing Lizette, the Queen of Hearts, the keeper of the keys, of house heart. All stand." He cleared his throat again as everyone exchanged confused glances. "Queen Lizette will preside over this meeting in the absence of her husband, Terrance, the King of Hearts. You may take your seats."

Carson sat down, and the turtle next to him turned and whispered, "He announces that like the queen isn't the one who usually makes all the decisions."

Carson just nodded. He'd never talked to a turtle before. The turtle straightened his bowtie and leaned back in his chair.

"It's true," said a voice behind him. Carson turned to see the Mad Hatter. "The queen's word is law. The king is only there to be a pretty face at her side."

"The king is far from pretty," said the March Hare, who was sitting next to the Hatter.

"Everyone is entitled to their own opinion," the turtle muttered under his breath.

"I thought you weren't allowed to leave your tea party," Carson whispered.

"We aren't," said the Hatter. "Not unless the queen summons us. Her word outranks everything else."

"I suppose you are all wondering why we are here," the queen said. "The reason this trial has been called is that this woman and her friend have been prancing around the kingdom with no regard to where they place their feet."

Lottie's eyes widened, and she glanced at Carson. He shrugged.

"We cannot have that in our lovely land. They trampled all over the clover and left it in a disgraceful mess."

The crowd gasped.

"They stepped on our clover?" someone moaned.

"What monsters!" said the turtle, scooting as far from Carson as he could.

"We didn't mean to," Lottie said. "We didn't even realize it."

"Likely story," said the March Hare. "How can a person step on a clover and not know it?"

"Because it's small?" Carson offered.

"So am I!" said the turtle. "Does that mean you might step on me?"

"We didn't realize the clover was special," Lottie said, wringing her hands. "We're sorry."

"Didn't realize it was special?" the queen asked, fire flashing in her eyes. "Off with their—"

"If I may, Your Majesty?" broke in Captain Card.

The queen pointed a long, slender finger at the card. "You interrupted me. I hope you have a very good reason, or your head will join the others on the chopping block."

Captain Card gulped. "When we were bringing them here, they mentioned Terry."

The queen spun around and pointed at Carson. "You, join your friend."

Carson jumped up, climbed past all the animals, and stood next to the stand where Lottie was sitting. The queen's face had lost all color, and her red lips were pressed into a firm line.

"What do you know of Terrance?"

Carson ran a hand through his hair. King Terrance was Terry? Then, that might mean that the queen was the person Terry had fallen in love with.

"We are looking for him," Carson said.

She crossed her arms and frowned. "Why?"

Lottie leaned forward. "Haven't you noticed the way everything has been messed up around here lately? Terry might be the only person who can fix it."

"Messed up? The only thing around here that is messed up is the clover that you so unceremoniously smashed."

Carson glanced at the crowd. The only person, or creature, that wasn't blinking in and out was the Hatter. "Don't you see how all the people are flickering?"

The queen narrowed her eyes. "Of course I do. What does that have to do with anything?"

"It's not natural. Something is wrong."

"What does any of it have to do with Terry?"

"He is the reason it is all messed up. That's why we need to find him and get him to make it right."

The queen's teeth made a horrible grinding sound, and she walked up to Carson and poked him in the chest with her finger. "You cannot blame Terry for this mess. If anyone should be blamed, it is that horrid fairy and her ridiculous friends."

"Nancy?"

She poked him again. "Yes. Are you one of her minions?"

"No."

"I don't like you." She spun around to Captain Card. "They lose their heads now."

Carson was surprised at how casually she could say that.

Captain Card looked from Lottie to the queen and fidgeted.

"Wait," Lottie said, getting the queen's attention. "We can help you find Terry."

The queen walked to the stand and gripped the top. She leaned toward Lottie. "What makes you think you can find him? I've had this entire kingdom searched and there is no sign of him."

"We don't know exactly where he is, but we know something that could help. Maybe if we told you, you would know where he is."

"Tell me," she demanded, staring into Lottie's eyes.

Lottie stared right back. "Not unless you agree to let us go, and no more talking about us losing our heads."

The queen was quiet for a moment, and she drummed her long red nails on the wooden stand. "Very well. If you help me find Terry, I will let you live. Now, tell me everything you know."

Carson tilted his head. "How do we know we can trust you?"

She smiled sweetly. "You don't."

Lottie pulled her hood over her head and fastened the cloak around her neck. The queen had provided her with a brown cape, because apparently the queen was the only one allowed to wear red. The queen was putting on a bright red cape and arranging her silky black hair over her shoulder.

Carson rolled his eyes. "We need to get going."

"We will go when I am ready," the queen said in a light airy voice. "Now, open the door."

Carson bowed sarcastically as he pushed open the back door of the castle.

"Oh dear," the queen said, glancing at the ground outside the door. "It would seem the hedge has shrunken. Odd for this time of year."

Lottie looked down to see a hedge maze that was no more than two inches tall. It went on for as far as they could see.

"It won't be a problem," Carson said. "It isn't big enough to be an obstacle." He started forward, and the queen grabbed his arm and pulled him back.

"What do you think you are doing?" she demanded.

"I was going to search for Terry."

She poked him in the arm. "You cannot step on the maze."

Carson arched his eyebrow. "Why?"

"Are you really that stupid?" She waved her hand in dismissal. "Of course you are. You trampled the clover, after all."

"Well, what are we supposed to do?" he asked.

She poked him again. "I am growing tired of your ignorance."

He crossed his arms. "And I'm growing tired of you poking me with your dagger fingernails."

The queen reached into a small pouch she had over her shoulder. She pulled out a small bag and reached inside. She handed them both a bright blue piece of candy.

"What is it?" Carson asked.

"Eat it. It will shrink you down so you can fit into the maze."

"It would be a lot faster if we didn't do that," Carson said, looking at the maze. "We don't know how far we need to go and being small can't be helpful."

The queen poked him once more and ignored the anger flashing in his eyes. "The only other way is to walk on the hedge and we will not be doing that. Have you no respect for nature?"

Lottie rolled the candy around in her hand and sighed. The woman didn't hesitate to chop off a person's head, but she wasn't willing to ruin a plant?

The queen popped a candy into her mouth and immediately shrunk down so small it was hard to see her.

Carson looked at Lottie. "What do you think?"

She bit her lip. "I don't know."

"The queen doesn't even know where we need to go. What if the maze doesn't lead us to the right place?"

"We don't have any other plan," Lottie said.

"I guess," Carson said, sticking the candy in his mouth.

Lottie followed his lead and felt herself shrink. It happened so fast it made her stomach roll.

The queen was folding her arms and tapping her foot. "It took you long enough. Now, let us be off."

"Off where?" Carson asked. "We haven't even told you what we know."

"Does it matter?" she asked, walking over the large door frame. "Wherever we have to go is not in the castle and so we must go this way."

Carson frowned as Lottie followed the queen. She was right. It wouldn't do any good to stay in the castle. The walls of the maze looked to be about ten feet now. They must be tiny.

"Now, tell me what you know," Queen Lizette said, as they walked.

"Terry is in a tower somewhere near the castle."

Lizette stopped, and her face turned red. "The tower? You mean he's been so close the entire time? I never thought of looking there. How is he being kept there?"

"He's in a magical sleep," Lottie told her.

The queen nodded like that was the most normal thing in the world and started walking again. "It is too bad the hedge is so small today. If not, we could be there in less than thirty minutes. Being this size will take quite some time."

"How long?" Carson asked.

"No more than a couple of days."

Carson muttered something under his breath. Lottie didn't want to spend a couple of days in the maze, but arguing with the queen seemed pointless.

"Will you be able to find the tower?" Carson asked. "Do you know your way through the maze?"

"You cannot know your way through the maze. It changes as it wishes. Luckily, it is a rather lazy hedge, and it has very few wrong turns. It would prefer to put its energy into growing beautiful leaves, not tricks."

Lottie watched Lizette walk confidently ahead of them. She was surprised the queen was up to doing this. She seemed like the type to be afraid of dirt. There was plenty of that here. She sighed. She shouldn't be judging someone like that. It hadn't been long since Lottie avoided dirt at all costs. Ever since she had been playing the role of the wicked stepsister, she had avoided the outdoors and anything requiring effort.

Lizette was obviously real. She hadn't flickered once. Who knew what type of person she was when Nancy wasn't manipulating her? She could be anyone from anywhere.

"Your... um, Highness?" Lottie felt ridiculous. She didn't know how to address royalty.

The queen glanced over her shoulder. "What is it?"

"I don't know what you know about Nancy, but—"

"What I know about her is that she is an evil fairy. If I had my way, she would lose her head."

"Very original," Carson said, his mouth turning up at the corners.

Lottie thought everyone had a right to know what they were up against, even this woman. "Nancy took people from their real lives and brought them here. Nothing here is real."

Lizette raised her chin and kept walking.

"People who aren't real are flickering. Some people forgot about their former lives but are now regaining their memories."

They walked for a moment in silence. The queen's mouth was in a tight line, and it didn't look like she was going to respond.

"Do you remember another life?" Carson asked her.

"That sounds like nonsense to me," she finally said, picking up the pace. She turned a corner and pulled her cloak tighter.

It was hard to take the queen seriously with her blue teeth. They probably all had blue mouths from the candy she'd given them. Lottie ran her tongue over her teeth, hoping to get any blue that might be lingering there.

The queen kept walking briskly in front of them. Lottie glanced at Carson, and they shared a look.

"We're from Boston," she said, hoping to draw the queen out. "I was on my way to Hawaii when Nancy sent me here. What about you?"

The queen didn't answer.

"Carson was getting off the subway when Nancy sent him. I guess I wasn't cooperative, so Nancy gave up on me. She made me into one of Cinderella's stepsisters. I repeated that story a lot. I hate reflecting back on it because I was such a horrid person. I was glad to find out that it wasn't my real life."

Carson turned and mouthed to her, *What are you doing?*

Lottie shrugged. She hoped if she kept talking, it would get Lizette to remember something from her real life, if she didn't already.

"We hope Terry can help us turn things around and get us all back to the real world."

Lizette spun around and her eyes flashed with anger. "Perhaps some of us don't want to go back to the *real* world. All of us didn't live in an ideal situation. Have you ever thought about that?" She turned back and kept walking. Her posture was even more rigid than it had been before.

"So, why did Nancy bring you here?" Carson asked. Lottie was wondering the same thing, but she didn't want to push more than she had.

Lizette clenched her fists, then took a deep breath and relaxed them. "My father was a drunk. He wasn't mean, but he was useless. I decided I didn't need someone to drag me down in life. I could succeed on my own."

"So, Nancy brought you here?" Lottie asked.

She nodded, her pace still brisk. "I'm stubborn. I refused to follow Nancy's little scenarios. Over time, I forgot who I was."

"And you slowly became the Queen of Hearts?"

The queen laughed. "No. I became a fairy."

"What was the story?" Carson asked.

"*Sleeping Beauty*. I can't even tell you how many times I played through the story. I couldn't remember when it started over, and I didn't realize it had until recently when I started having memories."

Lottie jumped over a root as she tried to keep up. "How did you get here?"

Lizette came to an abrupt stop and turned to them. Her mouth trembled, and she covered it with her hand. "Terry."

"He brought you here?"

"Terry was the prince in *Sleeping Beauty* that last time. The girl Nancy had dropped into the story was impossible. She was the worst Briar Rose of them all. I was feeling like something wasn't right. Terry was trying to keep the story going, but the girl wasn't cooperating. He kept persisting, and one day, he came to our cottage. I was the only one home, and I invited him in for a drink and a muffin. We started talking, and we hit it off. Of course, the story didn't like that, so the day repeated, and I didn't remember anything."

Lottie frowned. It was hard to keep up with the way Nancy worked. "But Terry remembered?"

She rubbed her heart locket between her fingers and smiled. "Yes. He came back day after day. I never remembered it, but he fell in love with me. Nancy told him he needed to stay away from me, but he refused."

"Something needs to be done about Nancy," Carson said.

Lizette snarled. "She ripped him away from the story, and the poor man couldn't get over it. It wasn't bad for me because I didn't remember anything. Terry did everything in his power to get even with Nancy. After some time, he realized he could do magic."

"How is that possible?" Lottie wondered.

"I don't know. He came and found me. He told me everything, and we left together. We worried the story would pull me back, but it didn't. Then, I started to have memories. I began remembering my former life, and I remembered all the time Terry and I had spent together. I also remembered what Terry had been like before, and it pained me to see what Nancy had done to him."

Lottie leaned forward. "What had she done?"

Lizette sighed and started walking, this time at a reasonable speed. "She broke his spirit. Taking me away from him was the last straw. He was a little strange after, but when my memories returned, I realized I loved him."

Lottie walked at one side of her, and Carson was on the other. "How did you get here?"

"Terry learned how to move through stories. He could go wherever he wanted. He brought us here. The King and Queen of Hearts were the first characters we noticed blinking as if they weren't real. Terry figured it all out and told them to leave. They did, and we took their place."

"And Nancy allowed it?" Carson asked.

"She had little choice. Terry is powerful, and he was angry. She fears him."

Carson glanced sideways at her. "So, you just took over and started chopping heads?"

"I haven't really," she said. "No one here is real, except maybe the Hatter."

"Still, it's weird."

She nodded. "I suppose it is. Still, it's better than my former life."

Up ahead was a large patch of flowers. They were as tall as a person. Lottie shook her head. They weren't tall; she was short.

Lizette held up her hand to stop them. "Quiet," she said in a near whisper. "You do not want to wake the flowers."

Lottie squinted toward the bright blooms. "Why not?"

"Trust me on this."

Chapter 14

The flowers were blocking the entire path. Carson wished he had a camera. All the flowers had faces, and they were all sleeping.

Lizette motioned for them to follow her as she stepped carefully around the plants, making sure she didn't bump them. She navigated her way through them like she had been doing it her entire life. Lottie followed her, and Carson brought up the end.

A snapdragon snored, and he jumped back, knocking into a small pansy. He put a hand to his mouth as the pansy yawned. It stretched its leaves and mumbled to itself. Carson felt his heart stop, but the pansy's head drooped back down.

Lottie and Lizette watched with wide eyes. Carson didn't think he should be scared of a flower, but they were big. Lizette stepped out of the garden, and Lottie was right behind her.

Carson was almost out when something wrapped around his foot, and he tripped. He tried to stand, but something had a tight hold on his ankle.

"Where are you going in such a hurry?"

Carson looked straight into the face of a daisy. She released his ankle and put her leaves on her hips. Did flowers have hips? Carson wasn't sure. The daisy reminded him of his fifth-grade teacher, Mrs. Mitchel. He got to his feet and faced the flowers. They were all awake, watching him curiously.

"We don't have time for this," Lizette said.

"Well, if it isn't the queen," a purple pansy said. "You people never have time for anyone."

"Yes," the daisy agreed. "No one ever cares to come and talk to the flowers. It's rude. It isn't like we can get up and go visiting now, can we?"

"Come on," Lizette said. "We don't have time to debate with this lot. They'll only try to make you feel guilty and waste your time talking nonsense."

"I've never spoken nonsense a day of my life," protested the pansy.

"That's a lie if I ever heard one," said a snapdragon. "All we do is sit here and listen to your nonsense."

"Exactly why we need visitors," said the daisy. "We are tired of our own company."

"We are busy," Lizette told them. "If you would like, I can come back and pick every one of you and put you in a vase in the castle. Then, you can talk to anyone you please."

The daisy shook her head. "If you pick us, we won't last long."

Lizette gave them a mocking grin. "Yes, I know."

Carson shivered. He better try to stay on the queen's good side. She might remember who she was, but that didn't make her less creepy.

"Do you want to hear a joke?" a tall orange lily asked.

Carson shrugged. "Sure."

"Why did the flower sell all her pots?"

"I don't know."

"Because she was a peddler."

They all stared at the lily.

"Get it?" the lily asked. "It sounds like petal."

"We get it," said the daisy. "It isn't funny."

"And we are leaving," Lizette said.

"You promised to send people to talk to us," the pansy whined. "Only a few came."

Lizette cocked her head. "Yes, and the ones who came will never come again. You are all too needy, and you complain and fight until you drive everyone away."

"We don't fight," said a different pansy.

"Of course we do," said the daisy. "You try keeping it nice when you are stuck with this bunch day and night."

"Like you are any better," said a red rose. "You're probably the worst."

"Me? What about you? I can't be worse than you."

"You are always complaining," a pansy said.

Lizette motioned forward with her head, and Lottie and Carson followed. Carson could hear them arguing behind him.

"Are they always like that?" Lottie asked.

Lizette nodded. "Every time I've been near them. I wouldn't mind coming for a visit every now and again, but I can't handle their bickering. Perhaps I should have the gardeners thin them out, or plant some of them in different places."

Carson didn't say anything. If things went the way they hoped, they would put an end to this world and send everyone home.

"You know this would all be faster if we were our normal size," Carson said. "Even if we step on the hedge, it won't hurt it. I'm sure it will spring right back up."

Lizette turned and focused on him. "Yes, the hedge would be fine, but what if we step on something that lives in the hedge? There are lots of creatures, not just the flowers."

Carson nodded. When she put it that way, it made sense. Maybe the Queen of Hearts wasn't as heartless as she wanted people to believe.

Lottie hated sleeping outside. Her cloak wasn't keeping her warm, and the ground wasn't a comfortable pillow. The hood of her cloak kept her head from touching the dirt, and it kept in a small amount of heat. She wasn't sure how long she'd been trying to fall asleep, but it felt like hours. Lizette was breathing deeply to one side of her, and Carson was quiet on the other. She couldn't tell if he was asleep, and she didn't want to wake him.

She rolled to her side and placed her head on her arm. That would only be comfortable for a few minutes, and then her arm was going to ache. She tried to make out Carson's features, but it was too dark to see anything more than his outline.

Carson hadn't kissed her again since that first time. She tried not to feel insecure about it. They had been busy, after all, and it wasn't like she had tried to kiss him, either. Still, after wishing for Carson for so long and finally accepting it was never going to happen, it was hard to believe he meant it. He had held her hand. That had to count for something.

"What are you staring at?" Carson whispered.

Lottie startled, and then smiled. "You can't see my eyes. How do you know they are open?" she said quietly.

"I'm guessing. You've been rolling around so much I figured you weren't asleep."

"I can't sleep. It's so cold. I wish I had the cloak Aspen gave me. It was a lot warmer."

"The one the queen gave you is pretty thin. Come closer to me."

Lottie hesitated as she stared at his dark shape. What did he mean by closer? Closer could mean so many things.

Carson chuckled under his breath. "A few years ago, you wouldn't have hesitated."

"A few years ago, we were... different." Lottie knew it didn't make sense to say it out loud, but it made sense to her.

The queen snored with the force of an elephant, causing Lottie to turn and look at her. Carson laughed quietly and Lottie's stomach jumped when he put his arm and cloak around her shoulder. "You wouldn't guess someone like the queen could make a noise like that."

Lottie nodded into the darkness and tried to relax in Carson's arms. It was the place she'd always wanted to be, but now it made her nervous. The queen snored again, and Lottie let a small giggle escape. It was funny to know that the sound was coming from the beautiful woman.

"It is impressive," Carson said close to her ear. "My dad doesn't even snore that loud, and that man can snore."

Lottie giggled again. "I remember it used to scare me when I was little and he would fall asleep when we were watching movies."

"I probably shouldn't make fun," Carson said. "I could have inherited it from him, and I just don't know."

Lottie smiled, but it quickly turned to a frown. What if she snored? She didn't have any siblings to let her know, and her parents had never said anything. Roco and Earl probably would have told her if she did. Carson would have teased her. She was probably safe.

"Are you warmer?" Carson asked.

"Yes." Lottie was a lot warmer, but she was going to have a hard time sleeping this close to him, and an even harder time sleeping with his arm under her ribs. She should probably ask him to move it, but she didn't want to make him feel bad.

"Good. Try to get some sleep."

The sun shone into Carson's eyes, and he sighed. He'd gotten almost no sleep. When he'd wrapped his arms around Lottie, he'd only been thinking about keeping her warm, but now his arm was numb and his shoulder ached. He'd been careful not to move for fear of waking her up.

186

It was hard to ignore the doubt that kept creeping into his mind regarding her. If she had fallen in love with him years ago, that meant she had fallen in love with him when he was different. In middle school and high school, Carson had been a bit of a class clown. He loved making people laugh. He was also a bit of a showoff, but that was usually to get a laugh as well.

Since there was no way to know how long he had been here, he had no idea how long he'd been growing cynical. It could be one year or five. He had no idea. Would Charlotte have fallen in love with him if she'd met him here? He seriously doubted it. She definitely hadn't seemed impressed with him when she didn't remember him.

Carson moved slowly and carefully pulled his arm out from under her. He moved his neck from side to side, hoping to get the kinks out.

Lottie sat up. "Finally, morning," she mumbled, pushing her hair from her face.

He shook his arm and felt a painful tingle that went from his bicep to his hand. He stood up and helped her to her feet. His hip hurt, and his eyes were blurry. This must be what it felt like to get old.

Lottie yawned and glanced around. "Where's Lizette?"

Carson jerked his head from one side to the other. "Oh man. She must have run off on us. I don't know if we'll be able to find Terry without her."

Lottie's eyes widened. "And how will we ever grow to our normal height?"

Carson's heart sped up, and he tried not to panic. If they were stuck at this size, they were in for a lot of trouble.

"It is about time you woke up," Lizette said, as she rounded the corner of a hedge.

"You came back," Carson said, relief flooding through him.

"I've decided walking to the tower an inch tall wouldn't do, so I called on the caterpillar. He is in charge of the size and placement of the maze."

"Of course, a caterpillar," Lottie said, gazing up at the sky. "That makes total sense."

"It does in this place," Lizette said. "I bribed him, and he said he will move the maze."

"Why didn't you do that yesterday?" Carson asked, rubbing his stiff shoulder.

"I didn't realize how long it would take being this small. I overestimated our speed."

"And our supplies," Lottie said, side-eyeing the woman. "We should have brought blankets and food."

Lizette shrugged. "Yes, well, next time we'll know."

Carson smiled as he watched Lottie clamp her mouth shut. She was holding something in.

Lizette pointed at the hedge. "Look, it's happening already."

Carson followed her gaze and watched as the hedge started shrinking. It kept going down until the dirt devoured it. There was no sign that it had ever been there. They were now standing in grass that towered over their heads and was as thick as they were.

"Great, now what?" he asked.

"Now we eat these," Lizette said, pulling some red candies from her pocket. She handed them each a piece. Having bright red teeth would be more unsettling than the blue they had had before.

Carson smiled and popped the candy into his mouth and began chewing. Sucking on it would probably only make his tongue red, but this was going to make a mess. He felt a weird sensation in his middle, and in a flash, he sprung into the air and was back to his regular height.

Lottie and Lizette were right there with him. Lottie took the candy from her mouth and threw it. She turned to him and her eyes widened. He smiled bigger, making sure she saw his red teeth.

Lizette looked horrified. Her brows came together, and she frowned. "That's disgusting."

Carson tilted his head. "What?" he asked, fainting innocence. Lizette rolled her eyes and walked toward a clump of trees. He looked at Lottie. "What's she talking about?"

Lottie's eyes sparkled, and the corner of her mouth twitched. "You're such a dork."

"Why? What did I do?"

"Come on, we don't want to lose Lizette."

"Don't you want a kiss first?" he asked, taking a step toward her.

"No!" she squealed, as Carson wrapped his arms around her and buried his face in her neck. She giggled and pushed him away. "Your teeth are so nasty!"

Lizette turned around and placed her hands on her hips. "I thought we had a purpose here? Are you going to come or act like a couple of fools?"

Carson placed his arm over Lottie's shoulder. "I'll have to think about it."

Lottie shot him a warning look, but Carson could see the twinkle in her eyes. "We're coming."

Lizette tossed her hair over her shoulder and started walking again. Carson and Lottie followed.

"You seem more like yourself today," Lottie said, glancing up at him. "You must have slept well."

"Not really," he admitted. "I wasn't meant to sleep on the ground. Maybe if I'd had a pillow."

"Me either. I mean, I enjoy camping, but having a tent and a sleeping bag makes a difference."

"I was always jealous that you and your family camped so much. My parents hated it, so we only went a few times."

She smiled at the memories. "My dad loves camping. Vacations are the only time he actually relaxes. You should see him fish. He will sit for hours without making a sound."

"I can't picture your dad being quiet."

"Yeah, it's weird. He probably fishes and thinks about how he can turn it into a story later on."

Charlotte's dad was one of the funniest people Carson knew. Once you got to know him, you caught on to which parts of his stories were true and which parts he had embellished for other people's entertainment.

"Almost there," Lizette said over her shoulder.

They entered the forested area, and Carson glanced behind him. He could see the castle. He shook his head and tried not to be irritated with their shrinking adventure. It would have saved time if Lizette had talked to her caterpillar friend yesterday.

Lizette weaved around some trees until an enormous tower came into view. It was made of stone and was narrow but tall.

"It looks like Rapunzel's tower, except the stone is darker," Lottie observed.

"This isn't Rapunzel's tower?" Lizette asked. "I thought it was from the moment I saw it. That was one reason I've ignored it. I assumed it wasn't anything I needed to deal with, as it wasn't this story."

"We spent a short amount of time in Rapunzel's tower," Lottie muttered, touching her hair. After they had left the tower, her hair had gone back to normal, but she must still think about it.

Carson inspected the tower. "How do we get in?"

"No idea," Lizette said. "Like I said, I've ignored it. I do know Terry kept Nancy inside for a while, but I didn't come near it."

Lottie walked around the tower, rubbing her hands over the stone. "Right here," she said. "There's a door, just like Rapunzel's." Carson hurried over and helped her pull it open. It was heavy and thick, and the hinges made a loud creak.

Lizette pushed past them and scurried up the stairs, holding her long red dress in her hands. Lottie glanced at Carson, and he shrugged. If Lizette was in love with Terry, she was probably in a hurry to get to him. They followed her up the spiral staircase.

When they reached the top, they saw a small stone room that stood empty except for a glass coffin. It sat in the middle of the room. Lizette was circling the coffin, her hand placed over her mouth. She dropped to her knees and placed her hands on the glass.

"So, this is Terry?" Carson asked the obvious. The man inside appeared to be asleep. He had sandy brown hair and wore a tunic and cape. It looked like the clothing Carson had always worn when he had been a prince, right down to the knee-high boots.

"Open it," Lizette commanded in a whisper.

Carson studied the coffin and leaned over to lift the lid. It was heavy and awkward. Lottie grabbed the other side and helped him slide it off. They placed it gently on the ground.

"Now, how do we wake him?" Lizette asked.

Footsteps sounded behind them, and a voice answered. "You don't."

Chapter 15

Lottie spun around to see a beautiful young woman with long red hair and a long blue dress standing with her arms crossed. Her fiery green eyes took in each of them, and she drummed her fingers against her arms.

"You will not wake Terry," she said through clenched teeth. "I will not allow it."

Lottie frowned at her. She didn't look like someone who could stop them. "Who are you?"

"She's Nancy," Carson said, crossing his own arms and glaring at the woman.

"Nancy?"

"Yes, I'm Nancy," the woman said, walking toward the coffin. "Get away, Lizette."

Lizette jumped up and backed away to the wall. She held her chin high, but her eyes showed fear. Lottie was confused. Nancy was an old lady. This woman didn't look any older than she was.

The woman glanced down at Terry. "Of all the stupid things you could all be doing. It's a good thing I spotted you all coming in. Don't you know this man is dangerous?"

"Terry isn't dangerous," Lizette protested, wringing her hands together.

"Isn't dangerous?" Nancy walked up to Lizette and stopped inches away from her face. "Terry is the most dangerous person you will meet here. Have you not seen what he's done to my world?"

Lizette cast her eyes to the floor.

Nancy spun back around. "I understand why Lizette would want to wake Terry, but Carson? What do you think you are doing?"

Carson wouldn't let Nancy intimidate him. "We need to get out of here. If you can't fix things or send us home, then maybe he can."

Nancy pointed a threatening finger at Carson. "What makes you think he would help you? Before I placed him here, he was not trying to help anyone but himself. He wanted to take over this world, not save it."

Lottie didn't want to listen. She wanted to go home. "Maybe we can reason with him."

Nancy laughed. "Reason with Terry? Believe me, I've tried. You remember the last girl that played the part of Cinderella?"

Lottie nodded. "Yes. I remember everything."

"Her name was Olivia. She fell in love with a man here named Jerron. They helped me trick Terry. He had some weird fascination with Olivia, so I put her under a spell. We applied a sleeping spell to Olivia's lips, and when he kissed her, he fell into a magical sleep."

"Kissed her?" Lizette squeaked.

Nancy's eyes jumped to the queen. "Kissed her. You see? He wasn't loyal to you at all. There is no reason to wake him."

Lizette's eyes narrowed. "You drove him mad. He was in love with me, but he wanted to go home so badly. Then, you ripped us apart. That was more than he could take. The next time I saw him, he was different. Sometimes he acted normal, and sometimes he didn't make any sense."

"Please," Nancy said with a sigh. "You can't blame me for Terry's behavior."

"If I speak with him, and he has the power, he will help." Lizette said. "He hates you, though. It wouldn't be wise to stick around. You don't want us to wake him because he will retaliate against you again."

Nancy's eyes flashed, and she pulled her wand from a pocket in her dress. "Listen to me, Lizette. You do not know what you are dealing with. You do not want to make an enemy of me."

"That's what you said to me right before you turned me into one of your silly side characters."

"Yes. You were much more pleasant as a fairy. More obedient, to be sure."

"Only because I didn't have my senses about me."

Nancy twirled a piece of hair around one finger and pointed her wand at Lizette. "I have more than I can deal with right now."

Lottie's eyes widened. "Don't do anything you're going to regret."

Nancy glanced sideways at her. "Come now, Charlotte. What do you take me for? I am not the enemy. I built this world for people like you, and you are all so unappreciative."

"It's not exactly a lovely Grimm's fairy tale, is it?" Carson asked. "Things are wrong, and you need to face up to your failures."

Nancy slammed her wand against her leg, and her eyes shot daggers at him. "A lovely Grimm's fairy tale? Are you kidding me? Never bring the Brothers Grimm or any of those other foolish tellers of tales into a conversation with me! Have you ever read their work?"

Carson shook his head.

"They took stories—*my* stories—and they turned them into horrifying tales with horrible endings and geared them toward children!"

Lottie frowned. "How are they your stories?"

"I am not *a* fairy godmother. I am *the* fairy godmother."

Carson and Lottie shared a confused look, and Nancy let out a long sigh.

"It's far too long of a story to tell you right here. The short of it is that I have always wanted to help people find love. Even before I created this place, I helped people. *Cinderella* was based on an experience I had while helping someone. I realized these events were marvelous stories, but I'm no writer. I found others and told them my stories. I told them to write them down because I knew they would inspire people. Instead, the authors of my stories took every creative liberty that they could and changed them into things only vaguely resembling the truth. They made them morbid and horrible. I tried to pretend they were alright just to comfort myself. When I created this world, I wanted to stick to the original written stories because people knew them. I hated them so much, but thankfully, after some years, better versions of the stories surfaced. I changed and went with some of the more beloved tellings. Now, if I even hear the names of those Grimm brothers or Hans Christian Anderson, I cringe."

Carson narrowed his eyes. "So, what made you go from helping people in their lives to bringing them here?"

Nancy tapped her lip with her wand. "Well, it didn't happen overnight. I wanted to create one of these worlds, but my father didn't think I was ready. I had the plan for a long time before he finally relented and let me do it. He must have realized how brilliant it was because he hasn't interfered."

Carson coughed behind his hand. It looked like he was trying to hide a smile. It was probably not a great idea to let her know her father was interfering.

Lottie couldn't believe the lengths some people would go to try to help people that didn't want their help. "I don't understand why you spend so much time doing this."

Nancy cocked her head. "Don't you? Now that you and Carson have found love, you should understand."

"So, you were so deeply in love with someone that you wanted everyone else to be that way?" Lottie was trying to understand.

Nancy bit her lip and looked at the stone ceiling. "Well, I... That's not exactly it."

Carson threw his arms in the air. "You've been messing with all our lives and you've never been in love?"

Lottie frowned. If that was true, she had a few choice words to say to the fairy godmother.

Nancy's brows came together. "I never said that."

"So, you have been in love?" Lottie asked.

Nancy took a deep breath and glared. "No, I haven't."

Lizette's eyes flashed with what Lottie could only call rage. "You've never been in love? What a hypocrite!"

Nancy pointed her wand at Lizette. "I am not a hypocrite. Trust me. I believe in love with everything inside me. I don't force people to fall in love. What I do is get them to believe in love. There is no time for it in my life because I'm so busy helping people like you."

"You might need a taste of your own medicine," Lottie said, crossing her arms. "Why don't you stick yourself in a story? It might be a great learning experience for you."

Nancy stepped toward her. "I told you. I want people to believe in love. My entire heart loves love. That's why I do what I do. I'm sure I'll fall in love someday. I am young, after all."

Carson snorted. "Young? You've been doing this for hundreds of years."

"Yes," Nancy said, fixing him with a stare. "Hundreds of years. Not thousands. If I get to thousands, then there might be a reason for concern. I'm barely old enough to get married."

Lottie wanted to argue, but what was the point? She didn't know how fairies worked.

"So, every story, every fairy tale, is based on something from your life?" she asked.

Nancy frowned. "Of course not. Some were, and some weren't. I use whichever one's fit my fancy. I haven't caused any tales in a long time now that I have this world going strong."

"It's a mess," Carson said.

Nancy rolled her eyes. "Yes, but it won't be for long."

"We are going to wake Terry," Carson said. "You don't have the power you used to. We need him to get us all out of here or to fix this place so you can get us out."

Nancy's brows knit together. "Who says I don't have the power I used to? You do not understand the problems Terry can cause."

"You've caused some of your own problems," Lottie accused.

Nancy blinked. "Yes. I know. But there are things you don't understand about Terry."

Carson shrugged. "So, tell us."

"Terry isn't actually here. Terry is in Boulder, Colorado, in a coma. That means his body is on Earth and his consciousness is here. He cannot be fully defeated here if he comes out in rebellion."

Lottie scrunched her forehead. "Shouldn't it be easier if his body isn't here?"

"No, because he isn't tied to this place the way some others are. To kill him, he would have to be killed here and on Earth."

"Whoa," Lizette said, her eyes wide. "Let's not talk about killing him."

"I'm trying to help you understand. There are things I don't even fully comprehend when it comes to him."

"Our bodies and our consciousness are both here, right?" Lottie asked.

"Yes. Some people I bring here I take from a spot in time, and I can return them to that same spot without anyone noticing. I do that a lot more than the coma thing. It's a lot less traumatic to wake up to."

"Why would you put anyone in a coma?" Carson asked.

"I like to experiment to see what works best."

"If it's only Terry's mind that is here, can he cause that many problems?" Lottie asked.

"Since this world is magical, it makes him capable of a lot more than if he were actually here."

"Just let us wake him," Lizette pleaded. "How do we do it?"

Nancy shrugged.

"Only Nancy can wake him," Carson said. "Or true love's kiss."

Lizette stepped toward Terry.

"Don't do it," Nancy said. She waved her wand around her head, and a stream of pink smoke filled the air. "I'm sorry to do this, but I need you out of the way until I clean some things up. Enjoy the memories for now."

"What—" Carson began, but that was all Lottie heard.

The smell of apples and cinnamon filled Lottie's nose, and she yawned. She was so tired. She'd been tired since she woke up, but now she couldn't keep her eyes open. Lottie sank down to the floor and yawned again. If she closed her eyes for a few minutes, she might feel better.

Chapter 16

Carson and Brandon drove home in silence. Carson was glad his friend sensed he wasn't in the mood to talk. He stared at the window and watched the houses pass by and tried to ignore the horrible feeling he had in the pit of his stomach.

Brandon pulled his car into Carson's driveway. "You alright, man?"

Carson rubbed a hand over his face. "Fine."

"I'm sorry I encouraged you to ask her to the dance. I never would have if I'd known she'd act like that."

Carson sighed. "It's not your fault. I never would have believed Char would do that. I think the cheerleading got to her brain or something."

Brandon cocked his head. "Are you sure you're going to be okay?"

Carson scowled. Didn't Brandon know guys didn't have to sit around and talk about their feelings? He knew that wasn't fair. Anyone would be lucky to have a friend like Brandon.

"Do you want to talk about it?"

"Not really," Carson said. "I mean, what is there to say? If all these years of friendship mean nothing to her, that's fine by me. She can go off with her cheerleading pals and chase after the football team. It doesn't bother me. I don't need her."

Brandon shook his head. "That's a lie. Charlotte's your best friend."

Carson stared out the front windshield. "*Was* my best friend."

"No, don't do that. You don't know why she reacted the way she did. Don't get all weird on her."

"Weird?" Carson laughed. "What do you mean? She laughed in my face. In front of everyone. You don't do that to friends."

Brandon frowned. "Maybe you don't know everything. Don't dump years of friendship over this."

"Why do you even care?"

"Because I'm your friend, and I like Charlotte. Maybe she was having an off day."

"I don't care. I'm done. She can't fix this. I doubt she'll even try. She's probably been trying to figure out how to drop me since she joined the squad."

"You know that isn't true."

"Do I?" Carson grabbed his bag. "I gotta go. I need to take a shower and work on my chemistry paper." He opened the door and gave a quick wave. Brandon was still frowning.

Carson hurried to his front door and opened it quietly. His mom might be home, and he didn't need her prying.

"Hey," his mom said when he entered. Her blonde hair was falling out of its ponytail, and she had on the jeans she always wore when she was doing a project. She was holding some nails and a hammer. "Good timing. Can you hold this nail for me? I'm trying to put this shelf together, and it's giving me trouble."

Carson dropped his bag and held the nail where she pointed. His mom was good at a lot of stuff, but using a hammer was not her thing. She tapped on the nail, and he closed his eyes. If she was going to hit his fingers, he didn't want to see.

"There we go," she said. "Thanks." He let go of the nail, and she grabbed another. "How was the track meet?"

"Fine."

"Really?" She looked at him and studied his face. "You look upset. Is anything wrong?"

"Nope. I just need to go work on my homework."

Her eyes narrowed. "Something is wrong. I can tell."

Carson clenched his jaw. "I don't want to talk about it."

She frowned. "I'm your mom. If you don't talk to me, I'll worry."

He sighed. "I had a fight with Charlotte. I don't want to talk about it."

She put a hand to her heart, and he fought the urge to roll his eyes. "You never fight with Charlotte."

"Yeah, and I never will again. I'm pretty sure I'm never going to talk to her again."

"No! What did you do?"

Carson threw his hands into the air. "What did I do? Why do you assume it's me?"

"You've been through plenty together. I'm sure you can work it out."

"I don't want to work it out. I don't want to talk right now, alright?"

His mom frowned and nodded. "Okay."

"I'm going to do my homework." Carson grabbed his bag and stomped up the stairs. He slammed his bedroom door and locked it. He tossed the bag on the floor and stood in the middle of his room.

He stared absently out the window and told himself he didn't care. Telling himself that was pointless, though. He cared way more than he would ever admit. How could Charlotte be so unfeeling? A nice *no thank you* would have been fine. It still would have crushed him, but not the same way.

He wanted to throw something, but that would only have his mom rushing upstairs to check on him. He wouldn't cry. That would be a stupid waste of time. He'd always hoped something would happen with Charlotte someday, but he'd never admitted that to anyone. He always acted like it was crazy if anyone ever hinted at it.

He shook his head. It would be fine. He'd take a shower and finish his homework and never think about Charlotte again.

Charlotte sat in her car in the garage and rested her head against the steering wheel. Tears ran over her cheeks, and she wiped at her runny nose. She couldn't believe Carson had asked her to the dance. She was glad she knew he was only joking, so he ended up looking bad and not her.

She sniffed. That wasn't true. No one else knew he was joking, so she looked like a big jerk. Even her friends on the cheer squad had been shocked at her reaction.

It would be silly to sit in the car crying forever, so she pushed open the door and bolted into the house. She ran to her room and shut the door, even though no one was home. She threw herself on her bed and wrapped her gray and pink comforter around herself.

Her parents wouldn't be home for over two hours, so she would give herself time to cry, then she would get herself back together before they came home. She squeezed her eyes shut and tried not to picture the look of betrayal she had seen on Carson's face when she'd laughed and told him no. He was probably just upset that his trick had backfired.

There was a pounding on the front door, and Charlotte paused. She didn't want to answer it. Her face was probably blotchy and red. She walked cautiously to the door and looked through the peephole. Brandon stood outside. He ran a hand through his short black curls and then knocked again.

Charlotte opened the door a crack. "What is it?"

"That was cold, Char."

"You heard what he said the other day. He did it as a joke." She tried to keep the trembling from her voice.

Brandon peeked through the door. "He wasn't doing it as a joke. He thought it would be fun if you went as friends."

"I wasn't going to sit there and let him make me look like a fool."

Brandon frowned. "You did that on your own."

She swallowed hard and resisted the urge to punch Brandon in the face. Brandon was a nice guy. Everyone liked him. He wasn't going to fix this, though. Charlotte was hurt in a way that wouldn't be fixed.

"Sorry, Char. I shouldn't have said that. Will you forgive me?"

"Fine, whatever. Can you just leave? I'm not in the mood to talk."

"Sure, but I want you to think about this. Carson is really upset. He never dreamed you would say no. Not only that, but you laughed at him. You should apologize, or you're going to lose all those years of friendship."

She shut the door and wiped at her eyes. If Carson had wanted to go to the dance with her, she had made a huge mistake. Still, she could remember his words in the car the other day. No, Brandon was just trying to be a peacemaker again.

She made her way to the pantry and climbed onto the bottom shelf. She ran her hand over the top shelf until she touched something. Her mom always kept the good stuff up too high. Grabbing what felt like a candy bar, she jumped to the floor and ripped the wrapper from the caramel filled chocolate.

More unwelcome tears fell from her eyes as she bit into the bar. It was her opinion that a gooey mouth full of caramel and chocolate fixes everything. Not this time. She was having a hard time swallowing. She dropped the candy bar to the floor and covered her face with her hands. If she didn't go talk to Carson, she might never recover.

Carson held his game controller in his hands and focused on not running his car into a wall. He was usually good at this game, but he'd been at it for two hours and never done better than third place. It was probably fair to blame that on his lack of sleep from the night before.

"Charlotte is here," his mom said, popping her head into the room.

Carson didn't look away from the screen. "Tell her to go away."

His mom sighed and came toward him. "I don't know what happened between the two of you, but you need to work it out."

"I don't know why you care," he said, throwing the controller to the floor after his car hit a tree.

"Why wouldn't I care? You're my baby, and I don't like to see you unhappy."

He rolled his eyes. "You've always taken Char's side. Ever since I can remember."

"You can't throw away that many years of friendship because of one little argument."

"We didn't have an argument."

She folded her arms and frowned. "Perhaps if you told me what happened—"

"I'm not talking about it. Ever," he said, leaning back in his gaming chair.

"Please talk to her."

He shrugged. "Fine, whatever." He knew he was being a jerk, but he was having a hard time controlling his emotions. She disappeared behind the door, and he waited. Charlotte peeked around the door frame, and he stared blankly at her.

"Hey," she said, entering the room. She stepped over a pile of laundry and stood in front of him. She twisted her bracelet and glanced at him.

He wasn't going to make this easier on her. He didn't say anything.

"I'm really sorry, Carson. I acted horrible yesterday. You caught me off guard and—"

"And I'm not a football player," he interrupted.

Her eyebrows came together. "What?"

He glared up at her. "Nothing. You apologized, so you can leave."

She kept twisting her bracelet. "But I need to know you aren't mad at me."

He chuckled, but it wasn't a happy chuckle. "That's too bad." He was angry... and also feeling the weirdest sense of déjà vu. A panicked feeling settled in his stomach, and he leaned forward and covered his mouth with both hands. Something wasn't right.

"I am sorry." She turned to walk away.

"Wait."

She turned and stared questioningly at him. Unshed tears sat in her eyes, but he barely noticed.

"Something's wrong. We've done this before."

She tilted her head but didn't speak.

His mom looked in. "Everything okay in here?"

"No, it's not," Carson said, getting to his feet. He put a hand to his head and tried to remember. "Nancy," he said, as his memories came flooding back.

"Who's Nancy?" his mom asked.

"She's the one that's messing with us." He stepped forward and grabbed Charlotte's arm. "Do you remember Nancy?"

"I don't think I know anyone with that name."

He smiled. "We had a misunderstanding. Everything is going to be okay. We have to wake up."

His mom frowned. "I think you need to go back to bed."

"You don't remember Nancy?" he asked Char. She frowned and shook her head. "She's a fairy godmother. Nancy took us to some crazy world and then she put a spell on us or something. I think we fell asleep, and we are dreaming about a memory."

Charlotte's eyes widened, and she glanced at his mom.

"Maybe you aren't you," he said, taking a step back. "Maybe you are having your own dream." He began pacing across the messy floor. "That could be it. It would be more convenient if we were in this together. I'm not sure what I need to do." It was strange that he could go from despair to hope in such a short amount of time. This was all in the past. In the future, Char loved him.

"If this is a joke, it's not funny," his mom scolded. "If it's not, you need to see a doctor."

He turned and focused on Char. His mom wasn't real, so she didn't matter right now. "You turned me down because you overheard something I said to Brandon. We had a huge misunderstanding and went our own ways."

Charlotte frowned. "Brandon promised he wouldn't tell."

"He didn't. You told me. In the future."

His mom ran a hand over her eyes. "Carson, you aren't making any sense."

Carson took a step closer to her. "Lottie, you have to re-member."

She took a step back. "Lottie? No one has ever called me that."

He reached out and gently took her face in his hands. "Re-member. Please be you. We need to wake up." He leaned down and kissed her. She jumped at the surprise, but then wrapped her arms around him and kissed him back.

"Carson! What is going on?" his mom demanded. He blocked her out. If she was really his mom, he might pay at-tention, but she was only a dream.

Charlotte pulled back and opened her mouth to say some-thing, and then closed it. She sank down to the floor and stared blankly ahead. Carson gave her a moment to think.

"We have to get out of here," she finally said, looking up at him. He reached his hand down and grabbed hers, pulling her to her feet.

His mom stood there with her mouth hanging open.

"No time to explain," he said, smiling at her. "We have things to do." He kept Charlotte's hand clasped tightly in his and pulled her from the room. He didn't know where he was going, but he knew they needed to wake up.

He pulled open the front door and almost plowed into Brandon.

Brandon jumped back and looked from Charlotte to Car-son, then at their joined hands. "Oh, good. I came here to knock some sense into you or something. I'm glad to see you've resolved it on your own."

"We have gigantic problems," he said. "We might need your help, but let me try something first. NANCY!"

Lottie jumped, and Brandon cringed.

Carson grinned. "Sorry. I should have warned you. NAN-CY! WHERE ARE YOU? COME TALK TO US!"

Brandon was covering his ears and glaring at him. "What the heck, dude? Who is Nancy?"

Carson scanned the yard. No sign of the fairy godmother. "It doesn't matter if she isn't going to appear."

Lottie glanced around. "Now what?"

Carson rubbed his chin. "We need to go to Boulder, Colorado."

Brandon's eyebrows jumped from his head. "Why?"

"Yes, why?" Lottie asked.

"Because Nancy said that Terry was in a coma in Colorado. If we find him, we might find her." He started walking, but Lottie grabbed his arm and pulled him to a stop.

"If this is a dream, what is the point of traveling that far? Can't we will ourselves there?"

"Hmm," Carson muttered, glancing up at the sky. "My dreams have never worked like that."

"Even if we find Nancy, it might just be a dream Nancy. She might not be able to help us, and even if it really is her, she will probably refuse."

Carson scratched his head. "Do you have a better idea?"

Lottie shook her head. "No."

"How real do you suppose this dream is?" he asked. "If Nancy is behind it, it could be more real than a normal dream. It feels more real. I even remember dreaming last night. That's like dreaming in a dream."

Her eyes widened. "What if we aren't in a dream? What if she sent us back, but in the past?"

Brandon grabbed both of their shoulders and looked from one to the other. "Is there a gas leak in your house or something? Do I need to get your parents out?"

Carson laughed. "No. It's too hard to explain."

"You both sound crazy."

"We might be. So, Colorado?"

Lottie shrugged. "I suppose."

Brandon crossed his arms. "I can't let you run off to Colorado like this."

"We're fine," Carson insisted. "We wouldn't mind a ride to the airport."

"Do you have tickets?"

"Nope."

Brandon sighed.

Lottie ran her hand over Carson's arm. "Why do you seem so optimistic?"

He gazed into her eyes. "Because this morning, my heart was broken. Having the memories flood in made such a huge contrast in my feelings that I feel like I can take on anything. We are going to find Nancy, and we are going to wake up and fix everything. Well, maybe not everything, but we are going to get back to our world, and not only in a dream."

Lottie smiled and went up on her toes and kissed him gently on the cheek.

"Now that's what I've been talking about," Brandon said. "Now, get in the car, and I'll take you freaks to the airport."

Chapter 17

Lottie jumped out of Brandon's car and turned to look at the airport—only the airport wasn't there. They were standing in front of a hospital.

Brandon slammed the car door and scrunched his forehead. "What? Where are we? What happened?"

Carson took a step forward. "I guess this dream isn't going to make us waste any time traveling."

"You know you sound crazy, right?" Brandon said. "Still, the airport was here a minute ago."

"Don't even try to make sense of it," Lottie told him. "It will just confuse you."

"I'm already confused," he muttered, his eyes glued to the hospital.

When they got inside, they rushed to the front desk. A woman with a dark brown braid and a big wad of gum churning around in her mouth glanced up at them.

"Are we in Colorado?" Carson asked her.

The woman stared at him for a minute, her bright green gum rolling around as she chomped with her mouth open. "Yes."

Lottie leaned against the tall desk. "We are looking for a woman named Nancy. She volunteers here."

The woman whose name tag said Jess rolled her eyes. "Volunteers can't have visitors."

Carson leaned in. "Nancy helped my friend, and we want to thank her."

"That doesn't change the rules."

"Yes, but..." Lottie grabbed Carson's arm and pointed down the hallway. Nancy, the old version of Nancy, was walking toward the front desk.

"Nancy," Carson said, catching her attention as she was about to walk past them. Nancy stopped and studied the three of them. There was no sign of recognition on her face.

"There really is a Nancy?" Brandon asked. "That's a weird coincidence."

"Do I know you?" Nancy asked.

Lottie crossed her arms. "Are you going to start with that?" She raised her brows.

"We need you to wake us up," Carson said.

Nancy looked at them all again.

When her eyes landed on Brandon, he shrugged. "Sorry, they aren't making a lot of sense today."

"I'm afraid I don't know what you are talking about," she said. "Perhaps you've confused me with someone else." She smiled and exited the automatic doors.

"You have to help us," Lottie said, as they followed her out. "We're from the future, and we need you to take us back. We're stuck in a dream."

Nancy stopped and frowned. "I'm listening."

"You waved your wand and made us fall asleep. We need to get back to where we were. Your crazy world is in danger, and we need to get back to our real lives."

Nancy sighed. "I hate it when my future messes with my past."

"Is everyone crazy?" Brandon asked.

Nancy ignored him. "If I put you to sleep, I must have had a reason. I don't want to do anything that might interfere with what my future self is thinking. That could cause a catastrophe."

Lottie glared. "We're already dealing with a catastrophe. We need to go back. Or maybe you could fix everything by not taking us into your world in the future."

"If she doesn't, we might go on having that misunderstanding between us forever," Carson said.

Lottie hadn't thought of that. If going to Nancy's world was the only way she could be with Carson, then she would stay there forever if she had to.

Nancy tilted her head and smiled. "I can see I'm still doing good in the future, although this isn't really the past, you understand. This must be a dream of the past, which means anything I do here will not affect the future. I might remember the dream, and so might your friend, but to us, it will only be a dream."

"This is the weirdest day of my life," Brandon said. "It would make sense if it was only a dream."

"It feels real," Nancy said. "All the dreams I make do, so it's hard to tell for sure. I've never been in one of my dream creations before. It's interesting."

"Please wake us," Lottie pleaded. "If you don't, something bad might happen."

"If I'm part of a dream, there is very little I can do to help. I wish you the best, though."

Lottie placed her hands on her hips. "Really? That's all?"

"My dream spells don't last long. No more than a day or two. Enjoy it while you are here." Nancy pulled her wand from her bag and swished it. Pink smoke was the only sign she had been there.

Brandon rubbed his eyes. "Whoa! She disappeared! I'm convinced this is my dream now."

"So, what do we do?" Lottie wondered.

Carson let out a breath and stuck his hands in his pants pockets. "I guess we wait until we wake up."

Lottie moved her mouth from side to side. He was probably right. She couldn't think of any solutions.

"Do you think Lizette is here?" Carson asked.

"Lizette?" Brandon asked, his brow scrunched.

"She was another person who is probably in one of these weird dreams."

Brandon pulled his phone from his pocket and started scrolling and muttering to himself. He flashed his phone at them. On the screen was a picture of a woman with long black hair, wearing Christmas tree pajamas and hugging a dog. It was Lizette.

"That's Lizette," Carson said, grabbing the phone. "She looks a lot less... creepy."

"Do you know where she is?" Brandon demanded.

"How do you know her?" Lottie asked.

"She's my cousin," Brandon said. "I haven't seen her in years."

Lottie frowned. "That's low if Nancy is making people disappear."

"She didn't disappear," Brandon said. "My uncle, her dad, was always a bit of a jerk. She left a note saying that she was sick of her life and she was going to live in Jamaica, or possibly Ireland, and she didn't want any contact with the family."

Carson frowned. "Why Jamaica or Ireland?"

"Our grandparents were from Jamaica, and her other grandparents were from Ireland. She'd always wanted to visit both places."

Lottie tapped her lip. "So, Nancy made it look like she moved when she was actually taken to Nancy's world."

"Is she alright?" Brandon asked.

Carson nodded. "Yes. She's the Queen of Hearts."

Brandon looked confused but didn't ask. "Can you take me to her?"

"I doubt it," Carson said. "We can't even figure out how to get there ourselves. We'll tell her you're looking for her when we wake up."

Lottie's vision was blurring. She yawned and stretched her back. It seemed odd to be tired in a dream.

"Are you alright?" Carson asked her.

"I think I'm waking up," she said, as the stone tower room formed before her eyes. She yawned again and sank to the ground.

Lottie sat up, and her eyes whipped around the stone room. Terry's coffin lid had been replaced, and Carson and Lizette were peacefully sleeping on the ground. She crawled over to Carson and shook his arm.

His eyes popped open, and he sat up. "I hope Brandon isn't freaked out without us."

"Oh, I am totally freaked out!" Brandon said, popping up from the other side of the coffin. "What just happened?"

"Oh no," Carson said. "How did we bring Brandon with us?"

"It's still a dream," Brandon said. "Still a dream. Lizette!" He hurried to his cousin's side and shook her awake.

"Brandon?" she muttered, looking around. "How did you get here?"

"It's a dream," he said, crushing her in a hug. "But I am glad to see you again."

Lizette hugged him back, then pushed her hair behind her ear. "Terry!"

"Who?"

Lizette jumped to her feet and grabbed the glass coffin lid. Carson and Lottie helped her lift it and place it on the floor.

Lottie cocked her head. "You better hurry before Nancy shows up again."

Lizette nodded and leaned down, pressing her lips to Terry's. His eyes slowly opened, and he placed a hand on his head. "Lizzy? What happened?"

Lizette sobbed and pulled Terry's arm as he climbed from the coffin. She wrapped him in a hug, her face pressed into his chest.

He rubbed his hand over her hair and frowned. "My mind feels cloudy. How did I get here?"

"Nancy," Carson said.

"I should have figured."

"Now what?" Lottie asked.

"Can you get us out of here?" Carson asked Terry.

Terry looked around the room. "Have you tried the stairs?"

"I mean out of Nancy's world."

Terry frowned. "Can I have a moment to think? My memories are muddled, but I believe I'll be able to sort them out if you give me a minute."

Lizette guided Terry over to the bed, and they sat down. He wrapped his arms around her, and she leaned into him, sniffling.

"Could this day get more bizarre?" Brandon asked.

Lottie smiled. "This is tame to some things I've seen here."

"Why couldn't you let things be?" Nancy said, as she stepped up to the top step. Nancy was walking up a flight of stairs? Perhaps her father was right, and she was losing her magic.

"It's time to let everyone go," Carson said. "You know it just as well as we do."

Nancy pushed her red hair over her shoulder and shot a dirty look at Carson. She pulled her wand from her dress and pointed it at Terry.

"Nancy?" Terry said with a small grin. "Who knew you could look like that?"

She rolled her eyes. "Yes, everyone is impressed. Now, can we discuss the matter at hand?"

Terry stared ahead and frowned. "My mind is clearing up."

Nancy pursed her lips, and if Lottie wasn't mistaken, she looked scared.

"I was so tired," Terry said. "After you took Lizzy away from me, I couldn't sleep. I never do well without sleep. I was so angry."

Lottie watched the man. He didn't seem like a threat.

"I remember everything I said and did, but it feels like it was someone else. I regret my actions."

Nancy nodded and rubbed her fingers over the wand. "I'm glad you've discovered the error of your ways."

Terry raised an eyebrow. "You aren't innocent yourself."

"No, she isn't," King Henan said, appearing in the middle of them all.

Nancy placed a hand on her chest. "Father! What are you doing here?"

"It's time."

She crossed her arms, and her lip came out in a pout. "What do you mean?"

"I've been a horrible father," he said, straightening his crown. "I've spoiled you and let you do things I didn't agree with because I wanted to let you live your dream."

Her eyes narrowed. "I am not spoiled."

He sighed. "I let you make this place, and I let you do things that weren't in the best interest of others because I wanted you to be happy and to believe in yourself. That was wrong. I've tried to help you here and there, but it stops now."

"Help me? How have you helped me?"

220

"I led you to people that I thought would play better into your plans. You didn't think Carson and Lottie just happened to be chosen by you and know each other, did you? That would have been a very unlikely coincidence. And what about Mara and Stephen? I helped you put people together that had the greatest chance of falling in love."

Nancy crossed her arms, and fire flashed in her eyes. "You cannot take credit for my achievements. What about Olivia and Jerron? That was all me."

The king sighed. "The idea to place two real people in the same story was sent to you in a dream, was it not? I'm not trying to take credit for your work. I tried to help you without anyone knowing, but you already had so much in motion here it was too hard. This place confuses me."

"Why couldn't you just tell me? Is that hard? I'm not bad at taking suggestions, you know."

The king let out a slow breath and studied the ceiling. "You have never been good at taking suggestions. This has to end. You have too many problems here, and I know your magic isn't what it should be. If it was, you wouldn't have appeared here in your actual form."

Nancy's green eyes were on fire. "You didn't need to interfere."

"I'm going to take this place from you if you can't fix it."

"No!" Nancy protested, rushing to her father. She placed one hand on his arm and looked up, her eyes pleading. "Please don't! It's mine. I made it. There is a lot of potential here. I just messed up a little."

The king leveled her with a hard stare. "I will let you keep this place, but you must fix it. You will also follow my rules."

Nancy's teeth made a small grinding sound. "What rules?"

He held up one finger. "First, you cannot bring anyone here unless you have their permission."

Nancy pursed her lips but didn't speak.

"Second, you send everyone home that you've already brought here against their will."

"I don't want to leave," Terry said. "It's grown on me."

"Neither do I," Lizette said, locking her fingers with his.

King Henan waved a hand in dismissal. "We will come to you later." He held up three fingers. "And finally, once you get the mess sorted out, you will come here without your magic and live here until you learn your lesson."

Nancy's eyes widened, and her mouth hung open. Lottie smiled. It would serve her right.

"Father! This... is... unacceptable!" she sputtered.

He crossed his arms. "Then, you surrender this place."

"No! It isn't fair. I can't do some of those things!"

Lottie and Carson shared a look. So much for the calm and composed fairy godmother. She was acting like a spoiled toddler.

"What can't you do?" the king asked.

"I can't send everyone home. My magic is pathetic at the moment. There is enough magic tied to some people that they might go back if they follow a story and fall in love. Mara and Stephen were sent back home, but Jurry and Meena ended up in the swamp."

The king rubbed his chin. "What was the difference?"

"I tried to send Jurry and Meena back myself. They weren't even together at the time. Mara and Stephen fell in love, and they kissed each other. That might be the reason it worked because that is how it's supposed to work."

Terry shook his head. "It all sounds confusing and messy to me."

"It has gotten that way," Nancy muttered. "A lot of that is your fault, though."

"Mine?" Terry asked.

"Yes," she said, glaring at him. "You've messed everything up. You traveled through stories, and that is not something you should be able to do. It's messed up the flow of the world. Now people are disappearing and reappearing in strange places. Trees are the wrong color. Everything is confused."

"Why can Terry do that?" Lottie asked.

King Henan tilted his head and studied Terry. "Years ago, my sister fell in love with a human. She left to be with him."

"I hope you aren't about to say that Terry is my cousin," Nancy said.

"That's exactly what I'm telling you."

Terry stood, pulling Lizette up with him. "You're saying my mom is a fairy?"

"Yes."

Terry ran a hand over his head. "So I'm like part fairy?"

"You are. That's why you've been able to manipulate Izla's magic."

"Izla?"

Nancy threw her hands into the air. "Father!"

He shrugged. "Sorry. I've never been able to see you as a Nancy."

Something was turning in Lottie's head, but she couldn't quite place it.

"Izla?" Carson said. "Wasn't that the name of the woman Earl met at the gym?"

That was it. Nancy was the woman Earl had been crushing on. He would be mad if he found out.

"We are not talking about this!" Nancy said. "Cousin or not, Terry cannot stay here."

"Why?" Terry asked.

"Because you mess things up, and your body isn't here. It might be okay for a time, but after a while, it will cause problems."

"So, bring my body here."

"I can't. Not until my magic gets stronger."

King Henan ran a hand over Nancy's head. "I think you need a break. You need to take some time to rest and get your magic back where it should be."

"But what about us?" Carson asked. "We don't want to be stuck here."

"I wish I could send you back," the king said. "If I did, it wouldn't be the way it should be. One fairy cannot understand the weaving of another, and so the results could be disastrous."

"I don't see why. All you would have to do is send us back," Lottie said.

The king shook his head. "It sounds easy, but Izla made the magic by tying you to this place with a link to your former time. If I try to copy it, you could end up in the wrong place or time."

Nancy's mouth turned down, and she glanced at Terry. "Terry can probably take himself home. It's different for him. I'm not sure if he could get back into his body, though."

Terry disappeared, and they all gasped.

Lizette's eyes widened. "Where did he go?"

Terry popped back in. He had a huge smile on his face. "I went into my body and brought it here. I feel so much better. Everything is a lot more clear."

"That didn't seem hard," Carson said. "Can Terry send us home?"

Nancy shook her head. "He would have the same problem my father would. How did you find your body?"

"I could feel it pulling at me. I've felt it calling me for a while, but I didn't understand what was happening."

She gritted her teeth together. "You should take yourself home."

Terry frowned. "I told you I want to stay."

Nancy put her hands on her hips. "Well, I don't want you here."

"But I can come and go. What are you going to do about it?"

"If you keep up the way you have been, the world will never stabilize."

"What if I promise to stay in Wonderland? Me and Lizette. We won't change stories, and you don't send anyone else here."

The king patted Nancy on the shoulder. "That sounds reasonable."

"Fine," Nancy muttered.

Terry grinned. "And I'll keep my dravuls around to make sure no one bothers us."

King Henan frowned. "What is a dravul?"

Terry's smile widened. "I could tell you, but it would be more fun to show you."

Chapter 18

Carson's impatience was about to spill over as he waited for Terry to come out of the castle. King Henan kept looking at the sun the way an impatient man would look at his watch. Nancy pouted like a little kid that had lost their ice cream. If she frowned any harder, it might become permanent.

Brandon didn't know when to be concerned. He was staring at the castle like it was the greatest thing in the world. Every few minutes, he would turn and tell Lottie something about medieval times. She was being polite and nodding, but Carson would bet her mind was somewhere else.

Lizette was pacing back and forth, her long red dress whipping around behind her. She seemed nervous. Carson supposed she could have a lot of reasons. Who knew what Terry was thinking? From what he'd been told, Terry wasn't the most stable person to come here. Lizette seemed to think he had changed from when she first met him, and if she was concerned, they all should be.

"There he is," Brandon said, pointing.

Terry was strolling toward them. There was nothing near him or in his hands, so what was a dravul? Terry also appeared to be talking to himself.

"Maybe he couldn't find whatever it was he was looking for," he said.

Lizette laughed nervously. "One does not misplace a dravul. They are probably behind him. He's the only one they listen to."

A chill ran down Carson's spine, and Lottie rubbed her arms and shivered. If the dravuls were a type of animal, they must be small because there was still nothing to see.

Small puffs of smoke were coming up from the ground behind Terry. The smoke strands didn't rise higher than a foot, and they were only a few inches wide.

"Do you see this?" Nancy asked her father. "What do you suppose is causing it?"

King Henan narrowed his eyes as he studied the scene. "I am uncertain. I'm sure it isn't good, though."

Lizette shivered. "Not good at all. You needn't worry. They obey Terry."

Terry reached them and spread out his arms. "Here are my dravuls."

"Where?" Brandon asked.

"All around me. You can't see them, but they leave footprints." Terry pointed at the ground, and Carson leaned in to see a large red paw print in the grass. Smoke rose from the print. Another one appeared. The creature was walking.

"What are they?" Brandon asked. He was the only one that didn't seem nervous.

"They are almost like a wolf. When I figured out the way Nancy was making people here that weren't real, I figured it out. Of course, I failed miserably and made them invisible. That was a lucky mistake. They are very loyal to me."

Lottie rubbed her arms and took a step closer to Carson.

"You don't need to worry," Terry assured them. "Leave us here in peace, and you never need to see the dravul again... Or I suppose you never don't see them again? You're never around them again? You know what I'm trying to say."

Terry's eyes danced with amusement, and Carson wondered if they had made a mistake in waking him. He was threatening them in a casual manner.

"I wish you hadn't made them," Lizette said, eyeing the paw prints as they moved around the group.

"Yes, but I've explained it to you. They are necessary."

She sighed. "I suppose."

King Henan crossed his arms and stared pointedly at Terry. Carson would hate to be on the other side of that stare. Terry seemed unaffected. "We will allow you to stay here for now. I'm not sure whether it's a good idea. I will talk to your mother. She knows you are here, and she's worried."

"So, if my mom is your sister, does that make her a fairy princess or something?" Terry wondered. "She never seemed very princessly to me."

The king nodded. "She is a princess."

"I might need to go visit her. She has a lot of explaining to do."

"Do not leave Wonderland," the king commanded. "As for the rest of you, I suggest you try to end your stories and go home."

Brandon raised his hand. "Does that include me?"

"No, you aren't really here," Nancy told him.

"You mean I'm like Terry was before he got his body back?"

"No. You are just having a dream," she told him. "I'm not sure why we can see you, or why we can speak with you, but it is a dream."

"That means I can wake you up without causing any problems," the king said. He waved his hand in front of Brandon, and Brandon disappeared. "I wish I could do the same for the rest of you."

"Well, I'm sure I've been missed at the castle," Terry said. "I know the dravuls missed me. They were sorely neglected while I was away. Should we return?" he asked Lizette.

She dropped her head and took his arm. She nodded to the others, and the two of them made their way back to the castle. The red paw prints followed them, and Carson let out a sigh of relief.

"I need to be going as well," the king said. "Remember what I told you, Izla. Fix this." The king disappeared. He didn't leave a poof of smoke like Nancy usually did. He was just gone. Nancy must do it for show.

"Now what?" Lottie asked.

Nancy sighed and bit the inside of her lip. "I need to get you to a story. The magic is the most powerful when you act out the story, fall in love, and kiss. That is your best bet because I can't manage any new magic."

"Are we close to any stories?"

"No, but once I realized you had a connection, I linked you together. If you kiss, you might end up in a new story. Do your best to get through it. I don't think it will make you redo days if you mess up. That was something I had to focus on to get it to happen."

"Um... but we've a... we've kissed since we've been here, and we didn't disappear," Lottie said. Her cheeks turned a light pink, and Carson smiled.

"I don't have a lot of magic right now, but I can focus it all on you. It might work." She pulled her wand from her pocket and spun it in the air. "Well, go on. Kiss."

Carson didn't need to be told twice. He bent down and kissed her. Almost the second his lips met hers, he felt himself spinning. He hated the feeling. It reminded him of not so pleasant times. He wasn't sure where he would wake up, but he hoped Lottie would be near.

Lottie squeezed her eyes shut as a thick liquid splashed into her face and she slammed into the soggy ground. She pulled herself up onto her hands and knees and lifted a hand to wipe her eyes, but she stopped when she realized her hands were covered in mud. She shook her head, hoping to get the goop off.

Lifting her arm, she wiped her face with the upper sleeve of her dress. She sat back on her legs and surveyed her surroundings. She had found the swamp. There was a small river of dirty water to one side and a forested area to the other. Plants she didn't know were all around. Five inches of mud squashed under her. This was just great. Now what was she supposed to do?

A moment ago, Carson was kissing her, and now she was in the middle of who knew where, covered in mud. She grabbed a handful of goopy wet earth and threw it. She wished Nancy was there to get it right in the mouth. Part of her wanted to stay where she was until someone came by, but it was possible no one else would ever come. No one would do it on purpose, that was for sure.

Getting to her feet required sticking her hands back into the mud. Once she stood, she shook her arms and watched globs of mud fall to the ground. Her dress was more brown than blue, but she tried to clean her hands on the skirt.

Where was she supposed to go? There was mud as far as she could see. Even the trees were surrounded by the stuff. She would avoid the river. If the water was clean, that would be a different story. It would be nice to wash her hands.

Something in her peripheral vision caused her to turn. She couldn't see anything, but she knew there was movement. Refusing to blink, she took slow steps backwards. The mud shifted, and she let out a shriek. An alligator covered in mud took a step closer to her. It was fifteen feet away, but with the thick mud, she might as well be in its mouth.

Lottie turned and did her best to run. The mud was so heavy she didn't have a chance. She thought she heard a roar, but alligators didn't roar, did they? Alligators weren't things she had studied. It could be a crocodile for all she knew. She wasn't going to ask.

She focused on moving forward. There was no reason to look back. If it ate her, she would rather not see it coming.

Something red jumped in front of her, and she screamed. "Max!" she yelled. "Run!" The fox looked up at her and then ran toward the alligator. Lottie spun around and fell. She was a goner, for sure. She looked up into the face of the alligator. It was only a few inches from her face. She closed her eyes and prepared for the inevitable.

"Are you hurt?" Roco's voice asked. Her eyes popped open to see Roco bending over her, his eyebrows knitted together.

"Where's the alligator?" she asked, hopping up. She spotted the animal. Max was sitting on its back, licking his paws. She took a step back.

"That's Horace," Roco said. "You don't need to worry about him. He's harmless."

Lottie wanted to scream at the top of her lungs. She wanted to hit something, possibly Nancy. She pushed her hair from her forehead and saw a group of about ten people standing in the trees watching her.

"Did all those people see that?"

Roco shrugged. "Probably. Don't worry about it. They all got here the same way. Some of them more than once. The swamp seems to pull people in. Nancy might want to rethink this place."

Lottie scanned the faces. "Is Carson here?" She could see Earl and Kirk. The other people were unfamiliar.

Roco grinned. "He's hiding off somewhere. He landed on a prickly plant so he's pulling some pokies out of his backside."

Lottie supposed she was lucky to have landed in the mud. She was having a hard time keeping her eyes off Horace. He didn't look harmless to her with his creepy eyes and sharp teeth.

Roco's eyes scanned the landscape. "Some of us are going to leave the swamp and hope we don't get pulled back in. A few are going to stay because they keep ending up here and figure it isn't worth it. What do you want to do?"

Lottie began walking toward the people, and Roco followed. "I'll go. I don't care how harmless the alligator or crocodile or whatever it is supposed to be is. I'm not staying around to tempt him."

"Horace is an alligator. Crocks have V-shaped snouts, and alligators are more U-shaped."

"Interesting," Lottie muttered, as they neared the group. She stepped on something and winced as it poked her foot. "I lost one of my boots."

"It's gone for good," Roco said. "If it's in the mud, there's no way we're going to find it. Come on, we have a fire going and some stew."

"It's good to see you guys again," Earl said. "Come sit down. It's not as muddy over here."

Logs had been laid in a circle around the fire, and now that she wasn't causing a spectacle, the people were all sitting around the flames. None of them looked clean, but she was the only one covered in mud from head to toe. She scanned the area for any snakes or alligators, then sat on a log.

A man was stirring something over the fire. He was short with a bushy beard, and something felt familiar about him. He ladled some stew into a bowl and handed it to her.

"I'm Jurry, if you don't remember. We saw each other briefly when you came to Carson's castle."

"Right," she said, accepting the bowl, trying to ignore her dirty hands. "You're Earl and Roco's brother."

"Something like that."

Lottie nodded as she took a bite of the stew. They were only brothers here. Not in the real world. She cringed. The stew was burned and had little flavor.

"This is Meena," Jurry said, pointing at a smiling redhead seated across the fire from her. "She's my... uh..."

"I'm his betrothed," she said with a huge grin. "We're getting hitched the moment we get out of this dump."

"Congratulations."

"Char!" Carson said, entering the area. "I'm so glad you ended up here." He carefully sat next to her, cringing as he sat. "You look good in mud."

Lottie rolled her eyes. "How did you stay clean?"

"I'm not," he said, motioning at his boots.

She arched her brow. "Wow, dirty boots."

He chuckled. "It does look like you challenged the swamp and lost."

Lottie gave him a half-hearted smile. "Ha ha."

Jurry handed Carson a bowl.

"Thanks."

"So, when are we leaving?" Lottie asked Roco.

"Soon. I've had more of this swamp than I can take."

Kirk sat down next to Meena. "I don't see any point in leaving. Every time I do, I end up falling back in."

Earl grinned. "No one has fallen in as thoroughly as Lottie."

A scream pierced the air, and everyone froze.

Carson dropped his bowl and stood. "Everyone stay here. I'll check."

"I'm coming with you," Earl said, grabbing a large stick.

"Be careful," Lottie called behind them.

Carson and Earl ran toward the scream. They shifted direction slightly when the scream repeated. They rushed around a tree to find Nancy trying to climb a tree while an alligator watched from below. Her long red hair had as much mud in it as Lottie's. She held on to a branch, and her feet were slipping against the tree's trunk.

"Don't worry, the animals are all friendly," Earl said, stepping closer.

Nancy turned and fixed Earl with a glare. "These animals shouldn't be here!" She dropped to the ground, scaring the alligator. It retreated into the trees.

Earl stood with his mouth open, staring at Nancy.

"What?" Nancy barked, brushing off her dress.

Earl rubbed his eyes. "Izla? How did you get here?"

Nancy paused, and her frown deepened.

Carson leaned toward Earl. "Izla is Nancy."

"WHAT?" Earl roared.

"She's lost most of her magic, so she can't make herself look old anymore."

Nancy had the decency to look down and at least appear ashamed.

"You're Nancy?" Earl said through gritted teeth.

She nodded and rubbed her arm.

"All your talk about wanting to help people and you tricked me! You made me like you just so you could reject me and then decide I needed to come here."

Nancy glanced up through her eyelashes. "No, it wasn't like that."

"Then, what was it like?" he demanded.

"I... wanted to go to the gym. It's important to know what humans like to do to better help them. I enjoyed your company, but I wasn't planning on anything besides having a gym buddy. I was shocked when you wanted to spend time with me."

He clenched and unclenched his fists. "So, you sent me here. You have more issues than I ever imagined."

Carson watched the emotions play across her face. There was some regret and more than a little embarrassment.

"Let's go," Earl said, motioning with his head. "She can figure this out on her own."

Carson wanted to agree, but Nancy looked so helpless.

"Don't leave me here!" she begged. "Please, take me with you."

"That sounds familiar," Carson said. "It sounds like the same thing everyone in this place has been saying to you. Probably for hundreds of years."

Nancy's shoulders drooped, and her lip trembled.

"You can come with us until we get out of the swamp," Carson said.

"What?" Earl protested. "Fine, whatever. Just don't let her talk to me. Or look at me. Or come near me." He turned and stomped off in the direction they had come.

Nancy kept her head down and followed. Carson shook his head. He wasn't happy with Nancy, but he didn't think she'd done anything malicious. She actually thought she was doing people a service. Maybe this little trip to the swamp would open her eyes.

When they came into view of the others, Nancy sucked in a breath. "Please don't tell them who I am."

Earl snorted. "Why? You don't want to take responsibility for your crimes?"

Her lips formed a thin line, and she mumbled. "They weren't crimes."

Earl frowned. "You keep telling yourself that."

"Everything is fine," Carson said to all the curious faces. "This is Izla. She wants to leave the swamp with those that are going."

Lottie's eyes widened, but she kept quiet. She was probably the only one that recognized Nancy in her true form.

Carson returned to his place by Lottie and carefully sat. It was hard not to grimace. He must have missed some of the pokey weeds he fell into because it still felt like needles poking him. He was going to have to deal with it because it wasn't something he was going to ask anyone to help him with.

Lottie's eyes sparkled as she looked at him. "I heard you had a rough landing."

He grinned. "Says you. You're the one covered in mud."

She rubbed her hand over his cheek, probably trying to make him dirty. It felt rough against his face as some of the mud had become caked on dirt. "At least I can wash it off. It doesn't affect my ability to sit."

Carson shook his head. "Yeah, I would prefer mud."

"I wonder why Nancy made the swamp," Jurry said, handing *Izla* a bowl of stew.

She didn't sit, just looked into her bowl. "She probably didn't make it. If every spot in a fairy made world isn't filled with something, then swamps or strange areas appear."

"She should have filled it all," Meena said, tapping her lip. "It seems clumsy to leave something so critical."

"It's hard to fill it all," Izla said. "It could take a thousand years to get it all right."

"She should have started smaller," Earl said, glaring at her.

Izla frowned and sat down. She took a bite of stew and frowned harder. Carson hoped this would make her think things through more in the future. Perhaps if she were to see things from the other side, she would realize what a mistake she had made.

Chapter 19

The swamp was vast, and Lottie's foot hurt. They had set out first thing in the morning, and it was well past noon. She wasn't used to walking around barefoot. With every step through the mud, she worried about stepping on a snake or some other swamp creature. When they stopped for a quick lunch, she had ditched her other boot. Wearing one was making her walk funny and hurting her leg.

Carson put a hand to her back. "Are you alright?"

She glanced at him, then turned away. "Fine." They were falling behind. The more her foot hurt, the slower she walked, and Carson must be falling behind to be with her. Not that she'd been great company. She hurt too much to make casual conversation.

Earl, Nancy, Roco, Jurry, Meena, and two men she didn't know were about fifty feet in front of them. The other five people had stayed where they were. Earl had tried to convince them to come, but they all figured it was a waste of time. It might be, but Lottie didn't want to sit around waiting for something to happen.

Something scraped against Lottie's foot, and she cringed. Tears sprang to her eyes, and she tried to blink them away. Maybe waiting would have been preferable.

"What's going on, Char?" Carson asked quietly.

If she talked, she was going to cry, and having sore feet seemed like a lame thing to cry about. She shook her head and took another step.

"Char?"

Tears leaked out of her eyes, and she turned away from him.

He grabbed her arm and stopped her. "What's going on?" He gently turned her head so she had to look at him.

"It's stupid," she said with a shaky laugh. "I keep stepping on things so my feet hurt."

"Are your boots wearing out?" he asked, looking down to where her feet would be if there wasn't so much mud.

She pulled one foot from the mud and showed it to him. "I'm not wearing any boots."

Carson frowned. "Where are your boots?"

"I lost one when we first got here. I left the other one because I couldn't walk lopsided."

"Why didn't you say anything?" he asked, scooping her up into his arms.

She wrapped her arms around his neck. "All I did as Cinderella's stepsister was complain and act snotty. I don't want to be that way."

He started walking. "Asking for help when you need it isn't complaining."

"I've been complaining in my head all morning."

"About your feet?"

"That and the dry dirt caked on me. It feels itchy and uncomfortable."

He nodded. "I bet. I only have mud to my knees, and it feels pretty annoying."

"You can't carry me for long."

Carson smirked. "Are you calling me a wimp?"

She smiled. "No, but carrying someone is going to get hard in less than a few minutes."

"Once my arms get tired, you can get on my back."

She glanced around at the trees and mud. "How big could a swamp be? What if it takes us days to find our way out?"

"Everything okay back there?" Earl called. The group had stopped, and they were all watching them with curious expressions.

Carson trudged the rest of the way to them. "Lottie doesn't have anything on her feet."

Roco hit himself on the head. "Sorry, Lottie. I forgot you said you lost your boot. We should have figured something out before we left."

"I should have said something," she said.

Nancy pulled a lacy white handkerchief from her pocket and tried to wipe the mud from one of Lottie's feet. The handkerchief wasn't up for the job, but Nancy got most of the bottom clean.

She sighed. "It's bleeding. We need to stop and take care of this. Does anyone have anything I can use to wipe the rest of the mud off?"

Everyone felt in their pockets, but nothing turned up.

Earl glared at Nancy. "It's almost as if everything we have disappears every time we get moved around."

"Almost?" Jurry asked. "That's exactly what happens. I wish Nancy would show her face. I've got a lot to say to that woman."

Nancy's jaw moved from side to side, but she didn't respond. She placed two fingers in her mouth and whistled.

Earl covered his ears. "Is that necessary?"

Nancy narrowed her eyes and kept wiping at Lottie's feet with the dirty cloth. A moment later, Aspen flew overhead. Nancy smiled and held out her arm, and the owl landed gracefully on it. Lottie's eyes widened. Nancy's expression didn't change with the weight of the bird. Aspen wasn't huge, but she wasn't small, either.

"Hello, beautiful," she cooed. She whispered something to the owl, and they all watched as Aspen flew away.

"How did you get her to obey you?" Meena asked.

"Animals in this world are usually helpful," Nancy replied. "I've known Aspen for a long time. Of course, that isn't her real name."

"I named her that," Roco said.

Meena grabbed Jurry's arm and jumped up and down. "Let's get a pet owl if we ever get home. Wouldn't that be fun?"

Jurry rubbed his long beard and frowned. "Owls probably don't want to be pets."

Meena punched him playfully on the arm. "Aw, you're just saying that because you don't want one."

Nancy arched a brow and crossed her arms. "Owls shouldn't be pets. They need to be free. If you keep them locked up, they won't be happy. That's the case with most wild animals."

"Something about your voice seems familiar," Jurry said, studying Nancy.

"I was thinking the same thing," said a man Lottie didn't know.

Nancy shrugged and searched the sky. "All the animals here are magical, so it shouldn't take too long."

"You know a lot about this place," Jurry said. "How long have you been here?"

Nancy puckered her lips and moved them from side to side. "Longer than anyone."

Jurry tilted his head. "I would think you would have plenty of men busting down doors to see you. Why did Nancy bring you here?"

Meena stomped on his toe.

"Ouch! What was that for?"

Lottie smiled at the clueless man. Carson shifted, and her smile slipped away. His arms probably hurt from holding her weight.

"Yeah," Earl said, crossing his arms over his chest. "Why did Nancy bring you here?"

Nancy cleared her throat and shot Earl a dirty look. "I don't want to talk about it."

"What a surprise."

One man pointed upwards. "There's the owl."

Aspen circled overhead and dropped something white. Nancy caught it and began unwrapping it and pulled out several white pieces of cloth. She separated out a few pieces and handed some to Meena.

Nancy went to work cleaning Lottie's feet. Lottie felt like a little kid. It didn't help that everyone was watching.

"You don't need to clean my feet," Lottie said. "Carson can't hold me up much longer, and I'm going to have to go back in the mud."

"I need to see what condition they are in," she muttered, as she cleaned.

Lottie sighed. It was good to know that even though Nancy was misguided, she cared.

"What do you mean I can't hold you up much longer?" Carson asked with a wink.

Lottie grinned. Her insides swarmed with butterflies. She wished everyone would disappear so she could kiss him.

"There are a bunch of cuts," Nancy said. "I wish the magic wasn't out of whack. This should be something easily fixed. I might be able to wrap them tight enough the mud won't get in. Wait…"

"What is it?" Lottie asked.

Nancy's lips turned up slowly. "The cuts are fading."

"Let me see," Roco said, moving in. "Wow. That's amazing."

Everyone else came closer to watch, and Lottie tried not to feel self-conscious. It was weird to have everyone fixated on her feet.

"Your hair is turning white," Carson said, staring at her head.

Lottie ran a hand over her head. "What? Why?"

"It's growing, too."

"Growing? What's happening?" she demanded.

Nancy's eyes lit up. "I'm not positive, but I have a theory. Give it a moment."

Roco pointed at Carson. "Carson has a crown! And his clothes changed."

"Everyone's clothes are changing!" Meera squealed and clapped her hands. "Look, I have puffy sleeves!"

Lottie's shiny white hair hung to her waist now, and she was wearing a long white dress. She touched her head and felt a delicate tiara. She was also wearing boots.

Nancy clapped her hands. "Terry's influence is lessening! I didn't realize it would happen so quickly. He must be sticking to his word and leaving things alone."

"You know Terry?" Jurry asked. "Isn't he still sleeping?"

"I know everyone," Nancy said, clasping her hands together. She let out a small giggle and turned to Carson. "Let Lottie down."

Carson let her drop to her feet, and she cringed as her clean boots sank into the mud.

Nancy pointed to the river. "Lottie, go touch the lake."

Lottie glanced behind her. "Lake? Where did that come from?" A large murky lake spread out before her. She wrinkled her nose. "Touch it? Why? It's gross."

"Trust me."

Lottie slogged over to the water and arched her eyebrow. The murky water sat dormant, and she wondered how her touching it would benefit anything. It was probably full of disease. She bent over and stuck her hand in the water. Calling it water felt like a lie. It was more like liquid sludge. She gasped as the water near her hand became a clear light blue. She stood up and watched as the clean water spread.

"Whoa," Carson said, coming up behind her. The others all stood at the edge of the water with their mouths open.

It wasn't long before the entire river was clear and sparkling. Lottie squatted down and touched the mud. The ground began to harden and grass shot out of the earth. In no more than a minute, the entire swamp was transformed into a majestic forest.

Flowers shot up from the ground as well as bushes covered in berries. Butterflies fluttered around their heads, and a gray and white rabbit ran across the small clearing they stood in. Max came bounding toward them and ran around Lottie's legs.

"What happened?" Lottie asked. "And why do I have the sudden urge to walk into the water?"

"It's *The Lady of the Lake*!" Nancy said, covering her mouth and nose with her hands. Her eyes sparkled, and Lottie wouldn't be surprised if the woman jumped up and down with glee.

"Alright..." Lottie said, crinkling her forehead. "I don't know that one."

"I've wanted to have this story for years," she said. "It never worked out. I tried and tried, but it always faded away. I'm so excited!"

"Wait..." Jurry said, his brows coming together. "You're Nancy! How did you make yourself look like that?"

Meena frowned. "She's Nancy?"

"I am Nancy, and I'm feeling so good right now I think I can do magic!"

"If that's true, send us back, right now!" Roco demanded. "Don't wait until it's too late."

She beamed and turned to one man. "Alright. Greg, you've failed miserably, but I hope you will try in the real world." She waved her wand, and he disappeared. "Same with you Chris." He saluted as he disappeared.

"Did they go home or back to the swamp?" Jurry asked.

"Home, I hope," Nany said. "I'll check later. I always do. They aren't in the swamp. The swamp is gone, and look how beautiful this place is! It's going to be one of my favorites for sure."

Meena placed her hands on her hips. "Send us next." She turned to Jurry. "You remember my phone number?"

Jurry nodded. "Yep."

"Call me as soon as we get back."

Nancy waved her wand, and they both vanished.

"Now, you, Roco."

He grinned and turned to Lottie and Carson. "Look me up sometime."

Lottie gave a small wave. "We will." She smiled as he faded away.

"Where's Earl?" Carson asked. "He was just right here."

Nancy frowned, and her eyes scanned the trees. "I guess he wasn't ready to leave. I'm finished with him, though. He can't have gotten far. I'll be right back." She turned and darted toward the trees.

"Why didn't she send us first?" Lottie complained. "I guess I should be happy I'm clean and my feet don't hurt."

Carson touched the crown on his head. "So, who do you think I'm supposed to be? Probably King Arthur. He had something to do with this story."

Lottie ran her hand over her long, white hair. "What's the story about?"

He rubbed his chin. "I don't know. I just remember something about King Arthur and Merlin. Possibly Lancelot and Gwenevere. The Lady of the Lake hid them or something. I might be wrong. I'm only having vague memories."

"Is King Arthur a fairy tale? Isn't it more like a legend that might be real?"

"I don't think Nancy is picky. I think she uses any story she likes."

Lottie touched her silky white dress. "Who lives in a lake and wears white? I wonder if the dress is magic and keeps itself clean. That would be the best thing to happen in one of these stories."

Carson paused, and his eyes widened. "Did you hear that?"

Lottie's pulse sped up. "No, what?" she whispered.

He glanced at the trees behind them. "It sounded like a growl."

Lottie grabbed Carson's arm and followed his gaze. "Where's Max? Or better yet, Finn."

"I don't know." Carson focused on listening. Another growl came from the trees.

Lottie gasped and tightened her hold on his arm. "Is there a monster in this story?"

"No clue," he said, putting his hand on her back. "We still don't know if the stories are working right. It could be anything."

"Nancy should have sent us home!" she said, as a black and gray dragon leaped out of the woods. They took a step back, and Lottie let out a small yelp.

The dragon didn't look happy. Carson tried to decide whether to run or play dead. He hadn't ever been instructed on what to do if you met up with a dragon. If they ran, they had a good sixty foot head start. Did a head start matter with a dragon? It could probably fly, and who knew how far it could shoot fire?

The beast took a step forward, and Lottie dropped Carson's arm. She turned and ran near the lake. Carson followed. What was she doing? Swimming away from a dragon seemed less effective than running.

Lottie dropped to her knees when she reached the water, and she pulled out a shiny silver sword.

Carson's eyes grew wide. "How did you know that was there?"

She shrugged. "I just did. It's Excalibur."

He turned and looked at the dragon. It hadn't moved, but it was watching them curiously.

"Here, take it," she said, holding it up.

He gripped the hilt in his hand and turned the sparkling sword. "It says, 'Cast me away' on the blade. What do you think that means?"

"Does it say anything on the other side?"

He turned it over. "Take me up."

Lottie got to her feet and stared at the dragon. "I doubt any of that matters. I hope you can use it."

Carson spun the sword in his hand and made a swipe through the air. He grinned when Lottie's eyes opened wider.

"Where did you learn that?"

"I've been here forever. I've learned a lot of stuff."

The dragon put its head down and ran at them.

Carson pointed to the left. "Run."

"I'm not leaving you," she said with a slight quiver in her voice.

"Then, stay behind me," he said, running at the dragon. He didn't have time to argue.

The dragon lunged at him, and he jumped out of the way. The dragon hit the ground hard and rolled. Carson might remember how to sword fight from his days as a prince, but he had never practiced with a dragon. He ran back a few paces and swung his sword at the dragon. It moved, and he missed. The dragon circled around him, and he turned with it, not allowing it to get him from behind.

"HEY!" Lottie yelled from the side. The dragon swung around and growled at her.

Carson rushed in, swinging his sword at the back of the creature. The sword connected with the dragon's back and bounced off, causing him to smack himself in the forehead with his fists, and the sword fell to the ground behind him. He spun to pick it up, but Lottie had already grabbed it.

She grinned. "I wish I had that on video."

He reached for the sword, and Lottie shook her head. She turned to the dragon and held up her hand.

Carson tilted his head as he watched her. "I think that only works in movies."

She smiled again as the dragon watched her. "I had a thought," she said, not losing eye contact with the dragon.

"Nancy brought us here to learn to love, not to die. She's not going to put us in actual danger."

The dragon stood on its hind legs and a swirl of green and blue twisted around him. When the colors vanished, so did the dragon.

"It isn't completely fixed," Nancy said, coming toward them. "I'll have to work on the dragon. He should have been a lot more threatening."

"He was threatening enough," Carson said. "My heart only slowed down once Lottie said you wouldn't put us in actual danger. Do you have some sort of protection for things like that?"

Nancy looked sheepishly at her wand. "Right... protection. That would be a good idea."

"Wait," Carson said, narrowing his eyes. "You mean there isn't something like that? The dragon could have eaten us?"

Nancy shrugged. "I doubt he would have eaten you. Dragons aren't into that. Fried you, maybe."

"Seriously?" Lottie asked. "Have you ever had anyone die here?"

"Never. I don't think any of my creatures could actually harm you. At least, not much. The real ones, maybe, but not the others."

Carson scowled. "Well, that's reassuring."

"Did you find Earl?" Lottie asked.

Nancy frowned. "No, but I will."

"Are you going to send us back now?" Carson asked. He was ready. He'd been ready for a long time.

Nancy's frown turned into a smile. "Now that things are getting back to normal, you should be able to send yourselves back. I don't want to rob you of that opportunity. I'll even leave so you can have your moment."

"Wait, how?" Lottie asked.

Nancy rolled her eyes. "I thought everyone had that part figured out." She grinned when she looked at Carson. "Hopefully, you can handle a kiss better than a sword."

Lottie giggled, and Carson sighed. He had a feeling he was going to be hearing about the sword for the rest of his life. Who knew dragons were so springy? Nancy waved and walked away.

Carson held out his hand. "Ready?"

Lottie dropped the sword and nodded, taking his hand.

"You remember my phone number?" he asked, mimicking Meena.

"No. I never knew it," Lottie admitted. "It was always in my phone."

He smiled. "I love you."

She reached her arms around his neck. "Not as much as I love you."

He wrapped her in his arms and leaned down. He couldn't believe what it had taken to make his dreams a reality. Maybe he owed Nancy after all. He pressed his lips to hers and welcomed the spinning sensation that overtook his senses. They were going home.

Chapter 20

Lottie felt her head fall forward, and she jerked awake. Her eyes widened and her heart sped up as she glanced around an airplane. She rubbed her eyes and looked around again.

"Are you alright?" an elderly man sitting next to the aisle asked her. There was no one sitting in the middle seat.

"Um... I... I'm a little disoriented," she managed. "Where are we going?"

The man elevated his bushy white eyebrows and rubbed his neatly trimmed goatee. "Hawaii."

Lottie secured a loose curl behind her ear. "Hawaii, right."

"I don't think you've had a very peaceful trip so far," he said. "You kept muttering in your sleep."

Lottie held in a yawn. "I had a weird dream." She frowned. Could it have been a dream? It felt so real—and so long. Still, everything felt a little hazy and disorienting, like a dream.

"I assumed as much," the man said with a grin. "I tried to make some noise to wake you, but it's awkward trying to wake a stranger. Let me tell you, I'm a talker, so I usually spend a lot of my trips annoying my neighbors. You found a way around that." He chuckled. "I've been working on my crosswords," he said, holding up a book. "They get boring after a while."

Lottie nodded. "When I first sat here, there was a woman sitting next to me. Do you know where she went?"

The man rubbed the back of his neck. "I never saw a woman here. I watched you sit down, and I sat here right after you did."

Lottie unclipped her seatbelt and stood up. She scanned the passengers and frowned. No sign of Nancy. Not the young or old version. It was hard to see everyone from her position, and she wasn't ready to give up yet. It felt like so much more than a dream.

"Excuse me for a moment," she said to the man. He stood in the aisle and let her pass. She walked slowly down the path and glanced at every person on her way to the back. When she was satisfied none of them were Nancy, she made her way back the other way. The man stood again and let her sit. She sighed as she sank into her seat.

"My name is Joe," the man said, holding out his hand.

Lottie shook it absentmindedly. "Charlotte."

Joe started talking about his pets that were going to miss him while he was away, and Lottie tuned him out. If Nancy wasn't here, and none of her dream had actually happened, then that meant she hadn't had all those moments with Carson. It also meant he was still out there hating her somewhere.

It was real. It had to be. There was no way a dream could last that long. How could it feel like years, but at the same time like she had just boarded the plane? She glanced down at her jeans and t-shirt, and it felt like she had only put them on this morning. If she had been trapped in Nancy's world for years, it shouldn't feel like that. Still, Nancy was tricky. Very tricky. Lottie glanced at Joe and frowned.

Joe's smile slipped away, and he stopped midsentence. "Is everything okay?"

"Are you Nancy?" she asked.

Joe's eyes narrowed, and he scratched his head. "Nancy? No, my name is Joe."

She peered up at him. "Is it, though?"

Joe coughed awkwardly and pulled out his pencil. "I think I'm going to work some more on my crossword."

Lottie sighed. Great. Now she looked like a crazy person. She pressed her head against the window and gazed down at the ocean below. She wondered how long they had before they landed. Once they did, she could turn her phone back on and call Carson.

Her mouth turned down in a frown. What would she say when she called him? If it had been a dream, he would be confused, and she could add him to the list of people that thought she was crazy. She bit her lip and considered her options. She could wait and see if Carson called her. But what if he assumed it was a dream and didn't? Worst-case scenario was that it was a dream.

Her stomach dropped at the thought. She wanted it to be real with everything in her. If it wasn't, she almost felt like she might find it within herself to go visit Carson and beg him to forgive her. She sighed again and closed her eyes.

Carson hopped off the bus and sprinted down the sidewalk. His head was pounding, and possibly bleeding, but he didn't have time to worry about things like that. He'd woken up on the ground in the subway with a huge crowd circling around him. He remembered falling when he stepped off, but that had been so long ago. After he'd assured the crowd he was fine, he'd caught a bus and tried to settle his thoughts.

There was no way Nancy's world had been a dream. It was much too fresh in his mind, and he had been there for years. Time must have stopped here, or Nancy had brought him back to the same time she took him from. He jumped over a tipped bike and didn't even slow down. Being a runner was coming in handy.

He turned left at a corner and ran toward the only bright purple house in the neighborhood. The two story home stood out like a sore thumb. If the color didn't get you, the lawn gnomes would. People used this house as a landmark when they gave directions. He ran past two gnomes standing as sentinels at the beginning of the driveway, and he skidded as he tried to run on the rocks in the Xeriscape yard, but kept his footing.

There was no time for stairs, so Carson jumped past the three steps and landed on the welcome mat. He pounded on the front door, ignoring the 'solicitors will be cursed' sign. The sign usually made him smile, but not today. He rang the doorbell three times and concentrated on regulating his breathing.

The door opened, and Brandon peeked out. His eyes widened and he opened it the rest of the way. "Dude. What happened to your face? Do you wanna come in?"

"I need you to take me to the airport."

Brandon blinked. "Looking like that? Your lip is bleeding, and you have a huge knot on your head."

"I fell, but I'm fine. I'm in a big hurry. Can you help me?"

"You're going to miss a plane?"

He wiped his lip with his hand. "I don't have a ticket. I need to get one."

"Have you looked online? It's probably not the greatest idea to go to the airport and expect to find a flight at the last second."

Carson pulled his phone from his back pocket and showed it to Brandon. "Just take me, alright?"

"Who's at the door?" Brandon's mom called from inside.

"Carson," Brandon called back.

"Tell him to come in for a visit."

"Come on, man," Carson begged. "Take me before your mom tries to read my palm or something."

"She's into auras this week," Brandon said with a grin. "Hang on a minute." Brandon disappeared, and Carson did his best to not fidget. Brandon reappeared with his keys. "Let's go." Carson rushed over to Brandon's Mazda and jumped into the passenger's seat. Why was Brandon walking so slow?

Brandon got in the car and started it up.

"Can we hurry?" Carson asked, jiggling his leg.

Brandon looked over his shoulder and backed up. "We can go the speed limit. You know I don't break the rules. So, where are you off to in such a hurry?"

Carson stared out the window as they began inching forward. Brandon was the most careful driver on the planet.

"Hawaii."

"I'm slightly jealous. Your parents are there, right? I thought you said you couldn't go with them."

"I changed my mind."

"Don't you need a suitcase or something?"

Carson shook his head. "I don't care about that. I'm sure I can get something when I'm there."

"This is all a little strange," Brandon said, turning out of the neighborhood. "Not as strange as the dream I had about you the other day. It was the weirdest dream I've ever had." He chuckled. "It was so real I almost called you to see if it had happened."

Carson studied his friend. "It did happen."

Brandon laughed. "I wish. It was so odd. Char was there, too. I know you don't want to talk about her, but, man, it was so real."

"It was real," Carson insisted. "That's why I need to go to Hawaii. I need to see if Charlotte got out of that crazy place."

Brandon braked so hard Carson's seat belt locked. He turned and looked at him. "There is no way that happened."

"Then, how do I know about it?"

Brandon shook his head and started driving again. "You don't know about it. All you know is Char was there."

"And your cousin Lizette."

Brandon sucked in a breath. "Now you're freaking me out."

Carson gave him a half smile. "You aren't the only one. I wasn't one hundred percent sure it happened until you said that."

"Did you talk to my mom?" Brandon asked. "I told her about the dream. Are you messing with me? Is this like a late April Fool's joke?"

"It's not a joke." He turned to his friend and frowned. "Why would you tell your mom? She's the worst person to tell something like that."

"Yeah, I don't know. She told me it was something about my need to help people manifesting in my dreams. She said I never got over you and Char breaking up. Now, she's been making me drink some horrible herbal tea every morning to cleanse my mind."

Carson smiled. That sounded like Brandon's mom. "Char and I never broke up. We were never dating unless you count whatever we did in Nancy's world."

"Nancy," Brandon muttered. "It really happened."

"Yes, now stop driving like my grandma and get me to the airport."

Lottie tried to drink a thick smoothie through her straw. Smoothies were supposed to be refreshing, but if you had to work this hard for it, it wasn't worth it. She shifted in her beach chair and tried to enjoy the breeze. Her parents were busy talking to Carson's parents, and she couldn't think of a way to bring up Carson without making them question her. She'd been avoiding any conversation about him for a year, and if she brought him up now, it would raise questions.

This would all be easier if she hadn't lost her phone on her flight. Without it, she didn't know how to get a hold of Carson. She didn't know his phone number, and she was fairly certain it wasn't in either of her parents' phones. Asking the Johnsons if she could borrow theirs would be suspicious. She'd been here two days and wasn't any closer to talking to Carson.

The sun was setting and casting beautiful colors across the sky. The ocean reflected the colors, and Lottie couldn't help wishing Carson was there to see it. There weren't many people on the beach, and Lottie was glad about that. She turned and looked at the hotel behind her. If she couldn't think of a way to bring up Carson, she might as well go back to her room. Maybe after the sunset.

"Did you hear that, Char?" her mom asked. "Dana said that Carson finished his first year at the university."

Lottie's throat felt dry. She swallowed and tried to take another sip of her smoothie. "Oh." This was her chance, but nothing was coming to her. If the adults sensed her discomfort, none of them showed it. Lottie knew they were faking. They all knew about Carson and Lottie's falling out, even if they didn't know the details.

"It's too bad Carson couldn't meet us here," Carson's mom said, sipping her smoothie. "He needs a vacation."

Lottie ran a hand over her eyes, and her hand trembled. Why was she so nervous?

"Char, honey, are you alright?" her father asked.

This was it. She needed to say something. "I need to talk to Carson."

The four adults all paused and looked at her. She tried to smile but probably only appeared sick. They all glanced at one another with concern, and she fought the urge to roll her eyes.

"Since my phone is lost, I can't call him." The McLinns and the Johnsons all began grabbing for their phones. Dana was the fastest. She quickly pulled up Carson's number and shoved the phone toward Lottie.

She panicked. It was already ringing. Lottie jumped to her feet and ran away from their parents. Sand filling her sandals made her retreat clumsy, but she was not having this conversation in front of them.

The phone kept ringing, and she held it to her ear.

"Hey, Ma," Carson's voice came over the phone, filling her head.

Lottie swallowed. "No. I borrowed your mom's phone."

"Char?"

"Yes."

There was a pause, and Lottie heard movement behind her. She turned around. She gripped the phone in her hand as a red paw print appeared in the sand. She gasped.

"What is it?" Carson asked.

Another paw print appeared. It was coming toward her. "Dravul," she whispered.

"What? Where are you?" Carson demanded.

Lottie took a step back and dropped the phone. She had to get out of here and lead the dravul away from her parents. She turned and ran as fast as she could. With every step, the sand tried to steal her sandal, but she didn't care. All she cared about was protecting her family.

"Charlotte!" her mother called. "Where are you going?"

She didn't look back. Looking back would slow her down.

∼ℓℓ∼

"Char? Lottie?"

"What's wrong?" Brandon asked.

Carson dropped his phone onto the taxi floor and leaned toward the driver. "Please hurry."

The driver ignored him, and Carson tried to ignore his speeding heart.

"What?" Brandon asked again. He had insisted on coming with him to Hawaii. After waiting for hours at the airport, they had snagged some standby tickets.

"It was Char," he said, pushing his hair back with his hands. "She said Dravul and then nothing."

Brandon's eyes widened. "Oh no. Can you please hurry?" he asked the driver. "Our friend might be in danger."

Carson wasn't going to panic. He felt completely helpless. There was nothing he could do to get to Charlotte any faster. He needed to keep a cool head and wait. That was easier said than done. Sweat ran down his brow.

"Maybe you misunderstood her," Brandon reasoned. "How would a dravul get here?"

"She whispered it, but that's what it sounded like. Then, there was nothing."

The phone vibrated on the floor, and Carson scooped it up. He pushed the button and yelled louder than he meant to. "Char! What's going on?"

"This is Mom, and why are you yelling?" came his mother's voice.

"Where's Char?" he asked.

"She's running down the beach. I'm not sure why. She dropped the phone and took off. What did you say to her?"

"Is she alright?" he asked, ignoring the question.

"I'm not sure. Jeremy and Susan are chasing after her."

Carson took deep, even breaths. "Is anything else chasing her?"

She paused. "Why would anything else be chasing her?"

"I don't know," Carson said, running a hand through his hair.

"There are these really weird red paw prints in the sand. You should see them. They almost glow."

"Stay away from the paw prints!" Carson commanded. "Go to your room and stay there until I come!"

"Come? You're coming? To Hawaii?"

"Go to your room!" He hung up the phone and stuck it in his pocket.

"Now she thinks you're crazy," Brandon said.

"Probably. How would a dravul get here?"

Brandon shrugged. "Maybe it came with us when we came back."

Carson rubbed the light stubble on his chin. "You don't think Terry sent it after her, do you?"

"I doubt it. He didn't seem to have a problem with you guys. Only that fairy godmother. I'm kinda jealous you two got to go have all those adventures."

Carson blinked. "Jealous? It was not fun. It was awful."

"I don't know. It might have been terrible for you because it's not your thing."

"What do you mean?"

Brandon tilted his head. "You only watch action movies, and you don't care if they end good or bad. I only like happy endings. It would be fun to act out fairy tales."

"You saw things there," Carson argued. "It wasn't all happy endings. I'm hoping I get one."

The taxi stopped, and Carson paid the driver, then leaped from the car. He ran up to a large five story white and gray hotel. He hoped Brandon was on his heels. There was no reason to go inside, so he ran around the back. The ocean momentarily distracted him, but he shook his head and ran forward, scanning all the small groups of people.

"Carson!"

He turned his head toward the voice and saw his mom coming his way. She appeared happy to see him, and she didn't seem distressed, so Charlotte must be okay. His father was a few feet behind her and hadn't spotted him yet.

His mom wrapped him in a hug. "I'm so glad you decided to come. This is the best surprise. We've planned so many fun things. We're going to hike a volcano tomorrow."

"That's great, Mom," he said, his eyes running over the beach. "Where's Lottie?"

"Lottie?"

"Charlotte."

"She went that way," she said, pointing. "Are you two talking again? I was shocked when she wanted to call you."

"I need to find her. She might be in danger." He took off in the direction she had pointed, and before he could get far, he saw Charlotte running in his direction with her parents trailing behind her. She was turning and yelling something to them he couldn't understand. When she saw him, she made a beeline toward him.

Without warning, Lottie fell face down to the ground and screamed. The dravul must have jumped on her because she was struggling to get up. Her parents were close behind her, but Carson was closer. He aimed above her back and leaped at the space. He connected with the invisible creature and knocked it off her.

"What is going on?" Susan asked, as she helped Lottie to her feet.

Carson scanned the sand for a sign of the dravul. Slow red footprints appeared, circling around him. Susan let out a loud gasp.

"What is it?" Jeremy asked. Susan pointed at the footprints, and all the adults stared in horror. Great, now they were going to have to tell all of their parents, and what were the chances they would believe any of their story?

"Everyone needs to get back," Brandon said, joining them.

"How is that happening?" his mother asked. "Is this one of your pranks, Carson?"

Carson's eyes didn't leave the prints. What was the beast waiting for?

"It's not a prank," Lottie said. "You all need to go back to the hotel."

"Not a chance," his dad said, watching the prints burn into the sand. "What's going on?"

Carson turned in a circle with the prints. He didn't want it jumping on his back. A growl behind him caused him to turn, and his mom and Susan let out screams as Finn jumped into the group, baring his teeth. Carson stepped back and pushed his mom and Lottie back.

"He won't hurt anyone," he said, as they all backed away.

"It's a wolf!" Dana said. "What do you mean it won't hurt anyone?"

"He's a nice wolf," Lottie chimed in.

Susan's eyes jerked to her daughter. "You know this wolf?"

Finn fell back and started growling and snapping at the air.

"The dravul must have attacked him!" Lottie squealed. "We need to do something!"

A large stick dropped to the ground, and Carson looked up to see Aspen flying overhead. Lottie picked up the stick and swung it above Finn. It connected with a thud, and Finn was back on his feet. Out of nowhere, Max came barreling at them and jumped in the air. He seemed to float. He must have landed on the creature.

Lottie's eyes went from Finn to Max, and she held the stick like a baseball bat. Her hands were shaking, but she looked ready to attack again. Carson grabbed her elbow and pulled her back. Max looked like he was biting the dravul, and Finn rammed it to the ground, causing Max to fall. The dravul let out a loud growl, and the fox jumped up and ran toward it.

A gigantic cloud of blue smoke billowed near them, and Terry appeared wearing a red cloak and a golden crown. "Stop!" he commanded.

Carson wasn't sure who Terry was talking to, but Max and Finn stopped, and the dravul's footprints weren't appearing anywhere new.

"Sorry about that," Terry said. "I don't know how he slipped away. He seems to have your scent." He turned to where Carson suspected the monster to be. "Come on, Carson. It's time to go home."

"Carson?" Lottie asked, tossing the stick to the ground. "Its name is Carson?"

Terry put his hand out and petted the invisible animal. "What's wrong with Carson?"

Lottie shook her head.

"Well, I hate to run, but I'm a very busy person." He grabbed the creature and disappeared in another puff of smoke.

"That was crazy!" Brandon said. "We should probably start carrying a taser or something. Maybe a sword."

"What just happened?" Susan asked.

All four of the parents looked a bit dazed. Carson wasn't sure where to begin. He looked at Lottie, and she shrugged. Her long brown hair was blowing behind her, and Carson stared at her. He'd always loved her hair. Right now, it was covered in sand.

"What happened to your face?" she asked.

"I fell off the subway."

"Does it hurt?"

He smiled. "Yes."

They both looked at each other for a minute and then they started laughing.

"How is any of this funny?" his mom asked. "What even happened? I think I need my eyes checked."

"If we told you what happened, you wouldn't believe us," Brandon said.

Carson's dad shook his head. "After what we just saw, we might believe anything."

Carson wasn't in the mood to sit around and talk. He'd come here for a reason, and talking was not it. He turned to Lottie and opened his arms. She smiled and stepped into his embrace. He ran his hand over her sandy hair and kissed her forehead.

"I'm so glad it wasn't a dream," she said. "It didn't feel like a dream."

"I love you."

"And I love you."

"Kiss, kiss, kiss," Brandon chanted.

Carson smiled and leaned down. Lottie's lips met his, and he sighed. He would live through Nancy's fairy tales again if it meant being with Charlotte.

"I want this story, and I want it now!" Susan demanded.

"Why are these animals staring at us?" his father asked.

Carson kissed her a little longer and then pulled away. Lottie rested her head against his chest, and he kept her in a tight hug. Finn and Max were staring at them, and so were all of their parents. And Brandon.

"We don't care about what the animals are doing," his mom said. "We want to know how you went from never wanting to talk to each other to this!"

"Exactly," Susan agreed. "The rest can wait."

"Well," Lottie said, pulling back and looking at the two women. "It's a long story, and we have some friends we need to check on first."

"Right, let's hurry," Carson said. He wrapped his parents in a hug. "I missed you guys."

"It was only a week," his dad said, shrugging.

His mom squeezed him back. "A week is a long time."

"It was a long week," Carson said. "We'll catch up soon. Come on," he said, grabbing Lottie's hand. They ran toward the hotel. With luck, a cab would be waiting out front.

"Wait!" Susan called. "We need to hear the story!"

"Later!" Lottie yelled back.

Chapter 21

Lottie and Carson stood outside the school office. Lottie was nervous, even though there wasn't a reason.

Carson had his hand on the doorknob. "You ready?"

Lottie bit the inside of her cheek. "What if it's not the right Roco?"

Carson grinned. "How many Roco St. James who teach English do you think there are?"

Lottie shrugged. He was right. Trying to find Mara was going to be a lot more difficult. They didn't even know what her last name was or where she was from. When they'd searched for Roco St. James, the only result that had come up was in Tampa, Florida.

Lottie grabbed her phone and put it on vibrate. Her mom and Dana had been texting and calling since they'd run off. They had decided it would be better to wait and tell them everything at once. They probably should have explained before running off.

Carson pushed the door open, and Lottie followed. They entered a large office with enormous windows. The sun shone in, highlighting a woman with short black hair and glasses. She was on a computer typing.

She glanced up at them, then back to her computer. "Sit, and wait."

"We just need—" Lottie started and stopped when the woman glared at her.

Carson sat on a blue chair against the wall, and Lottie sat next to him.

Carson leaned toward her. "Why are school secretaries always so scary? Remember Mrs. Griffin?"

Lottie giggled when she thought about their middle school secretary. She hadn't been that bad. Carson had just gotten on her bad side.

"Shhh!" the secretary scolded. "If you're going to be loud, go back to class."

"Do we look like high schoolers?" Carson asked, looking offended. "We're here to see Roco St. James."

Lottie smiled. It was funny to see Carson upset over being mistaken for an age he'd been a year ago. Still, to them, it felt like it had been years.

The woman stopped typing and fixed them with a glare. "What business do you have during school hours that can't wait?"

"I guess it can wait," Lottie said, "But we don't know where he lives."

"He's busy right now," the woman said, waving them off with her hand.

"He's teaching?" she asked.

The woman looked at her over her glasses. "No, he's in his office. He doesn't teach anymore. He's counseling with someone."

"He's my uncle. I need to talk to him," Lottie lied.

The woman slammed her laptop shut. "Roco is an only child. That means he is not your uncle."

"It's a complicated family thing," Lottie said. She knew it sounded lame.

The woman adjusted her glasses and pursed her lips as she studied them. "What do you really want?"

"It's not any of your business," Carson said, standing. "It's between us and him."

"I think you should leave."

The door opened, and Roco walked past them. He held a mug in one hand and had a clipboard under his arm.

"Hey, Tyla," he said to the secretary. "Miss me?" He took a sip from his mug. The woman gestured at them with an annoyed expression. Roco turned to see what she was glaring at and spit out whatever he was drinking. His eyes widened, and he took a step back, wiping his mouth on his sleeve.

Tyla leaned forward. "You know them?"

Roco put his mug on her desk and rubbed a hand over his eyes. "No, no, no," he muttered. "It's happening again!"

Tyla jumped from her chair and rushed around the desk. She put a hand on Roco's shoulder and frowned. "What's happening? Are you alright?"

Roco covered his face with his hands and peeked over his fingers. "This can't be happening."

"Are you okay?" Lottie asked, getting to her feet. "Maybe we should talk in private."

Tyla frowned. "Anything that involves my husband involves me."

Carson snorted. "Husband? You got married that fast?"

Tyla's eyes filled with fire. "What do you mean fast?"

"We only got home a few days ago, and you're already married."

Roco took a deep breath and sighed. "Follow me." He rushed down a small white hallway and took them into a spotless office. "Sit," he commanded.

Carson and Lottie took seats in front of the desk, and Tyla closed the door and leaned against it. Roco sat in a black rolling chair behind the desk and leaned his elbows against it, steepling his fingers in front of his mouth.

"Why?" he asked.

Carson shot a concerned glance at Lottie. She frowned.

"Who are these people?" Tyla asked.

Roco's eyes pierced hers. "People that don't exist."

"We exist," Lottie said. "What's going on?"

"Roco's office is a lot cleaner than I would have expected," Carson said, looking at the neat bookcases that lined the wall.

"I have... motivation," he said, glancing at his wife.

She fiddled with her hands. "Roco, you're making me nervous."

He glanced at her. "You remember all that therapy I sat through?"

"Yes."

"These are the people. The people you were all convincing me didn't exist."

Tyla sighed. "These are real people. The people from your... dream, they aren't."

"We shouldn't have come," Lottie said. "Sorry. We thought you would want to see us. We wanted to make sure you made it back and didn't end up in the swamp or anything."

Roco leaned forward. "You said you've only been back a few days?"

Carson and Lottie nodded.

"I've been back for three years."

Lottie's eyes widened. "Three years? How is that possible?"

"Nancy said she could return people to the exact time she takes them from," Carson said, glancing out the window.

"No time had passed when I returned," Roco said. "We must have been taken from different times."

"Didn't you try to find anyone when you came back?" Lottie asked.

"Sure I did. Everyone thought I was crazy, so I tried to find you all to prove it happened. I couldn't find any of you. I didn't know your last names, and none of you have unique first names. Searching seemed pointless, so I gave up."

"Did you try Jurry?" Carson asked. "His name is unique, and you know he's a truck driver."

"I tried searching for him, for all of you. I even tried searching for a fairy godmother named Nancy. Nothing."

Carson rubbed his chin. "I guess we don't know when she took Jurry from. It could have been a long time ago, or even in the future."

Lottie typed 'Jurry' into her phone and 'truck driver.' She scanned the screen and turned it toward Roco. "Right here. Jurry Stevenson. It even has the phone number of the company he works for."

Roco grinned. "Well, don't that beat all."

Lottie smiled. It was fun to hear Roco use *don't* incorrectly again.

"Can you send me the phone number?" he asked.

Lottie grabbed a pen and post-it note from his desk and jotted down the number. She handed it to him, and he stuffed it in his shirt pocket.

"Any idea where to find Earl? I know they aren't actually my brothers, but it felt like they were."

Carson shook his head. "As far as we know, Earl is still there. When Nancy started sending people home, he ran off."

Roco nodded. "I guess he'll come when he's ready."

Tyla was still leaning on the door. "None of this makes any sense. Is this a joke? Do you know how much time and money we put into getting all that stuff out of your head?"

Roco nodded. "Yeah, and it was a waste of time and money because it all happened."

"Please don't do this," she said. "Those stories you told me never happened. They were impossible."

Lottie turned to her. "They seemed impossible, but they happened. You don't think all three of us could have the same memories and have them be dreams, do you?"

She frowned. "I don't know what is happening. I know there is no way any of that stuff is true."

"I wasn't sure when I woke up," Lottie admitted. "But now we know. Terry even came here because one of his creatures followed us."

Roco scrunched his brow. "If I start telling people about this, they are all going to think I'm crazy again."

"So, don't tell anyone," Carson said.

"Yes, please don't tell people you are one of the seven dwarves," Tyla said, rubbing her temples. "I thought we were past this."

"You can pretend like none of this happened," Lottie said. "Perhaps we shouldn't have come."

Roco shook his head. "No. I'm glad to know I'm not crazy. It felt so real. I don't know why I told people. I should have kept it to myself. The memories weren't bad. I actually enjoyed a lot of them. The only reason I got upset when I saw you was because I thought I must be hallucinating."

Tyla scurried around the desk and kneeled in front of Roco. She gripped his hand and looked up at him. "Please, Roco. You can't let these people confuse you."

Roco ran his hand over her cheek. "I wish there was a way to convince you."

A pink puff of smoke blasted across the office, and Nancy stood coughing in the middle of it. Lottie fanned the smoke away from her face, and Carson shook his head.

Nancy's green eyes scanned the scene in front of her as she continued coughing. Tyla's eyes were as wide as saucers. Nancy brushed her red hair over her shoulder and frowned.

"Does that convince you?" Roco asked his wife.

"I... What?" Tyla sputtered.

"Drat," Nancy muttered, straightening her long green dress. "I'm young again."

"How is that a bad thing?" Roco asked.

"My magic is still having problems. I wanted to check on the lot of you before I rounded up the next bunch to send home. I was trying to find Jurry, though, not you guys. It is nice to see you all found each other. Points for me."

Carson frowned. "Points for you?"

"Yes. None of this is turning out as horrid as it could have. Of course, I'm having trouble getting things to go the way I want, and Terry is already misbehaving again, but we are on the right track."

"So long as we aren't a part of it, I'm fine with it," Carson said.

Lottie nodded in agreement. She was glad she had Carson now, but that didn't mean she wanted to leave this world ever again.

"Congratulations on the marriage," Nancy said, glancing at Tyla. "You seem to be doing fine on your own."

"I am," Roco said. "Of course, I'm doing better now I know it all happened."

"I don't know that there is anything more the three of you need from me. I'm off to find Jurry. After that, I suppose I better search for Earl."

"When is your father going to make you go live one of your stories?" Lottie couldn't help asking.

Nancy's eyes narrowed, and she crossed her arms. "I doubt he'll hold me to it."

"This is so weird," Tyla said, looking at Roco. "When we get home, I want you to tell me the entire story again, only this time, I won't judge."

Roco grinned. "I'd love to."

Carson had never been so happy to be home. It had been so long. He sat next to Lottie on an overstuffed brown loveseat and watched his mom pace in front of them. Susan sat on a wooden rocker and kept her gaze fixed on them. His mom was giving them a lecture about running off and worrying everyone, but he'd stopped listening a few minutes ago.

"Are you even listening to me, Carson?" she asked, placing her hands on her hips.

He grinned. "No, not really."

She sighed. "Susan and I have been worried. You took off and ignored us with only the occasional text telling us you were fine and you would talk to us later. I know you are both technically adults, but we still worry."

"And what happened at the beach?" Susan asked. "It was like a ghost dog or something. What made those prints? And what happened with all those other animals? They were acting so strangely. Then, that man appeared... and disappeared."

Carson laced his fingers with Lottie's and looked into her eyes. They probably should have discussed what they were going to tell their parents once they stopped running all over creation.

"And when did you two get... like that?" his mom asked. "That's what I want to know. You know I'm not complaining. Susan and I have had hopes for the two of you since you were five."

Carson grinned. He knew that was true. Now what to tell them?

Lottie tilted her head and looked at the two women. "If we tell you, you'll never believe it."

"After the invisible animal in Hawaii, I think we might," his mom said.

"Well," Lottie said, "it all began when we were trapped in once upon a time."

About the Author

Kristy Dixon received a bachelor's degree in English. She started writing stories when she was seven and never stopped. She enjoys writing fantasy books for middle grade and teens. At home, she spends her time playing board games with her husband and kids and writing. Occasionally she takes part in a Super Mario marathon. She has six chickens and two cats that help keep life amusing. If she isn't playing with her husband and kids or writing, she is usually eating cookies, or wishing she was eating cookies.

Also By Kristy Dixon

Akkron (The Silver Eclipse Series Book 1)
Boztoll (The Silver Eclipse Series Book 2)
The Other Continent (The Silver Eclipse Series Book 3)
The Amethyst Crown
More Than Once Upon a Time